THO͟ͅ ͟ ͟RUST

MARIE JONES

To my beautiful family, whom I love so much…
tha gra dh agam ort

To Sam, for encouraging me every step of the way
and staying up past bedtime to read the final draft.
To Rebekah, for your unwavering support.
To Anna, my book editing wizard.
To my cucumber club girls, love you.

To all my fellow peakers, my global family, for encouraging and
supporting me to achieve my personal and fitness goals, while as a
community raising an incredible amount of money for charities
fighting to beat cancer. Every one of you is a hero.
www.mypeakchallenge.com

Bidh tu m' aisling anns an oidhche,
mo leannan, mo leannan.
S leatsa mo chridhe,
an-còmhnaidh agus gu bràth.

(Scottish Gaelic)

You are in my dreams at night,
my lover, my sweetheart.
My heart belongs to you,
always and forever.

(English translation)

AUTHOR'S NOTE

Every person we allow into our hearts and souls will change and define us. Some bring goodness and restoration to our souls, flooding them with light. They will strengthen our hearts, be a protective shield, a soothing balm to our deep wounds.

Then there are the others who bring nothing but darkness and despair to our hearts and try to blacken our souls until they are exactly like their own. They will drag us down into their pit with them.

But we must fight to rise again.

Until we are once more touched by the light of the dawning sun.

[1]

In my defining moment, each of my senses became aware of the smallest, most infinite detail. The distant cry of a wild, eager fox. The soft, rippling sound of crystal water stirring within the loch. The sweet scent of a pine tree moving lazily in the wind. The freshly fallen leaves dancing around our feet. The acrid, metallic taste in my mouth as I forced away its dryness. His warm breath on my neck, stirring the tendrils of my hair and sending a tremor through my body.

I had let my eyes drift closed to savour it all for one sweet second. My hand moved carefully behind me, so he could reach for it. As I felt his calloused palm cover mine, I squeezed hard, knowing without any words he would understand what I needed. We spoke a silent language, our bodies moving of their own accord.

Then, knowing all too well what would confront them, my eyes reluctantly opened. Yet still, the shock of meeting those eyes staring hard and dangerously at me caused me to stiffen and bite down hard on the inside of my cheek.

Eyes that had once looked at me with affection were now that of a feverish stranger, hell-bent on getting what was so desperately sought, regardless of what happened to me. Had I ever really known the person behind them?

As we stood there, suspended, each waiting for the other to make the next crucial move, I knew it was my choice now as to how this tale would end. Would I go back to the woman I had once been, full of self-doubt, low, hollow, and giving in to the inevitable? Or would I rise up and fight back, show my new strength and courage to protect the man I loved fiercely?

Had it really only been five weeks since I'd made a different choice to take up a seemingly kind offer to stay at a friend's flat? Had it been so short a time from when Aneella had smoothed her way back into my life after ten years of utter silence? When she became determined to have her way over my life, once again…

I t hadn't been the best of mornings.

The rain was coming down in lashes, hitting the fragile, paned glass windows of my flat in Buxton. A headache loomed viciously behind my eyes, emboldened by the tossing and turning of the last few nights. My body was trying desperately, even now, to adjust to the absence of Richard's reassuring bulk beside me.

Shivering a little, I reached for my black, woolly cardigan strewn on the chair behind me, muttering as I did, "It's May, for heaven's sake, it's not meant to be cold."

Standing up from the desk, I stretched out my body, stiff from sitting cramped over the computer, and absent-mindedly rubbed my painful forehead. My freelance work, writing and designing computer programmes, filled up what would otherwise be long, empty days, and I was very grateful for its lifeline. But today, it felt like a burden pressing down on me.

Letting out a sigh, I walked into my rather compact kitchen to search out some headache tablets, then filled a glass to swallow them down. As I did, I stared across at the computer. The thought of sitting in front of it again was almost unbearable, but I needed to, for my already restless client was growing more agitated by the hour.

I hadn't sat long, a large steaming cup of tea untouched beside me, when a loud, insistent rap at the door had my fingers freezing on the keyboard. Frowning, I swung to look at the door as if expecting it to tell me who it was. No one, except the odd delivery man, came knocking on my door. When the rap came again, I pushed back and walked over, smoothing down my hair as I went.

A woman stood there, strikingly familiar in her stance and the way she held herself proudly, her blond hair stylishly flicked away off her face even when drenched by the rain as it was now. I inhaled in a stunned, incredible gasp.

"Surprise!" There came a laugh so clear it reminded me of polished glass.

"Aneella, Ella... Is that you?" I stuttered out, hardly believing what I was saying.

"The one and only! I happened to be in town and thought, why not look up my old uni friend Sophia? And see, here I find you at home, what could be better! Pleased to see me?" she asked, smiling confidently.

I couldn't help but shake my head as I said, "Of course... of course, I am! And incredibly shocked... It's been so long! Ten years at least, and you've hardly changed... I..."

I found myself lost for words. Aneella stood there looking expectantly at me, her smile beginning to freeze. I could see a whisper of impatience in her eyes, and the familiarity took me straight back to our university days together. It was enough to compel me to say, "Would you like to come in, have a cup of tea?"

The smile returned. "Now, that sounds like a perfect idea. Don't suppose you've got something stronger than a tasteless tea bag dunked in water?"

A laugh escaped me, even as I once again shook my head in mild disapproval. "Some things never change, Ella. It's only two-fifteen in the afternoon!"

Aneella raised an eyebrow. "Anything past twelve o'clock is considered pre-dinner in my eyes."

"Now, *that* I do remember," I commented mildly. "But I'm afraid I don't have anything alcoholic to offer, at least nothing I'm prepared to give someone of your refined taste. Would a coffee go down better?"

She sighed. "Marginally so."

While I made her coffee, she wandered around my compact lounge, picking up family photos and well-thumbed books before replacing them. I could see the restlessness which had often led me into trouble at university still coursing through her, like an electric current refusing to burn out. The smartly dressed woman before me was still the scantily dressed girl of twenty who'd caught us all up in her wild adventures.

"Are you hungry? Can I get you something to eat?" I offered, carrying her mug over to where she stood before picking up mine from the desk.

Aneella shook her head. "No, no. Come join me over here," she ordered as we sat down on the faded blue sofa. "Tell me everything. What are you doing as a job?"

"Still in computers. I know, predictable and boring. But I work freelance as a programme designer, which is a nice perk. I can somewhat make my own schedule. How about you?" I asked.

She waved her hand dismissively. "Oh, in a bank... But it's too dreary to even talk about. I need a change."

"Is that why you're here? In Buxton?" I broached, curiosity biting away at me.

"One of the reasons." Before I had a chance to delve deeper, Aneella moved on, "How long has it been since we graduated from university? Ten years or more?"

Sipping my tea, I nodded. "We graduated in July of 2007. Don't you remember how we all nearly passed out from the heat, wearing those thick black gowns?"

"I hated that gown. Didn't you?" Aneella put down her mug. "But we had such riotous years together, didn't we? Life seemed... so easy and uncomplicated, like anything was possible if we believed hard enough."

Perhaps for you, came my unbidden thought. But I played along with her, spinning a happier tale than what had been reality. "I'm not sure the caretaker in our dorm ever really forgave us for that incident with the toilet paper and cold jelly in the bath!"

Aneella raised one elegant eyebrow. "I suppose it's no wonder we were told to find different student lodgings after that. Some people have no sense of humour."

We both laughed, the levity drawing us together.

"And how's Rich? In fact, where is he now, at work?" Aneella looked around as if expecting him to jump out from nowhere. "Can't believe the university sweethearts got married right away and lived the dream. We all envied you, you know."

My laughter died away. Unwanted tears pricked my eyes. Aneella must have seen, for her smile slipped. "Sophia?"

I shook my head. "He's gone. Please," I said, taking her hand in mine, "don't ask me anymore."

She stared at me, then slowly nodded. "Love can be a bitch, can't it?"

The unexpectedness of her words made me half laugh, half cry. "Yes, yes, a complete bitch."

She kept her hand in mine, and it gave me the courage to say, "I missed you, missed our friendship. After our wedding, it was like you cut yourself off from us."

Aneella said nothing, letting go of my hand. I began to fear I had said too much and opened my mouth to swiftly apologise, only for her to say, "I needed to find my own space, my own walk in life. I'm sure you understand."

No, not really. I forced a smile. "Yes... yes, of course, I do. No one wants to be around newlyweds."

My eyes must have deceived me. There was a streak of guilt in her own as she looked at me. "Now I feel awful because it's obvious I did upset you immensely," she said.

"Please, don't worry. I'm a big girl—"

Her eyes bore into me. "No, no, it won't do, especially as I can see how tired and... down you look. Depressed even, if that's not too strong a word."

Her stark, blatant words descended on me, stinging like salt on an open wound. With them, a crippling weariness I'd been battling to push away for months darkened over me. Right then, all I wanted was to cover myself with a blanket and sleep, just sleep, shut out the darkness swirling in my mind. Instead, I forced myself to smile and deny the evident truth. "A little tired maybe, but I'm okay."

Aneella shook her head impatiently. "You think I'm buying that? You're clearly in low spirits, and I'm not surprised, with Richard gone. What can I do to help? No, no, don't say anything. Let me think... Of course, I've got it! What you need is a little holiday, and I have the perfect solution for you. Why don't you go and stay at my apartment in Inverness? Rent-free naturally."

"*Inverness*? You live in—"

"Absolutely! You could relax, enjoy the Scottish Highlands, have some well-deserved R & R. Oh, do say yes," she cajoled.

I stared at her, mouth agape. This was moving too fast for me. "But where will you stay if I'm using your apartment?"

"Oh, I have to go to the south for a while. I'll be gone for a few weeks. In fact, you'll be doing me the greatest favour. I don't like to leave the apartment empty for too long. Come on; it will be fun! Maybe when I get back, we could spend some days together, explore the area before you head home. I've barely visited anywhere in Scotland, how shocking is that? It will be an adventure for us both."

She was pulling me fast into her persuasive plans. It sounded heavenly and almost dreamlike. But I vainly tried to resist. "What about my work? I can't let my clients down."

"Take your work with you. You must have a laptop. Work for a few hours, then put it away and enjoy what

Scotland has to offer. What do you say? Say yes," she said breathlessly.

We both knew I would. How could I refuse this unexpected gift? I wasn't in a great place, that much I could admit. I had shut myself off from everyone, even my parents. But I couldn't hold it all in for much longer; I wasn't strong enough. Perhaps a change of air, a short break, was exactly what I needed.

"All right, okay. Yes, I would love to. Thank you. Just for a few days." I smiled, relieved to have had the choice made for me. If I was being honest, though I'd toyed with the idea of a solo holiday, I would never have booked one. I just wasn't the brave, adventurous type embracing this new single life, though I yearned to be her with every fibre within me.

Aneella's eyes widened in delight. "I knew you would go with my fabulous idea! Oh, that's fantastic, Soph. Now I feel so much better for not being around these last few years." She pulled me into an unexpected embrace. I found myself laughing, returning the pressure of her hug, and revelling in the comfort of another person's arms around me after such a long time without.

We spent the rest of the afternoon planning my impromptu trip. Aneella ducked out to buy some wine, insisting I share a bottle with her. I began to unwind as we reminisced over those hazy days of university, digging out some old photos I still had, while playing our favourite songs to which we'd once danced the night away. After Ella's expensive wine bottle ran dry, we succumbed to my cheap supermarket bottle left over from Christmas. We grew drunker and louder by the hour, so much so that my disgruntled neighbours stomped on the floor to complain. The hours flashed by, and at some point we crashed on the sofa as on distant nights gone by, only without Richard stretched out between us.

It was like we had never lived these last ten years apart.

[3]

With my suitcase packed for the morning and instructions to go to Aneella's neighbour at number twelve to collect the keys, I settled down to get some sleep, aware I had a long day ahead of me.

Except my body, it seemed, had other ideas. Hot currents of electric pulses raced round my blood, despite exhaustion making my bones groan. I kept reliving last night and that exhilarating thrill of Aneella turning up so completely out of the blue, a much-needed reminder of my former, happier self. I hadn't laughed or drank that much in a long time. Far too early this morning, she had left in a whirlwind, promising to see me soon, looking all fresh-eyed and dewy—while I had looked like death warmed up on a really bad day.

I was also aware that Aneella had coaxed out of me my deepest fears and insecurities, yet stubbornly kept her own reasons for being in Buxton locked away. It didn't surprise me; it had always been in her nature to distrust others. Yet, if I were honest, truly honest, it had always stung a little how she never trusted me with her thoughts and fears in all the years we lived together, sharing lodgings but never anything of substance. Even after four years, so much of her had remained a mystery, an enigma that could never be puzzled out. Yet one thing had always been evident: her ambition to rise above her own rank, and a ruthless determination in that pursuit.

WHEN I DID fall into a restless sleep, my dreams were full of Aneella and Richard, entwining, moulding until they became one person. I was once again eighteen, so full of naïvety and wide-eyed innocence, walking into my dorm on that first day of university. Aneella was already there, stretched out on the bed she had claimed for herself, with her clothes flung carelessly into the wardrobe and dresser as if she had no concern for them. She looked up as I shyly walked in, dragging my heaving case behind me. I felt her cool blue eyes appraise me, taking in and calculating everything about me before I had even spoken a word. I tried to smile, failed miserably, and found myself unable to stop staring at her cascading ash-blonde hair streaming over her shoulder and the *effortlessness* of her. Breaking my gaze away, I shuffled over to the unoccupied bed, feeling wholly ordinary and colourless beside her, and wishing the ground would swallow me up.

After a few moments of utter silence, where I stared blankly at my case without taking one single item out, a voice as clear as crystal water remarked amusedly, "Do you need a hand? You seem a little... lost."

Her words instantly hit me hard in the chest, and I felt exactly that—lost. I forced out a smile as I turned to her. "I'm not used to unpacking. I know, a bit sad for someone my age."

Aneella climbed off the bed and walked over to me, giving me a sympathetic look. "Why don't you let me help you." It wasn't phrased as a question. "Clearly, I'm an expert in the art of unpacking." She waved at her messy wardrobe with a grin. I laughed in a wave of relief. "I'm Aneella, but my friends call me Ella."

My smile stretched out as I held out my hand without thinking, making Aneella burst out with laughter. I made a poor show of trying to change it into an awkward wave as if it were my intention all along, groaning inwardly. "Sophia."

"Sophia, I think you and I are going to have a lot of fun together…"

Her voice echoed in my mind before receding. My dreams then scattered and dispersed, forming again to take me back to the fateful night which followed that first day.

The night I met Richard.

I had found it impossible to resist Aneella and her determination to enjoy every minute of her newfound freedom away from the "shackles" of her home life, as she put it. She was tempting, persuasive, and addictive to be around, impossible to refuse. All this I quickly discovered.

We had gone to the local student bar where all the freshman had descended like a swarm of ants. If it hadn't been for Ella's firm grip on my arm, I would have bolted for the hills, feeling overwhelmed and hopelessly out of my depth.

We had pushed our way through to the bar, where the surfaces were crammed with empty glasses and sticky with spilt drink. A harassed girl not much older than us with stick-up neon pink hair was trying to keep up with the demand. Ella turned to me and shouted over the noise, "What would you like?"

"Ummm..." I tried to look like I was considering, when, in reality, I was completely drawing a blank. I'd never had an alcoholic drink in my life. What did the cool girls drink? I discreetly looked around me trying to clock one. There was one, wearing cut-off denim shorts and a wispy top, flicking back her super sleek hair and drinking... Smirnoff Ice. "I'll have a Smirnoff, thanks."

Ella raised her eyebrows, "Vodka? I'm impressed."

Vodka?! "Oh, well, you know. If you're going to drink might as well do it in style." I gave what I hoped was a confident smile.

While Ella made her presence known at the bar, I looked around, feeling conspicuous and seriously out of place. The urge to scarper was beating strong within me.

It was then, as I contemplated making a discreet exit and was turning to leave, that my eyes collided with his. My immediate untamed reaction to him, intense and disturbing, had him grinning with a self-assured confidence I desperately envied. He stepped closer to me and was about to say something when Ella appeared beside us, draping a casual arm around his shoulders and planting a kiss on his cheek. His arm came around her, and I found myself staring at them.

"I see Rich has wasted no time in introducing himself to the pretty girl," Ella commented, passing me my drink.

"You know me, sweetheart." Richard basked us both with his wink.

I found my voice. "Are you two together?"

Ella nearly spluttered on the mouthful of cider she had just taken. "Hell, no! Annoying childhood friend who followed me here more like. We would kill each other in seconds if we were together. Isn't that true, darling?" She turned and gave him an intense look that left me doubting her conviction.

"Too true. She is the devil incarnate."

"Shut up." Ella hit him, then let go of him, frowning hard. "Why do you always call me that?"

"Because it's true to the core, and you know it." Richard moved away from her, dropping his arm and giving me his full attention. I found myself nervously smiling as he took my hand and raised it almost to his lips. "What kind of a friend are you, anyway, when you don't introduce us properly?"

There was a flash of anger in Ella's eyes, before she smothered it with a too-bright smile. "This is my roomie, Sophia. Isn't she sweet, innocent, and adorable? This is my bastard of a friend, Richard. I'm sure she would be perfect for you. Maybe turn you into a decent human."

"Wouldn't she just?" His eyes bore into me, making my body feel hot and sensitive. The flush travelled across my skin, making me feel like I needed to breathe cool air. His lips still hovered over my hand, his breath warm, eyes alight with the challenge of conquering me.

No, let me walk away... why can't I... help me... don't

let him touch me, I'll be lost. His lips are brushing my skin—don't... No! Please—

It was my soft moaning that finally dragged me out of my fretful dream. I touched my hot, sweaty hand. The imprint of his kiss still shivered there, and I stumbled out of bed to wash it harshly away.

It had been the same cursed dream that had haunted me for weeks, and I was becoming almost familiar with its damnation. Each time I fought with myself to walk away before he could leave his kiss on my hand. Each time I failed. The inevitably of that continually left me feeling weak, frustrated, and useless. Could we ever change who we are, our reaction to another?

Yet, there was something new tonight that left me inwardly inhaling in surprise.

It was the first time I had dreamed of Aneella.

⁘

FINALLY, after tossing and turning with short, unsatisfying bursts of sleep for the rest of the night, I got up at 5:00 a.m. as the sun began to tease the horizon. After a quick breakfast, I showered, dressed, then packed up the car, determined to shake off my dream from last night. I think I knew if I stopped to think about the rationale of taking this sudden, unplanned holiday, I could easily talk myself out of going. I wasn't by nature a spontaneous person. I planned everything with meticulous precision, weighing up the pros and cons before committing to anything. Only when I was around Aneella did this hidden person erupt eagerly out of me, and now I wanted it to push me on, tell me to *go, go, go.* I badly needed to get out of my own turbulent head, just for a few days. I needed to escape from a heart not yet healed.

⌃⌃⌃

AS THE ROADS carried me away from the never-ending stifling greyness and into Scotland, even my tired eyes couldn't help but admire the ever-changing urban to wild landscape. From sweeping glens and gentle streams to lush green rugged rises and mist-covered mountaintops, its vastness and raw mystery swirled toward me, hitting my senses. The snow-capped Highland mountains peeking out of the clouds were still some way in the distance, yet, somehow, they dominated the skyscape, proud and magnificent and soaring. A need to reach out and touch them overpowered me, making me gasp softly. I wanted to walk amongst them, lose myself in them. Perhaps there, in their overwhelming solidness, I would be able to shake off my pain over Richard. Perhaps there, I could lose myself in their healing powers.

I was so absorbed by my thoughts and the pull of the mountains I didn't clock that I was approaching Inverness. I switched on my satnav, and, for the next twenty minutes, I followed the tinny voice to perfection until I found myself parked up in the apartment's car park, impressed with what I was looking at. The apartments were tasteful and newly built. Optimism swept through me. *Not such a bad place to stay for a holiday,* I smiled.

Taking a deep breath, I climbed out of the car, grabbed

my suitcase from the boot, and began to walk toward the glass-fronted entrance doors.

As I did, the hairs on my neck stood up. I turned around, expecting to see someone coming up behind me. No one was there but me and lots of parked cars. *It must be tiredness.* I shrugged it off, laughing a little at my own fanciful thoughts.

Pushing open the front door to step inside the cool air of the lobby, I pressed the button for the lift, a smile on my face with the thought of finally relaxing after a long, aching journey. With a smooth glide, the lift carried me up.

⁓

ONLY A FEW FEET AWAY, two men sat in the parked blue Volvo watching the dark brunette get out of her car, crank her neck to look up at the apartment block, then heave her suitcase out of her boot and slam it shut. She locked the car and walked up to the front doors.

The one with the camera had already zoomed in and taken a photo of her when she happened to turn and glance their way, a small frown creasing her forehead. The other wrote down her car registration number, then said, "We should let the boss know there's someone new on the scene."

With a nod, the cameraman pulled out his phone and began to dial. As he did, he looked sideways at his companion and commented with a wry grin, "Had a nice-looking arse on her, didn't she?"

For this, he was rewarded with a sharp flick to his

forehead and was told to, "Shut the hell up and focus. This one could be important to us."

Unaffected, he gave a short bark of laughter, winking suggestively as he waited.

The call was answered on the second ring.

[4]

With my ears still buzzing from picking up the key from the extremely chatty neighbour, Susan, I inserted the key into the lock and stepped inside. My mouth fell into a silent "wow."

The apartment was stunning. Putting down my suitcase, I gazed around the spotless, spacious modern rooms, all designed to give the impression of top-end luxury, if perhaps lacking a homely feel. Most striking was the tidiness of it. Aneella had been one of the most careless, messy people I'd ever known. It used to drive me mad and had me verging on a cleaning obsession when we lived together.

Most of what Susan had said to me, in her broad fast accent, had washed right over my bemused self. But I did pick up that no one, apart from the cleaner, had been in the apartment for some time. That had left me confused. I was sure Aneella had mentioned she'd only just left Inverness. Or was that the impression she gave from saying she didn't like to leave the apartment empty?

As if these thoughts were proving too much, a wave of dizziness came over, making me sway on the spot. It was no wonder really, I'd barely eaten or slept in the last twenty-four hours. I caught a glimpse of myself in the mirror overhanging the mock fireplace, then wished I hadn't. My wavy, auburn hair looked limp and tired against my shoulders. My blue eyes showed smudges of darkness within them. I felt and looked like I'd been ironed out all wrong.

A long, blissful hot shower followed by some food was what I needed. And then, *sleep*, blessed sleep.

It was when I was walking out of the bathroom, briskly drying my hair with a soft blue towel, that I spotted it. Cleverly concealed behind a panel painted the same cream as the walls was the distinct shape of a safe. Curiosity piqued, I crouched down and carefully peeled back the panel.

Flip me, it really is a safe! I stared at it, surprised. I didn't know anyone who kept a safe as normal practice in their home.

I leaned forward to take a closer look. The safe was small and discreet, no bigger than what you'd find in a hotel room. It looked perfectly innocent and plain. Yet inside lurked... what?

What indeed? I laughed at my fanciful thoughts. Something occurred to me then. It would be very handy to put my laptop in here when I was out of the apartment. After all, if my laptop was stolen containing my HTML codes, anyone who understood anything about computer languages would be able to copy and forge my programme for themselves.

Over the years, I had learnt to be obsessive about my security, ensuring everything was password protected and fire-walled to high heaven. My customers paid a hell of a lot of money to have unique programmes built for them. I had sensibly transferred every programme off the laptop except the one I was currently developing, and even then, that left me a little anxious. I had been working on this project for five months. It consumed my every working hour. I wanted to be done with it, once and for all, and get it out of my hands. My current client was from a powerful and influential bank and what he wanted from my programme left me feeling nervous, not an emotion I was used to feeling when it came to my work.

Mind made up, I grabbed my phone and texted Aneella, asking if it would be okay for me to have the code to the safe.

While I waited for her reply, I kept busy unpacking my clothes. Opening the wardrobe door, expecting to find some clothes of Ella's still hanging there, I was surprised to find it completely bare. It was the same story when I went to search through the pristine kitchen cupboards. The fridge I had expected to be empty, but not the food cupboards. Surely everyone had the odd sauce jar or packet of pasta lurking around? It was almost like she had never lived here. There wasn't a mark or scratch to be seen throughout the kitchen, the worktops and tiles shimmering with high gloss as if they were brand new.

With a mental note to go shopping for food tomorrow, I was drinking the only liquid available to me, tap water, when my phone beeped with an incoming text. It was from Aneella.

. . .

GLAD YOU GOT THERE! Hope you find everything you need. Surprised you spotted my safe— it's meant to be hidden! Anyway, I guess that's fine to use as there's only a few pieces of sentimental nonsense in there. The code is 080707 x.

I QUICKLY SHOT BACK a text thanking her. A couple of hours later, another text arrived from her.

PLEASE DON'T TOUCH the box in the safe.

I WROTE BACK to reassure her I wouldn't touch the box. After a while, with no further replies, I decided to go out to get something to eat, then relax in front of the TV, thinking no more of it.

It was only when I was dozing off to sleep, my thoughts rearranging themselves, did something in her response strike me as odd. If there were only sentimental pieces in the safe, why would she be concerned about the box?

Then there was the code itself to open the safe: 080707. Why was that so familiar to me… It was the date we graduated, forever etched on my mind, as Richard and I had married the very next day. I could have sworn Aneella asked me only the other night when our graduation date had been.

It was possible, very possible in fact, I was remembering our conversations wrong. After all, it had been a long couple of days, with many hours of focussed driving, and my mind was off kilter.

With a soft sigh, I allowed my eyes to drift closed, letting sleep carry me away.

OUTSIDE, the two men noted down the time of the bedroom light going out, waited half an hour. Then, with no further movements, they started up the car and drove off, only turning the car lights on once they'd left the car park. Two different men arrived at 5:00 a.m., parking in the same place, yawning loudly as they drank their coffee like it was their only saviour. They watched the window as the curtains were drawn back just as the sun ascended. It was 6.30 a.m.

I WOKE UP EARLY, feeling refreshed and renewed in my determination to make the most of this unexpected holiday in Scotland, somewhere that had always featured high on my bucket list. I drew back the curtains to welcome in the early morning sun as I enjoyed my first coffee of the day. The pull of those mountains I'd seen from a distance on my journey up was stirring strong within me, and I wanted to walk within them in the next couple of days.

I also needed food. Hunger was driving me crazy. I loved breakfast and knew I didn't function well without it.

When the clock finally reached 9 a.m., I grabbed my handbag and jacket and scooped up the keys from the table, heading out and making sure I locked the door behind me. As I descended in the lift, I had a niggling feeling I'd forgotten to do something, but frankly, my stomach was growling louder by the minute, and no way was I going back up again on the off chance I had.

Leaving the car behind, I strolled toward what I hoped was the city centre, composing a text to Aneella as I walked.

JUST GOING for an explore around Inverness. Hope you're enjoying it down south. Xx

WHEN NO REPLY IMMEDIATELY CAME, I popped my phone back into my bag and, for the first time, began to take in my surroundings. As I did, a smile spread across my face.

There before me was a wide, beautiful river, the River Ness, where it met the Beauly Firth. Behind the river, nestled by its banks, stood the proud spire of a cross and the twin towers of a cathedral. The bells began to clang as if calling to me, and I ventured toward it.

After ducking into the cathedral's tearoom to indulge in a steaming Scotch broth and crusty bread, I stepped into the cathedral itself. Its splendour took my breath away. The stained-glass windows and its jewel colours were lit up by the sun's rays flooding in. High stone arches curved protectively over the panes, giving a strong sense of security.

After walking around the interior of the cathedral, I sat on a wooden pew and allowed myself the luxury of being still and peaceful. Only when the 11:15 a.m. Friday Eucharist began did I slip back into the bright sunlight outside.

With the rays warming my face, I ambled amongst the streets. The distant sound of bagpipes gave the feel of a city that had stood firm against conflicts fought in the name of freedom. Colourful shops were crammed with enticing goods. Gaelic cafes were awash with charm and character. The Victorian Market was full of old-fashioned nostalgia.

With sore feet, but happy, I finally made my way back to the apartment, my hands full of bulging shopping bags. I dropped the bags down with relief on the lift floor and pressed for level four. As the lift efficiently took me up, I dug around for the keys. My ascent came to a silent stop, and the lift door opened. Hoisting up my bags, I headed toward the apartment's front door.

As I drew closer, it began to dawn on me that something wasn't quite right—the door wasn't completely shut.

Odd. I swore I locked it before I left.

Carefully dropping the bags as trepidation shot through me, I hesitated as I stared at it. It didn't look forced in. What should I do? Go in? What if there were a burglar inside? Or, maybe I didn't shut it hard enough when I left earlier.

Feeling bolder with this last thought, I pushed the door open, more firmly than I intended. As I steadied myself, I looked up.

Only later did I realise that the scream filling the air was my own.

[5]

The startled man spun round, nearly knocking over the side dresser he had been rummaging through. It wobbled dangerously before coming to a shaky stop.

We stared at each other, both too stunned to react. My heart thudded, my throat raw from the scream.

Moving cautiously into the room, I stammered out, "What are you doing here? I–I think you should go before I call the police—"

He took a step forward. I took one back. He was around my age, maybe a little older, and wearing a sharp, grey satin suit. He didn't look like a regular burglar, but I wasn't about to take any chances.

I forced out, "Please, just go—"

"Are you kidding me?" he said, angrily. "You're asking me to leave my own place?" He moved ever closer. I had nowhere to go; my back was pressed against the cold, unforgiving wall.

"Your place?" I managed to get out, while discreetly trying to reach for my mobile jammed in my back pocket.

"No, this is my friend's apartment, and she definitely won't be happy about you trespassing on her property like this."

He cocked his head, staring hard at me. "Your friend?"

The initial panic was turning to anger, surprising even me. "Yes, that's right. Now, I'm asking you to leave, whoever you are. I don't know how you got in."

"Isn't that obvious? With my own damn key. Which begs the question, how the hell do you have my girl-friend's key?" His anger was matching mine now.

My fingers froze over the phone. Something about his indignation began to impact my slow mind. My voice was careful as I said, "What's your girlfriend's name?"

His hands spread out as if to say, Why are you asking me such ridiculous questions?

"Ella. Why?"

I frowned, daring to move into the room. "Ella, as in Aneella?"

"Yeah, that's right. I'm Lyle—"

A sudden disturbance from outside the door forced him to break off. We both turned around. Two uniformed police officers burst into the room, accompanied by a tall, broad man, dressed casually in black jeans and a jacket, his wavy light brown hair swept-back, just on the wrong side of being neat as it curled over his collar. His piercing, blue-green eyes immediately locked onto my own startled ones as he flashed me his police badge.

"What the—" Lyle's voice broke off as the man spun round to him.

"I'm Detective Inspector Armstrong." His deep, rich, Scottish accent was surprising against his stern, unsmiling appearance. He turned to me again, his eyes scanning my face. I was struggling to keep up with spinning events and being the full and unblinking focus of this man's unnerving scrutiny was not helping. "We've had a report of a woman screaming. Was that you, ma'am?"

What could I say to that? I was acutely aware of Lyle watching me from across the room, as well as the presence of the other two police officers as they moved silently around the room, mumbling into radio mics attached to their protective jackets.

"Um, yes, yes, that was me," I admitted, before rushing on as he remained silent and watchful. "But it was a misunderstanding. I wasn't aware my friend's boyfriend was coming to the apartment." I waved a hand toward Lyle as I spoke. "He took me by surprise. Probably an overreaction." I tried to smile, failing miserably. "Sorry you got called out."

There had been a brief flicker of surprise in DI Armstrong's eyes as I spoke. Now he was silent for a few beats, eyes narrowed as he observed first me, then Lyle. I involuntarily shivered. His voice was clipped as he said, "Can I ask who you are and what your connection with the owner of this apartment is?"

I hastily nodded. "Sure, of course. I'm Sophia Meadows. My friend, Aneella Blair, invited me to stay for a few weeks to look after the place and..." I trailed off, unsure how to continue.

He began to move around the apartment, his eyes as sharp as laser beams, his presence filling the room.

"What are you doing?" Lyle demanded, his voice raised to a high pitch.

The answer was spoken over his shoulder without turning around, "Just routine when we've had a call out, to ensure everything is in order and nothing's been disturbed." Giving no opportunity to respond, DI Armstrong continued in the same calm manner, "And you are, sir?"

Lyle was visibly barely hanging on to his patience, and his voice was clipped and agitated as he gave a reluctant reply, "Lyle, Lyle Boyd. And before you ask, yes, I do have every right to be here seeing as I part-own this place with my girlfriend! You want proof? Here, see, my key!" He brandished it before us like it was a weapon.

DI Armstrong stopped and looked at him, until Lyle began to squirm under the scrutiny. "Where's Ms. Blair now, so she can confirm this?"

There was a deafening silence. Lyle's jaw clenched and unclenched as he stared at DI Armstrong before he admitted, "I don't know where she is."

I stared at Lyle, taken aback. How could he not know where his own girlfriend was?

I must have let out a surprised gasp, for the Detective Inspector turned sharply to me. "Do you have any better idea of where Ms. Blair may be, Ms. Meadows?"

I reluctantly shook my head, "Not exactly, only that she's gone south for a few days. I'm calling her later. Shall I ask her to contact you?"

He walked across to me, reaching inside his jacket to pull out a business card. Our hands touched, jolting me. "If you could, thank you. This is my direct number at Police Scotland station, here in Inverness. If I'm not there, someone will take a message for me."

I looked down at the card: Detective Inspector Marcus Armstrong. The card felt hot against my palm.

I raised my eyes to look at him. As I did, something flickered in his own as they searched mine, as if taken aback by what he found there. Something stirred deep within me. I found I couldn't look away, and, it seemed, neither could he.

"DI Armstrong."

We both turned at the sound of the voice, breaking our gaze. Almost immediately, on becoming aware of the presence of the others in the room, I was hit with the reality of my present situation. One of his officers was hovering near the bedroom door, and it seemed to trigger his professional mask to fall back into place. He looked at me again, but not as he had a moment before.

"Ms. Meadows, it would be a good idea to check the other rooms while we are here to make sure nothing has been taken."

Before I had a chance to respond, Lyle, angry sparks flying off him, burst out, "I know our rights! You can't just search our apartment without a warrant."

There was a faint smile on DI Armstrong's face as he mildly replied, "I'm well aware of the law, Mr. Boyd. Rest assured, we are not going to search Ms. Blair's apartment. I merely need to establish nothing has been taken of Ms. Blair's or yours without consent." Those eyes were back on me, as I stood uncomfortably in the middle of them. "Ms. Meadows, are you happy to show me around the apartment so we know it's secure?"

I cleared my throat a couple of times. "Yes, yes, of course. Everything seems to be in order here in the lounge from what I can see—oh, my laptop!" My hand flew to my mouth in sudden fear.

"May I accompany you into the bedroom?"

"Yes." I nodded, distracted, flying into the room without waiting to see if DI Armstrong followed.

The laptop lay in the same position as I had left it on the pillow. "Thank God!" I exclaimed, grabbing it hard against me. If that had been stolen... The thought was too unbearable to contemplate.

"This is your own personal laptop?"

I turned at the sound of DI Armstrong's voice, smiling my relief. "Yes, I brought it with me. I was going to put it in the safe"—my hand waved toward it—"when I left earlier but totally forgot. Don't worry, I won't make that same mistake again."

There was that faint smile of his again. "I'm sure you won't." His gaze moved off me to study the safe. "Are you aware if the safe is in use?"

"Why the hell do you want to know that?"

We spun towards the indignant voice. Lyle was blocking the doorway, eyeballing DI Armstrong.

"As I said, we want to rule out anything being stolen," DI Armstrong replied.

"And I told you, no one has been in here except her and me. No burglars stealing the crown jewels or whatever you think is happening here," Lyle said, waving vaguely in my direction at my mention.

There was silence following this. I dared to look at DI Armstrong as he met Lyle's blazing eyes. There was a sense of control in his face and eyes that I found admirable, despite the unease created by his presence.

"With all due respect, Mr. Boyd." DI Armstrong said, a firm note in his voice, "I only have your word for that." He shifted his attention back to me, making me jump a little. "Ms. Meadows, please, would you kindly contact Ms. Blair to ask her to come down to the station tomorrow? We need her to confirm all of this and fill out a report on any personal items possibly stolen. If it is impossible for her to attend in person, then would you come once you've spoken with her?"

At this point, I was happy to agree to anything, just as long as this disturbing man with his disturbing ways walked out, so I could calm down and lose the burning in my face.

"I will, yes. Thank you." I nodded, my words almost tripping over themselves in their haste to get out.

I forced myself to meet his intense eyes long enough to be considered polite, then looked away before I got caught in the confusing heat again. I felt a rush of relief as he finally headed to the door, officers in tow, telling me he looked forward to hearing from me tomorrow and to Lyle that he would be in touch. Why did those words, said in that way of his, feel like a soft threat? Or was threat the wrong word to use—more so a command he expected to be obeyed?

The door closed behind them, letting the room breathe again. My body felt weird, like something profound had happened I couldn't yet decipher and unpick. Though the conversations had been short and to the point, my brain hurt trying to recall them. My mind grappled with how this DI had managed so successfully to make me feel naked.

I was so gripped by these thoughts that when Lyle's voice cut through them, I jumped, having forgotten he stood there.

"Don't you think that was weird?"

I spun round to face him, "You mean how they turned up so quickly like that?"

Lyle's eyes were narrowed and dark. They looked deadly in this light. I shivered a little and hugged myself.

"Yep, seeing as you'd just screamed not two minutes before," he brooded. "I don't know about you, but I've never known the police to arrive so fast, and certainly never with a Detective Inspector in tow for a suspected break-in. He was way too interested in everything—"

"What exactly are you saying?" I cut in, frowning.

Lyle said nothing for a moment, his scowl making his face turn ugly. "I'm not sure," he said. "But I don't like what just happened."

I stared at him, trying to process what he said. I was acutely aware I was standing in an apartment of a friend who hadn't been in my life for a long time, talking to a man who claimed to be her boyfriend—and a sharp-eyed DI wanted me to come to him tomorrow with answers from her.

A thud of apprehension struck me in the chest, and I dragged in a calming breath to steady myself.

[6]

Sleep was not my faithful companion that night, but this time, it was not because of my recurring dreams.

After Lyle had finally taken the hint and left, I found myself unable to settle. I still felt jittery from having first Lyle, then DI Armstrong, come unexpectedly into the apartment. More crucially, this DI wanted me to reach Aneella, and that was no easy task. I had tried calling her a couple of times and leaving messages. I really wanted to speak to her before I went to the police station tomorrow. I wasn't sure what I could say in reply to DI Armstrong's queries.

Phone in hand, I gnawed at my lip, willing it to ring.

No surprise, it stayed silent.

⌃

I MUST HAVE FALLEN asleep because something woke me with a start, my heart pumping rapidly. My phone was ringing.

Aneella.

I grabbed it. "Ella, thank goodness! I've been trying to reach you!" My voice was breathless as I rushed on, "Listen, there's nothing to panic over, I just wanted you to hear it from me rather than the police or Lyle. When I arrived home earlier, the apartment was unlocked, and for one panicky moment, I thought you had been broken into—"

"Is anything taken? Is my box safe?" she cut in, her voice heightened as she misunderstood what I said.

"Yes, yes, I think so," I said with slight hesitation.

"You only *think* so?"

"No, no, I'm sure of it." I hastened to reassure. "The safe wasn't touched. In fact, nothing was. But listen, the police have been here asking questions about your personal belongings, wanting you to confirm nothing has been stolen. They asked your boyfriend too."

"*Boyfriend?* What are you talking about?" she cut in once more.

That stopped me short. "Lyle. He was here in your flat when I got back from the shops."

"Listen, Sophia," she said, a note of sudden desperation in her voice I had never heard before. "I don't have a boyfriend. I don't have a partner. Tell the police you couldn't reach me. And whatever you do, don't let Lyle back in."

"What?" Perhaps my mind was sluggish from sleep because she wasn't making sense to me. "I don't understand. Have you two had a falling out?" Silence. "He has his own keys, how the heck am I meant to stop him coming in?" I continued, feeling a little trapped.

"Just do what I ask, please." Her voice had grown faint and tinny, and I strained to hear her. Other background noises crackled on the line. "I have to go."

"No, wait!" I practically shouted to be heard. "I need you to come back home to talk to this DI yourself or call him—"

The low hum of the dead tone was my reply. Shaking my head, I called off, then tried ringing Aneella's number again.

It didn't surprise me at all when the phone went straight to her voicemail, but it still left me unsettled. Something about her reaction didn't sit right with me. If it had been my flat with unwelcome guests and police calling, I would have wanted to come straight home and sort everything out. In fact, the police could help Aneella get rid of Lyle, if they had had a violent break up and she was worried by him still having a key. A shiver went up my spine at the sudden concern Lyle had in fact been violent toward her, hence her strong reaction. *But surely, she would have mentioned that to me?* I was sure she would have. It still left me with a bigger problem. How was I supposed to explain her lack of concern to this DI Marcus Armstrong tomorrow when I barely understood it myself? Without doubt, he would be expecting to speak to Aneella, and he struck me as someone who did not let questions remain unanswered, nor was he afraid to pursue them 'til he got his answers. It must have been how he had managed to rise through the ranks to be a DI at such a young age: the tenacity to not give up his pursuit of the truth.

THE NEXT MORNING, after showering and dressing, I ate some breakfast to settle my stomach, which was a funny mass of nerves. I was trying not to think about why I was so nervous about seeing this DI again.

The Police Scotland station was easy to find. I pulled up and looked at its facade, looming high in the air. Its modern glass front and red brickwork was a surprise. I had been expecting to see an old-fashioned rundown building.

Heart tripping a little, I walked into the reception area.

"Can I help you?"

The voice, friendly enough, belonged to a polite-looking female officer sitting behind a front desk. Another police officer hurriedly brushed past me on his way out.

I cleared my throat. "Um, yes, I'm looking for Detective Inspector Armstrong."

The female officer gave a faint smile as she said, "Is he expecting you, Ms...?"

"Meadows, Sophia Meadows," I replied. "And, yes, I think he is. Or perhaps my friend, Ms. Blair."

She gave me a brief nod, then picked up her telephone. I heard her speak into her receiver and tried not to listen in. After a moment, she replaced the phone into its cradle and said, "I'm sorry, DI Armstrong is away from his desk at the moment. Why don't you take a seat, and I'll try again in a few minutes?"

The thought came fast. If I made an excuse that I couldn't wait, it would give me time to try to get Aneella to come after all. The disappointment that rushed through me on realising I wouldn't see him was a feeling I chose to ignore, pushing it hastily away. "Oh, no, that's okay, I won't trouble you. I am in a bit of a rush. Maybe you could let him know that I stopped by, and, unfortunately, I've not had any luck in contacting my friend yet," I lied. "He'll know what I'm talking about."

With that, my cheeks all flamed, I briefly smiled, then turned to walk back out of the door I had only moments ago come through.

The officer called after me, "I'm sure he won't be long, Ms. Meadows, if you wouldn't mind waiting."

I pretended not to hear as I pushed open the door.

The feel of the cool, fresh Highland air felt good against my burning skin. I let out a breath to calm the nerves that were still racing through my body. Only the guilt of one lie. With the best of luck, DI Armstrong wouldn't need to call me at all, so long as I convinced Ella to come straight back home. Simple.

Who was I kidding?

My hand was reaching out to open the car door when determined footsteps came up behind me, stopping within a hair's breadth from me. I could feel his breath caress the back of my neck, and I knew, in that gut-clenching moment, something acute and profound was happening.

"Ms. Meadows, I believe you were looking for me."

My outstretched fingers curled in on themselves. My eyes momentarily closed against the bright, glaring sun, and I could hear my heart pounding in my ears. My body turned to face him fully, in response to his deep, firm voice. His tall presence blocked out the light. His eyes met mine unwaveringly.

My breath caught.

He led me through a confusing maze of echoing corridors.

At last, we came to a bay filled with around ten people, all casually dressed and either answering the constantly ringing phones or speaking in hushed tones to each other. They looked up to stare at me as we walked past.

He led me toward a small office at the back, opening the door bearing his name.

"Please have a seat, Ms. Meadows. Can I offer you a coffee or tea?"

I shook my head as I gingerly sat down on one of two chairs facing his organised desk. "No, thank you. I'm fine."

"Good. I appreciate—"

"Sir, I need you to—oh, sorry, I didn't realise you had company."

We both swung our heads round at the sound of a female voice. A dark-haired, attractive woman stood in the doorway, looking at me in open curiosity and something else I couldn't quite put my finger on. They shared a quick look.

"I'll come and find you when Ms. Meadows and I have finished our chat," DI Armstrong said.

The woman nodded her pretty head and shut the door behind her. I was once again left alone with DI Armstrong, who leaned rather imposingly against the corner of his desk, his arms crossed.

I decided to plunge in while my nerve still held.

"Detective Inspector Armstrong, there's really no need to give up much of your time to speak to me. I don't have anything further to tell you from yesterday," I lied as convincingly as I could, avoiding that piercing stare for as long as deemed polite. "I haven't managed to reach Aneella, but if I do, I'll be sure to call you. I mean, thank you for your concern, but it's really not necessary, I assure you. It's all just a silly misunderstanding, mostly my fault."

I bit down further on any more words spewing out. I was babbling out of nervousness, and I was embarrassed by myself. A surprised breath forced its way out as he unexpectedly sat down beside me, close enough for our knees to almost touch and for me to become acutely aware of his physical presence.

"Ms. Meadows, I appreciate you taking time out of your day to see me."

His polite, calm voice—not what I was expecting—caused my eyes to fly to his.

"That's okay," I stammered, thrown.

"There's something I want you to answer for me."

I didn't reply. I couldn't.

"You seem like an honest, decent person. You have no record in the system," he said.

"You checked me out?" I gasped.

"Aye, I did. My instincts tell me you like to live on the right side of the law, to conduct a good, respectable life. Am I correct?"

I gave a faint nod.

DI Armstrong also nodded and leaned a little closer. "Tell me then, if that's so, why are you currently lying to a police officer?"

I stared at him, licking my suddenly dry lips. "What, uh, what makes you think I'm lying?"

He gave a small sideways smile, as if amused. "Let's just say I have a lot of experience in this area, and people only lie when they have something to hide. So, taking this into account, I'm at a loss here. What should I trust more, my instinct or experience? Because if you *are* lying to me, Ms. Meadows, it opens up a whole chain of dangerous thoughts in my mind as to why you'd feel the need to do so and what it is you're trying to hide from me."

His piercing eyes held mine, waiting for my reply, watching every flicker. What was I meant to say? I felt a little faint as I stared dumbly at him, biting my lip. The urge to tell him what little I did know was fighting to gain supremacy, the truth of my niggling worries about my friend dangling on the tip of my tongue. I even opened my mouth in readiness. But as I did, Aneella's words came back to me, loud and insistent, telling me not to say anything to the police. I couldn't go back on my word.

Standing up abruptly, forcing DI Armstrong to do the

same, I forced myself to meet his assessing, striking eyes full on.

"Look, am I being formally questioned here?" I asked.

"Should you be?"

"No! I've done nothing wrong. I don't know why you're so personally interested in my friend and her possible break-in, when you clearly have officers who could deal with this small, insignificant matter." I gave him a moment to respond, half hoping, half dreading his reply but was met with silence. I took a deep breath. "And you're obviously not going to answer me. So, in that case, I'd like to go home now, please."

He gave a short nod, finally looking away to my immense relief. My heart was still beating wildly, but at least I felt a little more in control.

"You can leave, for now. But I'll be in touch again. Soon."

I swallowed hard, hearing loud and clear what he was saying. I had merely been granted a reprieve.

I gave him a slight nod, absently running my fingers through my hair to draw it back from my face. His eyes followed the movement, his gaze lingering for a moment on my hair before turning away to open the door. I determinedly ignored the sudden warmth inside me and hastily made my escape.

Yet his voice followed me. "I'll look forward to speaking to you again, Ms. Meadows."

I RETRIEVED my car from the police station, purposely keeping my eyes from straying to the glass building and DI Armstrong within it.

As I manoeuvred my way back through the traffic to the apartment, my thoughts raced. The same burning questions were constantly revolving: why were the police so interested in speaking to Ella, and what exactly was in that box in the safe that had her so panicked at the thought of it being taken?

When I finally pulled up in the car park, I tried her number again. This time, it rang and rang without switching to voicemail. I swore aloud.

Letting out a breath, I climbed out of the car and locked it behind me. As I did, that strange shivering feeling came over me again, trickling down my spine and raising the hair on my neck. I looked around. Once again, I seemed to be alone. The air was silent, as was the car park.

Knowing rationally that I was on the verge of becoming unnecessarily paranoid, I nonetheless found myself walking faster than usual into the apartment's entrance lobby and into the welcoming lift.

⌒⌒⌒

MARCUS WAS SITTING at his desk early the next morning, rubbing his cheeks to wake himself up as he fought against the relentless tiredness. He'd come to accept it as an inevitable part of his life, but it didn't make it any easier to bear.

In front of him was his officers' latest notings of Ms.

Meadows' comings and goings into Ms. Blair's apartment. Nothing of significance since Tuesday afternoon, when, finally, his team had the perfect opportunity to gain entry into the apartment without needing a warrant. Marcus couldn't believe their good fortune and had acted quickly and boldly.

Now, he found himself staring at the photo of Ms. Meadows taken a couple of days ago by the undercover officers. *Sophia.* She had thrown them all with her sudden unexplained appearance. In the photograph, her warm blue eyes stared intently at him beneath a small frown, as they had when he'd passed his card to her in the apartment and again yesterday when she had sat in this very office, flustered and in a rush to leave him. *Why had that been? Why act in a guilty manner if you're innocent? Who exactly are you, Sophia Meadows? Should I believe you to be as innocent as you claim?* Her files were blank on their records, showing no previous convictions or warnings, substantiating her protests to this fact. But so was Ms. Blair's, and without question or any doubt whatsoever on his part, she was one hundred percent involved with this fraud. Now, it was down to him to get the evidence to back this conclusion up.

With no relieving answers to his questions, Marcus took her photo—along with Ms. Blair's, which had been taken when she'd hurriedly left the apartment without returning one week ago—and pinned them both onto his working case wall. He found himself staring once more at Sophia as his mind whirled back to when this case had been given to him. Two months to the day.

In truth, he had been restless and keen to make an

impression. His promotion to DI had been surprising and therefore unpopular with some of the detective sergeants, all decidedly older than him and expecting it to be their turn, they having paid their dues. Even now he sensed them muttering about him in the station, urging everything within him to prove his worth to the chief, who'd openly shown his confidence in his new DI. However, Inverness was not a hotbed of crime, and he'd been considering, with reluctance, a move to Glasgow despite his spirit craving the nearness of the mountains. These highlands were in his blood. They were where he had played and roamed as a child, enjoying a freedom many could only dream of.

So, when the call came in reporting unnaturally high activity on a new bank account right here in Inverness, Marcus had almost wept with joy and wasted no time in launching an investigation. Ms. Blair's apartment had been the address listed on the account. The bank activity appeared to have strong connections to a known criminal network whose blackened tentacles reached as far as Ullapool to Glasgow, from Belfast to Newcastle and beyond. Lyle Boyd's name had cropped up briefly before the suspected break-in. Now he was being treated as a suspect and was being followed by one of Marcus' undercover cops.

He felt the burden of solving this high-profile case. If he couldn't find out who the masterminds behind the fraud were, then without a doubt the guys at Glasgow head office would swoop in and take over, leaving him looking inept and incapable. Not to mention ridiculed by the whole station. More so, Marcus loved his country and wouldn't rest until the lowlifes contaminating it were brought to trial and successfully prosecuted.

He couldn't fail in this case. He didn't dare.

So, to that end, he wasn't going to dwell on why there had been a moment, a brief frisson of intensity, when she had looked at him with surprise in her eyes... Surprise, and something far more dangerous to him.

Determinedly, Marcus turned away from those blue eyes that reminded him of the deep, soothing water of the lochs and once more picked up the reports spread out on his desk.

THE WHISTLING of the kettle almost drowned out the knock on the door the following morning. I looked up in surprise, hesitating for the briefest moment, before going to open it.

"Oh!" I exclaimed, feeling immediately wary.

Lyle gave me a funny look as he lounged against the doorframe. "Expecting someone else?"

"Yes... No. That is, I wasn't expecting you." I tried to pull myself together and not show my apprehension curling around inside me, instead latching onto sarcasm. "Not using your key today?"

I recoiled as Lyle boldly gave me a long, appraising look. "I didn't want to catch you unawares. But I am expecting you to invite me into my own apartment."

And without waiting for an answer, he moved past me to force his way inside.

[8]

As I watched him make himself at home, I remained at the front door, trying to gather myself. There was something very different from the angry, defensive Lyle of yesterday. He had, once again, caught me off guard, putting me at a disadvantage. This he was all too aware of.

Now, he bestowed the full force of his smile on me. "Don't just stand there, come and sit down. This is as much your home as mine right now."

Carefully, I walked over to him and perched cautiously on the edge of the sofa where he was sprawled out. The fact that I was alone with an unpredictable man didn't escape my notice. Aneella's words of *"Don't let him back in!"* came back to me in a rush. Her warning was clear and something I had taken heed of. But what could I do?

Lyle looked at me with amusement, "I don't bite, you know."

"I'm sure you don't," I said.

He laughed. "Then try not to look like I'm about to pounce on you. Relax!"

I let out a breath. "You have to acknowledge that, although you're Ella's boyfriend, the first time we met was yesterday. And that was hardly in normal circumstances."

My eyes caught the clench of his jaw, giving me a sharp reminder of yesterday.

"Has Aneella been in touch?" I continued before he could reply, "I haven't managed to get hold of her today. Have you had any better luck?"

Lyle shook his head, seemingly unconcerned. "No, but, you know, we give each other space. She's not one to be tied down. We don't keep tabs on each other."

I frowned. "Surely you're as eager as I am to reach her?"

Lyle sat forward, his eyes fixing hard on mine. "Why?"

I half laughed, half gaped. "You're joking with me, right? Of course she needs to come home, so she can sort out all this misunderstanding and talk to the police."

He gave a scoffing laugh. "There's no need for her to come running back. We can handle it."

I shook my head, stunned, but didn't reply. There was a pregnant pause as we both eyed each other.

"Listen, we need to talk about yesterday, only not here. I don't know about you, but I've got a sudden thirst on. Get your bag," Lyle commanded.

I wanted to tell him where to go. The last thing I desired or wanted was to spend time with this cocky, perhaps dangerous man who seemingly cared little for my friend. Yet the more rational and sensible side of me forced its way through. He might be able to answer some questions playing on my mind if I handled this carefully.

⌒⋏⌒

THE IDLE AND Wild bar we pushed our way into was surprisingly full for 11:25 a.m. on a Thursday morning. I was immediately hit by the sound of loud chatter and laughter. Slick-looking office workers enjoying an early lunch jostled alongside indulged, privileged wives with no need to rush anywhere. Fresh-faced students leaned nonchalantly against the bar while slowly nursing pints of beer. In my jeans and striped top, and looking far older than the young and keen office workers, it was impossible not to feel out of place in this arena. My choice, if I'd been given it, would have been one of the more traditional, friendlier pubs we'd passed on our way here.

Lyle was already making his way to the bar. I followed behind, looking straight ahead to avoid the curious glances cast my way.

"What can I get you?" Lyle asked, turning to me with an expectant look. I played it safe by asking for a Coke and had to bite down on a smile when I saw his shocked face.

After collecting our drinks, we pushed our way back through until Lyle found us a spare table. I sat down. Taking a sip of Coke, I discreetly watched Lyle as he tapped his fingers on the table, his eyes on everyone but me. There was no doubt he was good-looking. I could see why Aneella would have fallen for him, with his slick-backed hair and smooth-shaven face. He was once again dressed in a suit and crisp white shirt, partly unbuttoned. Yet, he was so different from the men Ella had gone for at university. There, it had been all about ripped jeans and holey jumpers, leather jackets and trainers. She could never resist the bad-boy type. I remember one phase specifically during our first year of university, which was spent hanging round a grungy rock band. The lead singer had had the hots for Ella, and she'd been more than happy to encourage it, which meant that I was dragged along to countless rundown pubs so they could gaze, snog, and maul at each other while I pretended not to watch. That was, until Richard finally decided to put his claim on me after leaving me dangling, wanting him, in some kind of sick amusement.

Don't think about Richard.

I forced myself to the here and now. Lyle was giving me that assessing look again, and it wasn't a comfortable feeling. He leaned forward with his glass in his hand. "So, I want to ask you something."

"Go on," I cautiously replied, taking another sip of Coke.

"How come Aneella asked you to look after our apartment?"

How did I answer that? Not with the truth. There was no way I wanted him to know anything about me and why I had needed this break. "I think she wanted someone to stay in it while she was away."

Was that vague enough? I hoped so.

Lyle's eyes narrowed as he continued to appraise me. "If so, why?"

"I don't know. Sometimes we ask friends on a whim to do something for us, don't we?" I tried to keep my voice light and neutral.

"Perhaps. But that doesn't really answer my question."

I stared at him, then shrugged my shoulders. "I don't know," I repeated, refusing to be drawn in.

Lyle took a swig of his drink. I looked down and sought refuge in my own. The tart sweetness hit my mouth before sliding down my throat.

"Did she give a reason why the apartment needed a friend to look after it? Or perhaps to look after something within it?"

I had the distinct impression he was angling to extract information from me. Didn't he realise I knew no more than he did?

"As I said, I think it was simply a desire for your apartment not to be left empty, along with wanting me to have the opportunity to visit the Highlands. Kind of her, really, wouldn't you say?" I boldly added, "And of course, kind of you too," I smiled as charmingly as I could, lifting my Coke as if doing a toast.

Lyle was looking none too happy. Finally, I'd gained the upper hand. While the tide was in my favour, I decided to run with a couple of questions of my own. "So, how long have you guys been together? Ella never mentioned you to me."

A flash of anger sparked in those eyes before he smothered it and was charm parse. Admirable, fascinating, and a little disturbing.

There was a boastful smile on his face as he said, "I was a little secret, the tryst our bosses didn't need to know about."

I frowned. "You work together? Where?"

It was very clear that he didn't want to answer my

question, but having dug the hole, he now had to crawl his way back out of it. "A bank, in London. I doubt you would have heard of it."

"I often travel to London, so there's a good chance I have," I replied.

He ignored me. "We don't publicise our relationship, as you can imagine. I'm sure Aneella would prefer you didn't mention us to anyone."

"On that, I think you are both of the same opinion."

Lyle looked startled. "What has she said about me? About us?"

Suddenly, an overwhelming tiredness descended over me, and I wanted nothing more than to leave. I really didn't want to be mixed up in whatever somewhat twisted and toxic relationship existed between them. I also didn't like the look in his cold eyes. What I wouldn't give right then to disappear into the mountains and breathe in the fresh air.

Caught up with this tantalising thought, I found I was standing before my mind had fully realised my intention. In my haste, my hand caught my Coke glass and the last dregs of the drink spilled on to the glass table. Lyle caught his vodka before it also became a casualty, while I hurriedly grabbed a serviette to mop up the spillage.

He flew to a standing position. "What the—"

"Sorry, sorry," I rushed out as I dropped the wet serviette on to the table and grabbed my handbag. "I need to go. I'll speak to you soon."

As I turned to fly out the door, I caught the eyes of a man standing on the other side of the bar window. His intense gaze took in the scene: first me, then Lyle, seemingly spending a cosy time together.

Then, eyes narrowed, DI Armstrong gave me a brief nod before disappearing.

An unnecessary guilt overwhelmed me, slashing across my face and causing my heart to thud painfully.

[9]

The streets of Inverness were quiet as I touched over their surfaces, deep in thought. Although I looked straight ahead, I failed to notice the rustling canopy of leaves above me, the distant sound of ringing church bells calling its people to mass, or the sweeping brush of the hunched-over road cleaner as he passed me by.

What plagued my mind was that DI Armstrong had seen us together. And why was that? Was it because I didn't want to appear to be close to Lyle? Or that I cared far more than I should about what this detective thought of me. And if so, *why?*

I shook my head, hoping to clear my agitated thoughts away. When that failed, I abruptly stopped on the pavement, causing a young mother and child behind me to collide into my back. I rushed out an apology as the child burst into an impressive, ear-piercing wail of indignation. His mother gave me an angry, reproachful look before scooping up her bawling child and barging past me.

Deciding to give them breathing space, I waited a few minutes before continuing to walk, noticing my surroundings at last. I gazed around, enjoying the peace of the solitude and the feel of the sun. Spring, now in full flow as it neared its way to summer, had encouraged the lush green leaves to unfurl from their winter hibernation. The air had finally let go of the worst of the coldness and was enjoying an unseasonably warm temperature.

Feeling lighter in mood, I shrugged off my jacket and tilted my face up. The sun felt so good I could stay like this.

But a sudden, cold chill swept down my spine, diminishing the warmth. I shuddered, feeling a quake within me. Slowly I turned around to look behind me.

A man was watching me, unrecognisable, indistinguishable. On seeing me clock him, he swiftly turned and walked rapidly down the street where I had just come from.

I felt a gut-wrenching immediate fear, the kind I'd never felt before. This man, a stranger, had me in his sights, and I had no idea why.

Taking a deep breath, I attempted to calm myself by talking rationally. I was being paranoid—of course he wasn't watching me. Too many late-night crime TV shows were messing with my jittery thoughts.

I exhaled a half laugh, half cry. Wrapping my jacket tight around me, my feet began to speed through the now-crowded, bustling streets until they reached the safety of the apartment.

Standing in the middle of its chic sparseness, I still had

the oddest feeling that I was being watched. Feeling very silly but unable to stop myself, I checked all the rooms, making sure nothing had been disturbed, especially at the safe, aware of Ella's concern for the box within it.

The safe stood as silent and unassuming as ever.

No, wait, hold on.

The panel over the safe didn't look right. It was as if someone had tried to push it back into its original position but hadn't done a very successful job.

I knelt before it. I knew I hadn't opened the safe, Lyle hadn't given me the chance.

My mind raced with possibilities. Perhaps while I'd gone to grab my bag, Lyle had made his way in here. But, no, my bag had been in the bedroom, and I would have noticed if he had followed me in. Maybe I hadn't placed the panels back the first time I looked. *But I did... didn't I?*

I made myself walk into the kitchen for something to do and gazed without seeing into the near-empty fridge. An overwhelming urge to call DI Armstrong took hold. My hand hovered over his business card where it sat on the kitchen work surface.

The kettle I didn't remember switching on began to whistle, inadvertently stopping me. My hand dropped away, leaving the card untouched. Instead, I reached for the half-full bottle of wine sitting on the side and poured myself a healthy measure.

I WATCHED the sun rise early in the sky, as it did here in Scotland. 5:05 a.m. glared out from the bedside clock. After tossing and turning for a while longer, I got up around 6:00 a.m. I sat, nursing a coffee, curled up on a seat gazing out of the kitchen's apartment window over the stone-clad houses and lopsided chimney stacks, enjoying the view.

My phone alerted me to an incoming text. I reached over for it, hoping it would be from Ella. It had been nearly three days since she'd last messaged me, and I would feel a whole lot better if I heard from her.

Disappointment coursed through me as I saw it was from an unrecognisable number. Who else would be up at this ungodly hour like me? I clicked on it.

It's Lyle. Call me.

I GASPED, the sound reverberating around the echoey room. How had he got hold of my number? That fact alone was enough to shake me. I didn't want to read it, yet I found myself doing exactly that.

Underneath the command was a thinly veiled threat; I could feel it trying to drag me in. More and more, I could understand why Ella had warned me away from him. Apprehension mingled with anger. The anger won.

I slammed the phone down on the counter without replying, went to the bathroom to take a fast shower, and pulled on the first clothes my hands grabbed. All I cared about was escaping these walls.

It was exactly 6:35 a.m. when I firmly shut the apartment door behind me, a rucksack filled with drinks, snacks, and a waterproof jacket.

THE MAGNIFICENCE of the scene before me was mesmerising. The caps of the mountains were still stroked with snow, but the mountainsides themselves were bursting with new life. The richness of the green contrasted against the delicate, pale pink common spotted-orchid and wood anemone flowers. Once awash with spilt blood from battles against the English, these mountains were now wreathed afresh with these tiny flowers alongside gentle streams and roaring waterfalls. The slopes were solid, real, mighty, and proud, as they had been for thousands of years and would continue to be long after I had stopped walking on them.

I stood looking up, thinking, This is what matters, this ground beneath our feet, taking us far away from the small claustrophobic world we entrap ourselves in. Here, the earth didn't put any demands on us, it didn't care what we were wearing. It just wanted us to enjoy its stunning grace and walk over its soft-cushioned grass.

I needed to walk on that grass.

Determinedly, I switched my phone to silent before jamming it into my jeans pocket, grabbed my jacket to wrap against the chill of the early morning, locked the car, and then set off on foot toward the flat base of the mountain range, known locally as Munros.

I had a vague sense of where I was. I'd taken the road south from Inverness, hugging close to the famous twenty-four-mile-long Loch Ness, whose watery expanse was over a mile wide according to what I'd read on the internet last night. The water seemed to hold a mystery all its own. I had stopped to gaze over its misty surfaces, staring hard in case I might see the Loch Ness Monster rear up, all the while amused at myself. On a whim, I had carried on toward Cannich, travelling down what seemed to be "the beaten track." And I was so glad I did, for now I could touch the mountains instead of being teased with a distant glimpse.

As I let my feet carry me up the old rocky path that weaved slowly along the Munro, I began to feel a release, a sense of letting go. I'd never felt anything like this before. A sensation of a heavy burden being lifted away, effortlessly.

On I walked, though my legs protested, letting the narrow path lead me along its intriguing twists and turns, successfully taking my breath away as it teased me with the full vista yet to come. Occasionally, I caught the faint, twinkling sound of a gentle stream flowing nearby.

A little out of breath from the exertion—no doubt the result of too many hours spent hunched over a laptop—I forced myself to carry on until two hours later my weary feet finally reached the summit of the rugged mountain. Jubilation alongside staggering awe burst inside me as I was rewarded with the most magnificent view my eyes had ever feasted on.

Around me, everywhere I turned, were proud and dominant mountains, reaching far higher than where I stood on this relatively small one. It seemed as if they were touching heaven where the clouds invited them in. I couldn't see the tips of their sharp peaks.

A distant eagle gave a piercing cry. The cool, unrestrained breeze circled around me, cooling my hot, puffed out cheeks.

I could live here. I could feel at peace here.

I sank down onto the ground, hugging my knees, greedily drinking in everything being offered to me, the peace and solitude it afforded me with no demands of its own. My heart sang with thanksgiving. I so desperately needed this, a brief calm against a silent storm which raged inside me unnoticed.

A movement from the mountain closest to the one where I sat caught my eye. I frowned hard, trying to focus on what it was. I let out an astonished gasp. Before me stood a regal stag, its horns long, twisted, and dangerous; its body hard and strong; and its fur smooth and beautiful. It stood poised, unmoving, as it locked eyes on me, challenging me as to why I had stepped into its territory. I held my breath, not daring to move in case I frightened it away, though in truth I was more in awe of its presence than it of me.

Richard would have loved this.

The thought pushed its way in—uninvited, unwanted, and yet, so naturally.

A rush of acute, overwhelming anger swept over me, shocking me even while I embraced it. Anger at him for walking out on me and our ten-year marriage, as if I had meant nothing to him. Anger at myself for letting him bring me down so low, hollowed out and mistrustful of love yet needy for it. Anger that I had, until now, pushed all these emotions down to remain unacknowledged and unattended, but far from gone.

I let out a loud, anguished cry that echoed around the

silent mountains. Birds flew up in panic, the stag turned and bolted from me. But the mountains remained steadfast against my torrent, soaking up my pain.

"I hate you for what you've done, Richard," I cried out, "for what you've done to me. But I won't let you bring me down anymore. Do you hear me? No more!"

As the words tore their way out of me, I let the tears come for the very first time as I accepted Richard was gone. He was gone. He had taken his love from me, had gotten what he wanted. I wasn't enough; I had never been enough. It was time that I faced this brutal truth if I was ever to move on.

I'm not sure how long I sat there as the sun climbed higher into the sky and the new day became fully born, just as it had for thousands of years and would for thousands more. It didn't matter, not really. What mattered was that when I climbed slowly down the mountain, my heart felt stronger, my mind clearer, and my spirit lighter.

THE KNOCK on the car window jolted him crudely awake from the nice doze he was having. Vigorously rubbing his face, he stretched out and unlocked the door to let his partner in who was carrying, rather precariously, two coffee cups and fat-laden bacon rolls oozing with tomato sauce.

"What the hell are you doing sleeping on the job?" came the sharp rebuke as arms and legs clambered in beside him. As he reached out to grab his bacon bap and much-needed coffee, yawning and ignoring the biting comment, he happened to glance toward the apartment's front door. His mouth froze over the bap he was about to take the first bite from. He frantically waved his hands around, spilling hot coffee over them both, causing swearing and oathing to escape from them both for different reasons.

"What the piss—"

"Look, man!" he practically shouted as he pointed wildly toward the man they had seen entering before, now lurking near the entrance before sliding in through the doors. His partner swore again as he dropped his own bap onto his lap, tomato sauce spilling out over his leg.

"Call it in. And you'd better pray he never knows we nearly missed it."

⌒⌒

I ALMOST BOUNCED out of the car when I pulled up about an hour later, a smile upon my face even though my whole body was gloriously shattered. I began to whistle a tune, slightly off-key, as I walked in through the entrance doors to the apartments, amused at myself. This felt like the old me, a me who hadn't seen the light of day for a very long time. Perhaps the mountains held a magical, healing air.

Grinning, I entered the lift and waited for it to take me up. The lift swished to a stop and the doors opened. I stepped out toward the front door of the apartment where I stopped sharply.

It took me a full moment to understand I was not

alone. Still another for my smile to die away and my heart to start beating erratically as my eyes connected with his.

10

We stared in equal horror at each other. Then, he moved like lightning, barging past me from where he had been coming out of the apartment and raced toward the back stairs used only in emergencies.

"Wait! Stop!" I uselessly called after him, hearing the panicked note in my voice. I moved to the top of the staircase, but all I saw was the flash of a dark jacket. A dark jacket exactly like the one worn by the man watching me in the street yesterday. God help me, it was the same man. None of this was coincidence or in my imagination.

Icy fingers began to creep their way up my body.

I took careful steps back over to the ajar front door. Gingerly, I pushed it fully open, worried someone else was still in there. When no one jumped out at me, I breathed out in relief. But my heart thudded painfully as I forced myself to walk further into the chill of the lounge. Everything seemed exactly as it had when I left a few hours ago, nothing disturbed. After a few minutes of standing there uselessly, I carefully ventured into the kitchen. Again, all was as it should be. Lastly, I stepped into the bedroom.

I cried out sharply. In disbelief, I crouched down in front of the exposed safe where the panels designed to conceal it were now nothing more than broken, useless pieces of jagged wood. My hand flew to my mouth as I stared at it in shock.

"Hello? Ms. Meadows? Are you in here?"

My head flew up.

"It's DI Armstrong. Is everything okay?"

DI Armstrong! My feet scrambled to get off the floor, and I rushed to the doorway of the bedroom. He stood a few feet from me with a small frown on his face, looking solid, real, and unquestionably safe.

His voice was full of concern. "Your door was wide open, otherwise I would have knocked. I wanted to—"

Without thought or conscious decision, a gut-wrenching instinct took over. He caught me just in time as I flung myself against him, wrapping my arms tight around his neck. His body was still against mine for a moment. Then his arms were around me, holding me steady. I would have stayed like that, his warmth easing away my coldness, but he was already gently pulling me back to better scrutinise me with that piercing look of his.

Embarrassment washed over me. "I'm sorry, I–I don't normally fling myself at men like that. It was the shock and the man and the broken wood—"

"Okay, take a wee breath, there's no rush," he said, a faint smile hovering over his lips. "And ach, don't worry. It's not every day someone is genuinely pleased to see me arrive uninvited. More likely, they're running away from me as fast as their legs can carry them."

I broke out in a surprised laugh, taken aback by his desire to put me at ease. The faint smile grew a little wider.

"Feeling ready to tell me everything now?" he said.

I gave a shaky nod. "I think so."

"Good. Now start from the beginning and in your own time." DI Armstrong pulled out a notebook from the inside of his jacket. "Don't hold anything back. It's often the smallest of details which carry the utmost importance."

I began by telling him about the man I'd seen yesterday, and how I was sure it was the same man who'd been here in the apartment today. He gave nothing away, his face a professional mask as he asked me questions, all the time keeping his eyes fixed on me. We moved through to the bedroom. I was acutely aware of how intimate it felt, he and I alone in there. I stared at his broad back as he bent down to look at the broken panels, before pulling out his mobile phone to snap a couple of photos. When he had finished, he turned his head toward me as if sensing my eyes following his every move.

"The safe is still locked, so whoever it was gave up or you scared him away before he could decipher the code. What concerns me most is that he knew precisely where to find it."

He turned fully to me now, and I felt the breath rush out of me, already anticipating what his next words would be. "Have you managed to talk to your friend, Ms. Blair, yet?"

And so, it had arrived—my time to choose. Whichever route I chose, I would either be laying myself wide open to a barrel of questioning or a breaking down of trust between friends.

As if sensing this conflict, DI Armstrong rose up and took a step toward me. I searched his face as he held me in a steady gaze. In that moment, something gave way in me, an acute need to trust and not carry my worries for Aneella alone. I stepped closer still, making him frown, though he didn't move back.

"Marcus," I said. There was surprise in his eyes at the use of his first name, but he said nothing, letting me continue. "I need to know that I can trust you. Really trust you." Without conscious thought, for I would never normally dare to do such a thing, my hand reached out and laid itself on his chest as if it belonged there. My eyes didn't leave his face. "Can I?"

The air grew thick around us as he stared at me, a strange array of emotions clouding his eyes. In his hesitation, I began to regret my words, my bold touch. I went to pull my hand away only for his to cover and still it, his warmth radiating through my skin.

My eyes shot back up to him. There was a fierceness in his gaze I hadn't seen before, whipping away his normal cool reserve. His Scottish accent grew thicker as he said, "You can trust me, Ms. Meadows. You have my word on that."

There was no doubt of his sincerity. All I could do was take him at his word and pray this was the right choice. I doubted Ella would think the same when she found out about my cooperation with the police. But this was getting out of control and surely having the police on our side could only be a good thing? I had no way of knowing whether this burglar and stalker was an opportunist who wanted to hedge his bets on something valuable being in this safe, or if something more sinister was afoot here. I couldn't shift this feeling it was all connected to this mysterious box kept within the safe. I prayed Ella herself was safe. If her apartment had been broken into, then this could mean that whoever this man was might well be tracking her whereabouts even as we spoke.

My words rushed out of me like a tornado. "I had spoken to Aneella before I came to see you. I'm sorry I lied, sorrier than you know. But she asked me not to talk to you."

"Me personally?"

I shook my head, "No, 'you' as in 'the police.'"

"Aye, I see." I could see his mind whirling away, processing that. He eased his hand gently off mine then walked back over to the safe. "Ms. Meadows—"

"Please, call me Sophia," I rushed out while my courage held.

There was that faint smile again. "Sophia. Do you know if there is anything of value in this safe?"

I came to stand beside him. We both looked down at the safe, and as we did, gut instinct once again kicked strong within me. "I have the code," I found myself saying. "I don't know when Aneella is coming back, so I think it's time we opened it to check what is inside." I turned to look him squarely in the eyes so there could be no misunderstanding. "I'm willing to take full responsibility on Aneella's behalf for opening it and happy to sign anything you need me to testifying to that. Right now, her potential anger with me is the least of my concerns."

"Then, with your permission, let's open this safe."

11

Crouching, we both stared into the darkness.

I could make out a small box held together with a red ribbon, sitting all alone in the safe.

I realised then that I had been preparing myself for something much more... sinister. A short laugh escaped me. Marcus turned to me, a querying look in his eyes.

"I thought there would be something more dangerous in there," I explained with a small smile, shaking my head.

He frowned. "Don't be misled by a seemingly innocent box. Sometimes they carry the greatest harm."

"Oh," I faintly replied, feeling suitably chastised.

"When you're ready, bring out the box."

Nodding, I did, drawing it out and putting it down on the floor between us. Sitting back on my haunches, I untied the ribbon before pulling out the contents one by one. My eyes were immediately drawn to a pretty silver heart locket. I laid it in my palm to open the clasp. There, on one side of the heart, was a miniature photo of a man with sandy hair. He seemed oddly familiar, like I'd once known him. Bemused, I softly closed it and placed it back in the box.

Next to me on the floor was a photo of Aneella and me from our university days. We were standing outside the campus, arms around each other, grinning madly. In the background, you could make out Richard and a couple of other university friends pulling silly faces. Swallowing hard, I turned it over, not wanting Richard's eyes on me. When I did, I paused, thrown. There on the back were the words,

I'm sorry.

Sorry for what? To whom was the apology? And was it written by Ella herself? I wondered why she had kept it in the safe. It was only an old photo.

"Would you mind opening this book for me, so we can have a look?"

Happy to be dragged out of my thoughts, I looked over to see what Marcus had in his gloved hand, held out toward me. It was a small black address book. Reaching for it, I began to slowly flick through the pages. Each alphabetically indexed page had numbers scrawled along the top next to addresses I didn't recognise, hastily written by the look of them. The numbers seemed to be grouped into fours, some the same, others different.

"Any idea what those numbers may be alongside the addresses?"

I gave a slight shake of my head. "No idea. They seem too long for the numbers in a postcode and too short for phone numbers. It's a little strange, don't you think, to have this in your safe if it's only an address book?"

"Mm," was his non-committal reply. Then, "Okay, I'll need to take all of these items to the station with me."

"You want to take it all away?" On hearing this, my heart leapt in trepidation. How did I not realise this was what Marcus would want to do? I had conveniently forgotten he was a DI who'd come here for reasons he hadn't divulged. I'd been so relieved to see him, I never thought to ask why he was here in the first place. Now, I didn't know how to broach it without appearing odd, especially after he had been so patient and understanding when I needed it the most.

Marcus's eyes trapped mine. "This is probable evidence, Sophia, against a man who followed you yesterday and quite possibly on other occasions you weren't aware of. A man who then broke in and entered this apartment without your consent. That is concern enough for me to want to look further into this address book and other items within the box, and why I need you to come with me."

"What?" Still dazed by the starkness of his words, I struggled to follow what he was saying.

Patiently, Marcus repeated himself, "I need you to come with me to the station. We'll take your statement, starting from the moment Ms. Blair contacted you. I'll also need your fingerprints to rule them out and your signed permission as agreed." Seeing my look, he leaned a little closer, ensuring I was looking right at him. "When I said you could trust me, that wasn't a mind game to get what I wanted. God forbid I should ever be that kind of police officer. But that part about trusting me? I need it to begin now."

I felt myself give way to him. Surely, I wasn't wrong in trusting this man before me, who had gone from being someone to avoid to the only solid person in an ever-changing, fast-moving tide?

I stretched out my hand still holding the address book toward him. Marcus reached out to accept it with a nod, understanding exactly what I was saying without the need for me to utter a word.

MY HEAD WAS close to exploding from all the questions being fired at it. My back was crying out to be stretched and released from this hard-backed, plastic chair. My throat was as parched as a desert, and I could almost fantasise a cool glass of water filled with ice and lemon right there before me on the cheap Formica table.

We sat in a cheerless, nondescript room, with just one sorrowful-looking potted plant in the corner. There was one slightly streaked window looking out over the red rooftops from where we sat on the top floor.

Could be worse, I thought humourlessly. At least I wasn't locked up in an interview room being mistaken for a criminal.

I must have looked as I felt because when Marcus next looked up from the notes he'd been making, whatever question he had been forming died away on his lips. There was a sympathetic look in his eyes as he said, "Aye, you know what, I think we'll call it a day before you collapse on me. Not quite part of the service we aim to offer here."

I groaned in relief, my head slumping forward to

almost hit the table, with my arms rescuing me just in time. "Oh, thank goodness." I peered up at him through narrowed eyes. "I pity every criminal who has had the misfortune of being interrogated by you."

Marcus raised an eyebrow, amusement lurking in those blue-green eyes of his. "I'll take that as a compliment."

"You do that, you do that."

"Would bringing you a coffee I should have offered an hour ago help revive you before you head home?"

I managed to raise my head enough to nod in reply. "Yes, unless you want me slumped on your table all night."

This time Marcus laughed. The unexpectedness of it caused a strange sensation within me. I felt a smile tugging at my lips.

"I'll be back with that coffee," he said before walking out of the room.

Left alone, those throbbing doubts of whether I had made the right decision to trust Marcus began to rear their way back up again. To distract myself, I got up from the chair and began to wander around the small limiting room, arching my back as I did. The realisation that I had absolutely no idea what would happen next when I left here was too stark for even me to ignore.

Biting my lip, I pulled out my phone, half hoping, half dreading Ella would have texted or called me. There was neither... Which meant I would have to call her to confess what I'd done. I let out a shaky breath, nerves kicking painfully in my stomach.

The door swung open. I looked up with a smile, only for it to fall away in confusion. Instead of Marcus standing there with a mug of coffee, it was the young, dark-haired woman from the other day, who'd come bursting in when I had been in Marcus' office. She wore the same lanyard badge as Marcus, so it wasn't hard to guess she worked alongside him. For some reason, the smile on her face didn't quite meet her eyes, leaving a coolness to the air.

"DI Armstrong has been detained on a phone call. He asked me to bring you a coffee," she said, offering the mug to me.

I stepped close enough to reach for it with a polite smile and said, "Thank you."

"I'm Sergeant Morven Atkins. I work with DI Armstrong. Mind if I sit down for a minute."

It appeared not to be a question. Not waiting for my assent, Sergeant Atkins sat down while watching me in an unsettling way. I felt obliged to sit opposite her, cradling my coffee. I had the oddest sensation I had somehow offended her—no, that wasn't right. Rather, I had ruffled her feathers by stepping in her lair.

"DI Armstrong doesn't normally interview witnesses himself, certainly not twice. You must be a special case."

Her comment hit exactly where she'd intended it to. A frown spread across my forehead though I kept my voice neutral. "In what way?" I asked.

Her fingers tapped the table with an impatience that seemed to seep from her pores. I seemed to be annoying her but found myself not overly concerned as to what this woman thought of me.

She continued to stare at me. "Where are you from? You're certainly not from these parts."

"Near Buxton," I answered reluctantly. A slight

bending of the truth but close enough not to raise suspicion. I took refuge in my scalding hot coffee while giving the door a discreet look, willing Marcus to come back. To think I had thought he was a tough questioner. *Come back, Marcus, all is forgiven.*

The ticking of the clock filled the tense air. Still, I sipped my coffee; still, she stared at me; still, I willed the door to open, bearing the reassuring presence of Marcus. We remained suspended in this uncomfortable moment, waiting to see who would speak next. No surprise to find it wasn't me.

"So, what exactly is it that you're helping DI Armstrong with?"

That had me swinging my head up in surprise. I had presumed they were working together on this case but clearly not, from this comment. It was, however, evident she wasn't happy about being left out in this way. Knowing that Marcus hadn't shared this with her only made me trust him that little bit more.

My mind raced to think of an answer that would satisfy her but drew a big fat blank. I stood, causing the table to sway a little. With the threat of coffee spilling all over her tight-fitting trousers, Morven pushed back from the table in alarm, giving me the opportunity to say, "Do I have to remain here, or can I go?"

Her eyes narrowed as she took in my flushed cheeks. "No, you're free to go. You're not under arrest."

I nodded. "Please tell DI Armstrong I'll be in touch." Without waiting for a reply, I turned around and walked swiftly to the plain grey door to yank it open. Release swept through me with every step taking me farther away from those narrowed steely eyes.

I glanced at my watch. 3:30 p.m. How could it still be so early? I felt like I had lived this day already. Tiredness bit away at me, slowing down my pace. I wished for one tantalising minute that I hadn't come to Scotland. *But then I wouldn't have met Marcus—*

Where on earth had that come from? I couldn't afford to start having lingering thoughts about him, even if the feel of his chest beneath my hand still lived in my mind. Disconcerted, I quickened my pace and forced myself to think about what I should do next.

I needed to call Ella, that much I knew, even though my heart sank at the thought. She would see this as betrayal, and she would be right, even if her reasons for not wanting the police involved made no sense at all. Maybe, just maybe, I could convince her that Marcus could help her.

But even though I believed that wholeheartedly, I was still unable to explain why he was so interested in the items in her safe or why he had been there in the apartment moments after this second break-in. It was too late to ask him now.

All I could do was trust he was on my side.

MARCUS EYED his subdued officers standing before him with a look that would have sent most men cowering. They, at least, had the sense to look suitably nervous and scolded.

"Tell me, how the hell did this happen?! An unidentified man gains access to the apartment right under your noses, and you only report it *five minutes after*? You were meant to be watching over her—the apartment—every minute of every hour." *Too close.* Too close to unintentionally slipping out why he was really so angry with them, to the point he was fighting the urge to punch something. A vivid sense of her in his arms, clutching him tight, was making him clench his hands so hard by his side it was turning his knuckles white. "That is sloppy work. Sloppy, careless work. And aye, know this, no one on my team works at that unacceptable level. If they do, they'll find themselves back in uniform patrolling the streets of Inverness and picking up litter before they even know what's hit them. *Do I make myself understood?*"

"Yes, boss," they muttered.

"Sorry, boss," one of his men had the courage to mumble.

Marcus dragged in his breath, then when he felt calmer said, "Right, I want to know who this man is, who he's working for, and why he wanted to get into that safe. And I want to know what those numbers in that address book mean. Go."

They scarpered, fast. With a sigh, dragging his hair absently away from his forehead, Marcus turned back to his desk. His eyes connected with the photo of Sophia on his working wall.

"Damn!" He'd left her in the room. With Morven. And coffee. Most likely eaten alive.

With a sudden bounce to his step, he rushed out of the office and straight into Morven. She reached out to steady herself with a hand on his chest. The look in her eye when she touched him made him immediately wary. He stepped back carefully once she was steady, forcing her hand to fall away.

Her eyes turned cold. "Your suspect—sorry, *witness*—bolted. Must have been the coffee."

[12]

As I entered the apartment, it felt like the room was holding its breath too.

In a bid to put off the call to Ella, I walked into the kitchen to make myself a quick sandwich. My stomach was gnawing away at me, which was most likely because I'd forgotten to eat again.

My thoughts drifted to Marcus as I ate the plain ham sandwich without really tasting it. I was painfully aware of my constant thoughts of him.

I was pushing the now-empty plate away when my phone began to vibrate in my hand with an incoming call of "Number Unrecognised." I cautiously answered it. "Hello?"

"Was the coffee that bad you had to do a runner?"

I felt an unexplainable relief mingled with unexpected joy at the sound of his voice. Smiling, I said, "It was pretty awful. But no, that wasn't why I did a runner."

Marcus paused on the other end of the line, waiting on me. Should I speak the truth, I wondered, then found myself doing precisely that. "It was more to do with the questioning I received after you left."

"Ach, aye, Sergeant Atkins can be a little... intense. Apologies, I got tied up with something of importance, and she offered to take it in for me. I hadn't realised she would stay with you."

I sank down onto the sofa. "No, well, I take it all back about you interrogating criminals. You should leave it to your sergeant. She's like a terrier with a bone that refuses to let go."

I could hear him laughing quietly, though too professional to respond. There was a brief pause before he said, "I wanted to update you. I've been looking into Lyle Boyd. Has he, at any time, told you where he is working?"

I cast my mind back, trying to recall. "I think he mentioned that he and Ella met at the bank where they worked, but it had all been kept hush hush—their relationship, that is. Why do you ask?"

"An interesting piece of information has come my way, which I feel is right to share with you. Apparently, around two months ago, Lyle was fired from the same bank where Ms. Blair works."

That stunned me. *"Really?* He kept that quiet. I wonder why?"

"Aye, precisely. Has he been in contact with you?"

"Weirdly, he texted me this morning. I have no idea how he got my number," I said, pausing, thinking hard. "He wants me to call him. What should I do?"

Marcus' voice held a firm note to it when he said, "Call him, but when I'm with you. Can you swing by the station later today or tomorrow?"

I wanted to say, T*oday, I'll come today*. The thought rather unnerved me, so I made myself say, "Tomorrow is better. I'll come see you in the morning."

As I walked up the steep hill toward the police station the following morning, I felt my gaze turn with longing toward the tantalising view of the distant mountains. I knew I hadn't even begun to touch the surface of this beautiful area filled with mystery and solid earthiness. I'd read the lochs were a must-see. The water, it was said, was as clear as crystal glass shimmering in the light.

I could do with the environment's restoring powers this morning, especially after another restless night. Every night sound, it seemed, was determined to wake me. After talking with Marcus yesterday, I'd finally plucked up the courage to call Ella, my heart hammering the whole while. Yet, I needn't have worried. It seemed Ella wasn't answering my calls. Or couldn't, which was far more worrying. I left a rambling message to call me back urgently. *Please, just let her be okay*, I had repeatedly prayed in the night.

I stood in front of the police station. The now-familiar police officer at the front desk buzzed me through, and I made my way up to Marcus' small, neat office after a couple of helpful pointers along the way.

He was sitting in front of his laptop, his profile to me. I could see a frown creasing his forehead as he concentrated hard on what he was reading. His hair looked slightly rumpled, like he had been absently raking his fingers through it. His shirt sleeves were rolled up, exposing the skin of his muscled arm. In that unguarded moment, I felt something kick and stir in me in a way it hadn't since Richard. I saw him, truly saw him, for the attractive man who had the ability to make me react in this instinctive way. I was caught.

Staggered by my reaction, I stood still, unable to tear my eyes off him or move from the spot. Marcus, becoming aware of my presence, turned his head, and our eyes connected. For a breathless moment, we simply looked at each other. Then he smiled. My breath inhaled as I watched it transform his face. I wanted to feel that smile on me again and again.

He stood up, his smile drawing me into his office, drawing me to *him*.

"I wasn't expecting you this early on," Marcus said, indicating the chair I last sat on, only this time he sat opposite me.

"I know, I'm sorry," I apologised, feeling a faint flush on my cheeks. "I was up early." I looked away, before turning back to him. "I'm not sleeping so well at the moment," I admitted.

Concern flew into his eyes. "Why is that?"

I bit my lip. "Because every time I close my eyes, I think that man is going to break in through the door," I said, my throat closing up around the words. I think saying the words aloud, finally admitting them, hit me harder than I anticipated. I could feel tears prick my eyes and hastily went to wipe them away. As I lowered my hand, it was caught by his.

"I don't want you to feel afraid," his voice was strong,

earnest. "I'm not going to let anything happen to you. Remember the trust we talked about?" I nodded. "I want you to trust me on this. I'm only ever at the end of the telephone, any time, day or night."

"I presume you sleep at some time, though?"

"Aye, every once in a while, my AAA battery runs out. I just plug myself in, recharge, and I'm good as new."

I laughed. "Thank you," I said, my tone more serious again.

Marcus nodded, smiled, then let go of my hand. I had the briefest feeling of being watched from a distance but brushed it quickly aside, too much focused on this man before me to be concerned.

"Ready to do this?"

I took in a breath to collect myself, then nodded. "Ready."

Marcus led me to a different nondescript room than before, though with the same featureless, bland interior. I pulled out my mobile as soon as we sat down and grasped it tight to steady me. I watched him reach for his notebook.

"How should we do this? What do you want me to say? Strangely enough, I've not had a lot of practise at this," I said, giving a small humourless laugh.

"We'll let him lead the conversation. We're going to put it on speakerphone, and I'm going to record what you both say."

I was back to biting my lip, stalling. "What is it you suspect him of? Suspect them both of?"

Marcus drummed his fingers as he tried to form the

right words, finally saying, "I can't go into details with you, especially as you are a witness and possible…"

"Suspect?" I finished for him.

He gave a little nonchalant shrug. "But you're being incredibly helpful and cooperative. I really appreciate that, Soph," he finished smoothly.

I just had time to register the shortening of my name before he was down to business, once more the DI. "When you give the nod, we'll press record and dial Lyle's number. Make sure you connect it straight to speakerphone. Understood?"

"Yes, yes I've got that."

"Then I'll write down questions for you to ask as we go. Ready?"

I put my mobile onto the table and found Lyle's number in my recents. On my nod, Marcus pressed record as I touched the dial, hitting the speakerphone option. The phone only rang once before Lyle's brash, impatient voice filled the room.

"You took your time coming back to me."

I looked at Marcus as I replied, "Sorry, this is the first opportunity I've had to call you."

There was an annoyed sigh. "Why didn't you pick up last night when I rang you?"

"I had the phone on silent," I lied, Marcus giving a small nod of approval. I watched him scribble fast. His note read:

ASK HIM WHY HE CALLED.

. . .

"W<small>HY WERE</small> you trying to reach me? Have you heard from Aneella?"

"I was going to ask you the same. Even I'm pissed off now she's gone off the radar and not picking up. Who does she think she is leaving us hanging like this?" he said.

The force of Lyle's anger hit us through the phone's wire.

The scribbled words came fast:

H<small>E'S ANGRY</small>. Use that. Keep pushing him.

N<small>OT ASKING MUCH THEN</small>... "I know, it's completely out of order. The least she could do is tell us when she's coming back." A part of me felt shameful I was playing along with bad-mouthing Ella, worried as I was for her. Yet another part of me acknowledged that there was truth in what I said.

"You sure you don't know where she is? I really need to speak with her—"

"Why?" I cut in, acting on instinct. "What do you need from her?"

There was a pregnant pause. Marcus and I shared a tense look. Had I pushed too far?

"It's personal. Let's just say she's got something I need. Listen, I've gotta go—"

Panicking, I jumped in, "Hold on! Wait!" Marcus furiously wrote on his pad before holding it up for me to see. I stared at him for a long moment, then found myself speaking his words. "Will you not see Aneella at work? I thought you worked together."

"I've... had a change of circumstance. A difference of opinion, let's call it."

I ploughed on, unable to stop myself now, "So, what you're saying is, you haven't seen her since—"

"What does it matter? I haven't seen her, end of story. Remember to call me when she makes contact."

And with that, the phone line went dead, the low tone resonating off the walls. We turned and looked at each other, both frustrated and inwardly cursing. Lyle had managed, cleverly and precisely, to tell us absolutely nothing we didn't already know. We were still at square one. But one thing of which I was now certain: Lyle cared more about getting into the safe then his supposed girl-friend. His voice had been devoid of any concern for Ella.

And that unnerved me more than anything else.

⁓

MARCUS SAT BEHIND HIS DESK, staring without seeing, his thoughts full of her. His eyes drifted to where she had sat, the chair still warm from her presence. He again saw the tears in her eyes, seemingly genuine, affecting him far more than he could admit to. His mind was full of conflict, the need to remain professional and distant fighting against his growing concern for her safety. He was acutely aware she was placing her trust in him and by doing so, pulling him ever closer to her.

He'd meant what he said to her, that she was under his protection. No harm would come to her, not on his watch.

He was acutely aware of the exact moment this sudden, overwhelming need to protect her had begun. It had been the day he'd walked into the apartment to find her shaken up by the second attempted break-in. On seeing him, she had thrown herself into his arms as if he alone was her protector. Something had shifted in him then, something profound, which he had refused to examine more closely until now.

Yet how could he possibly protect her when he wasn't certain of her involvement in the case? Was it already too late? Were the lines blurred by his own unguarded reaction to her?

LATER, after leaving Marcus and grabbing some lunch, I jumped into the car and headed out toward Drumnadrochit, once more hugging the edge of the mysterious Loch Ness. The need to feel the refreshing air of the mountains and the calm it brought to my mind again was urging me on. The earlier downpour had cleared away, and now the sun was fighting its way back through the parting white clouds.

I felt my body begin to unwind as it let go of earlier tension. I wound down the window to breathe in the pine scent. The light shimmered like stars on the loch's water as it hugged the road beside me.

I found myself wishing I could have brought Marcus with me. Somehow, I knew he would feel as at ease in these mountains as I. There was still so much hidden behind those focussed eyes of his to unlock. So much I—

A magnificent, proud hawk chose that moment to sweep over the water, skimming it as it caught its unsuspecting prey of salmon in its beak. It was enough to jolt me from my ponderings, which in truth was no bad thing. I wasn't a fool. I knew I was no more than a helpful witness to him. I would be leaving soon. It would be better to keep this growing attraction for him buried deep.

Rather than going into Drumnadrochit itself, I took a snap decision to head away from Loch Ness. The road became narrower, twisting and turning as it pleased.

My breath stilled as I rounded the next corner. There in front of me was a stunning oasis of calm: a small yet majestic jewel of a loch. I parked up in the small car park and burst out of the car.

The small, discreet tourist sign proudly displayed the name "Loch Meikles." It helpfully showed me a route to walk around the loch, and on impulse I pulled out my phone to snap a picture of it. I noticed I had no signal, and rather than alarming me, this cheered me up. It was... liberating.

As I followed the slightly rocky, jagged path meandering around the loch itself, I gazed at the sapphire water reflecting the sky above. It was as if the skydome had been painted over loch's calm, flat surface. I stepped as close as I dared to its inviting edge. Its water was clear, and I could see salmon and smaller brown, speckled fish warming themselves on the surface, their mouths hungrily opening before diving back down again.

For the next hour, I allowed the surrounding beauty to absorb me and enjoyed the luxury of not being on guard or fearing I was being watched. The wind rustled the leaves in the canopy above, and the sun warmed my skin.

I found myself once more at the signpost. With no desire to rush off, I lowered myself onto the leafy ground, my back against the surprisingly comfy wood-framed sign, and took out my phone. I made a poor job of capturing the beauty of the loch and laughed at my appalling results before putting it back away.

I found that I couldn't keep my eyes open. No doubt the lack of sleep over the last few nights was finally catching up with me. The sound of the water and the gently rustling leaves lured me into a sleep I didn't attempt to fight against.

I'M NOT sure what jolted me awake—the crack of a branch, the hoot of a passing car perhaps. I scrambled up, my mind disorientated and my bones slow to respond. My eyes blinked against the brightness of the sun as my mind struggled to place where I was. I shook my head, rubbing my eyes with the palms of my hand.

Footsteps were coming toward me from behind.

The crunch of a stranger's feet had me spinning round, trying to see who it was. My heart beat wildly, erratically. Blood pounded in my head from getting up too quickly. Darkening clouds now eclipsed the sun, and I had to screw up my eyes to see through the dim light.

It was a man. Of that I was sure.

He was coming closer. He was coming straight for me.

My mind told my body to run back toward the car. But somehow my feet were uncooperative, and—

"Sophia? Is that you?"

At the sound of my name, I swayed on the spot and probably would have fainted if it wasn't for two arms reaching out to catch my fall.

"Well, that's a first and no mistaking."

Marcus was looking down at me, an amused smile curling the corners of his mouth as his eyes crinkled up. I found myself gazing up at him, dazed. Until, that was, the fog began to lift, and it dawned on me we were on the ground, I sprawled awkwardly over his legs and the beginnings of excruciating embarrassment flushing my cheeks.

"What?" I stuttered, trying to push myself up. The pressure of his firm legs against me was too evocative, and I needed to move away from him. Fast.

Seeing me struggle, he propelled me up until I was in a sitting position against him, his voice rich with humour as he explained, "Having a girl faint on seeing me. Aye, definitely a first." I groaned—because of his words or the fact the world still spun around me, who could say. Marcus, on a roll, kept his arms around me as he continued, "I had no idea my looks could cause such a reaction in a woman. It's either from being staggeringly good-looking or being so hideous it was too much to bear. I don't think I'll pursue which one is the truth."

Hearing me groan again, unable, it seemed, to form any intelligible words for fear I would reveal my attraction to him, Marcus frowned. "Are you hurt? You're looking a wee bit pale, if you don't mind me saying. And a bit odd. Sorry," he added on seeing my affronted look.

I found my voice then. "I mean, anyone would be!" I said indignantly, without explanation, brushing stray leaves off my grubby looking jeans. "What the hell are you doing here?"

"I could ask the same thing," he said.

"Going for a walk, of course." I glared at him.

"Then why were you sitting on the ground?" came his mild reply, completely unfazed by my look.

Ever the detective. I found myself justifying my actions. "I'd stopped to have a doze. I told you earlier I haven't been sleeping well—"

"I remember."

"Well, anyway, your footsteps must have woken me. Hold on." Eyes narrowing, I pointed an accusing finger at him, anger replacing my earlier embarrassment. "Are you following me?"

Rather than give me a straight answer, he subjected me to a piercing, intense scrutiny that left me feeling like I was being stripped bare. His voice was calm as he said, "Should I be following you?"

Frustration seeped out of me. I resisted the urge to stamp my foot like an impertinent child. "I'll let you be the judge of that. You have to decide if you can trust me, just as I made that choice about you."

With that, I scrambled inelegantly off the earthy ground and marched toward my car.

I was fumbling to unlock it when his voice stilled my hand.

"I live here. My house is a few minutes down this path."

I turned to him, eyes widening in surprise. Marcus shrugged a little, revealing a hint of vulnerability mingled with frustration in being forced to this point. "Is that enough demonstration of trust in you, Ms. Meadows?" he commented dryly.

I was taken aback by my own boldness urging us on to a new, deeper level as I softly commanded, "If you take me there, yes."

"You want to see my house?"

Too late to lose my nerve or examine my reasons. "Yes."

"Why?"

"Why?" *Why indeed?* "Because then I'll know with utter certainty that you're not following me because you believe I'm involved in whatever it is you suspect Lyle of. Because I'll know you trust me beyond a detective inspector befriending a witness to get what he wants," I said, swallowing as he stared at me, his eyes full of hidden thoughts I was not party to. My voice dropped to a low whisper, vulnerability replacing my previous pride as I forced myself to admit, "And because your home may be the one place, the only place, where I can feel completely safe."

Where those last words came from, I don't know, not really. Maybe, somewhere deep within me, I needed to grasp onto something warm and solid. As we stood there, surrounded by staggering beauty, something began to shift and stir between us that couldn't be pushed away.

I had laid myself bare before him, even though I'd vowed never to do that again. The next step was Marcus'.

⛰

A SENSE of nervous excitement coursed through me as I walked along the leafy, damp pathway beside my silent companion. I had left my car where it was parked by the loch.

We came to a stop. Before me stood a fairly large wooden lodge. It had a veranda, cleverly positioned to look out over the loch upon which I had spent the last hour gazing, and which was now within reach. I could see an outside fire urn next to two chairs covered with a warm and inviting red-and-blue tartan blanket.

"Wow," I gasped, staggered.

"Not what you were expecting from a stuffy-looking strait-laced detective?"

I turned to Marcus, who was looking at me, eyebrow cocked. I couldn't tell if he was teasing me or being serious, so I settled for middle ground. "Not what I imagined any detective from Inverness would be living in, strait-laced or not."

"And cunningly answered as any good detective would, neither confirming nor denying. Perhaps you missed your calling, Ms. Meadows." There was the tiniest of grins lighting his face.

"Perhaps I have, Detective Inspector Armstrong."

We both gazed at each other for a moment. Marcus

broke first, turning his head away to stare at his lodge, before returning his eyes to me. His smile was gone and was replaced with cautious, conflicting features, internally battling against this decision of his to bring me here. My smile faltered, acutely aware what position I'd put him in by my sheer will and determination. Guilt swept over me sharply. I needed to let him off. I wasn't playing fair.

His hands came to rest lightly on my shoulders, the warm pressure pulling me out from my confused, tumbling thoughts.

"You need to understand, before I take you inside, that we're stepping over a line. *I'm* stepping over a professional line I've always taken pride in not crossing—"

"Why are you?" I cut in, stepping closer to him.

When he didn't answer, stubbornly holding back, I sighed and stepped away. He caught my hand. I stared up at him as his thumb stroked over my fingers, making them tingle. His head was bent, watching the stroke of his own hand, and his voice strained as if his next words were costing him dearly. "It seems you've found a way under my skin, into my thoughts. Your trust, for reasons I won't allow myself to contemplate, has become very important to me," Marcus said, shaking his head before raising his eyes to meet mine, taking me in. "I want you to feel safe with me."

My heart contracted a little, and I found I had to swallow. My fingers captured his own. "I do feel safe with you, Marcus." After a pause, I smiled, wanting to help him relax. "And I'm really looking forward to finally having a decent coffee."

[14]

I gazed around as I followed him in. We walked directly into a lounge full of comfy sofas surrounding a large fireplace, dying embers still lingering in its grate. I took stock of books haphazardly sitting on walled shelves, an oak table with yesterday's mugs on it beside what looked like scribbled notes. Marcus switched on some modern lamps, as the light had begun to dim. Their light brought an added warmth and cosiness in which I felt immediately relaxed.

An open doorway led off to a bedroom—mostly taken up with a wood-framed double bed covered with a blue-and-grey striped duvet— with what appeared to be an adjoining bathroom. The kitchen, its pale wood in keeping with the flooring I stood upon, was beside the lounge and the whole area was open-concept. Throughout was the subtle feeling of a feminine touch: coloured, matching cushions, a warm wool rug on the floor near the fireplace, candles absently set in a couple of places.

But whose female touch?

My eyes flew to Marcus' left hand, as he waved it in the air to show me the lounge. I nodded, all the while searching his wedding finger. No ring. I let out a breath. So, not married, but that didn't mean he didn't have a partner.

"So, this is my humble abode. Ach, probably not the most glamourous place you've stepped into."

He gave me a funny, lopsided smile coated in self-consciousness. Wanting to put him at ease I confessed, "My flat in Buxton is hardly high class, trust me. My sash windows are something from the dark ages, letting in every conceivable cold draught, even in the middle of summer, and forcing me to wear arctic clothes 365 days of the year. Believe me, this is pure luxury in comparison." Marcus gave a short laugh. I hesitated, before adding, "I like it here, in your home."

He looked surprised for a moment, before giving me a warm smile that caused my insides to do a funny turn. "You should smile more," I found myself blurting. "It lights you up from within and everyone lucky enough to be touched by it."

As soon as the words were out, I regretted them, feeling ridiculously silly. My cheeks flushed.

Perhaps sensing it, perhaps not, Marcus' hand reached out to touch my cheek with the lightest of strokes, before falling away. "That's quite a compliment. Thank you, I think. Trying not to dwell on the fact you seemed shocked I can smile. Needless to say, I don't have much to smile about at work, so maybe it is a wee rarity to glimpse one."

I found myself relaxing again. "Perhaps that's why it's taken me aback. It's the same as Scotland suddenly encountering a heatwave or at least one day without any rain."

"No mocking of my birth country. We are a proud nation, remember that well." He gave me another of those raised eyebrows. I felt myself smiling as Marcus continued on his roll. "Tourists flock here in their thousands to sample all that earthiness our pure rain brings to our valleys and Munros. But before I turn all proud and noble Highlander on you, I should probably go make us some drinks. What can I get you?"

"What do you have?" I asked.

Marcus walked into the kitchen, his voice almost lost as he stared into his cupboards, "It's not looking too promising, I have to say." His head popped up. "Ah, I can probably stretch to an instant coffee, might even have some tea bags down here somewhere." His head disappeared into the cupboard again.

"Instant coffee is fine," I hastened to reassure, biting back a grin.

He emerged, looking relieved. "Let's just hope there's milk, otherwise it will be long black all round. I really need to do some food shopping," he muttered to himself.

"If I'd known, I would have brought my own supply," I quipped.

Marcus filled the kettle up then placed it on an old-fashioned Aga stove to boil. I raised an eyebrow in surprise. He shook his head, "Don't ask. One of those grand plans at the time, until it comes to the practicality of having to light the damn stove every time I'm in need of a coffee."

I laughed, all the while aware I'd never heard Marcus talk so much about everyday, mundane things. This meant he was either accepting of my coming into his home and trying to put me at ease, or still feeling tense in stepping over his own fierce professional lines and was now overtalking to compensate. I think I preferred the first option.

"Take a pew if you like," his voice carried to me. "As you're here, I might have a couple more questions for you, if that's okay."

"Oh, yes, sure. If I can help, I will."

I moved back into the lounge, unable to stop myself from doing a wide arc of the room, so I could have a nosy at some of his photos and books. Most of the books were factual, telling me how I could solve such and such, manage such and such, or delve into forensics and crime-solving procedures. But every once in a while, a well-thumbed fiction thriller or action book was thrown in the mix and somehow that made him all the more human.

I lowered myself into one of the sofas and found it invitingly comfy, so much so I had to resist the urge to curl up and close my eyes. Instead, to keep alert, I picked up the nearest magazine to hand, bemused to find myself glancing at a motorbike magazine. The kettle began to whistle, and I heard Marcus moving about as he made our coffees. His gaze fell on me a couple of times. I knew because my body became more alert, and I had to fight the vain desire to smooth down my hair.

"Do you take sugar? We're in luck by the way, there's milk and, even better, it's in date."

I looked up, eyes wide. "Oh-kay, going to trust you on that. One sugar, thanks."

As he came over with two steaming mugs, I put the magazine back where I found it. Marcus sat on the armchair near me, and it was evident we were both grateful for the excuse to sip our coffee for a moment as we gathered our thoughts.

I went to place my mug down on the table near me, and as I did, my eyes caught and fixed on a black and white photo. My heart dropped in sudden, overwhelming disappointment. For there before my stunned eyes was Marcus, dressed in a full, dazzling tartan kilt, kissing the cheek of a stunning bride as confetti fell like raindrops around them.

Catching my stunned, frozen look, which was difficult to miss, Marcus turned his head to follow my eyes. His body stilled.

"You're married!" I gasped, unable to help myself, feeling pain at his betrayal though he'd done nothing to justify it. Even so, ugly feelings of jealousy reared up inside me.

Without turning from the photo, as if he too were unable to look away from her beauty, Marcus swallowed hard and said nothing for a moment, as he tried to control an emotion I couldn't read. Then, "My wife, Lucy. She... passed away three years ago. Cancer."

The unconcealed pain and desolation in his voice told me everything. His heart was still grieving. Shock rippled through me along with immeasurable guilt that I had brought her up because of my own silly jealousy.

"I'm sorry," I whispered, turning to him. "So sorry you've suffered this huge loss, and I was insensitive enough to bring it up." I shook my head, seething at myself, looking down into my coffee.

Marcus closed his eyes for a moment, swallowing hard, "Don't be. You weren't to know."

"But even so…" I trailed off helplessly.

He breathed out, then turned to me. The effort it had taken to control himself showed in the strain of his eyes. I wanted to hold him, stroke those lines away, but instinct told me that this wouldn't be welcomed. So, I sat on my hands and gave him a few precious moments to compose himself.

When he had, it felt right to ask him what his questions for me were. Obvious relief swept through him in being allowed to move away from his wife and back onto firmer ground where he was in control.

"I need to ask you whether Ms. Blair ever talked about her job with you, such as what role she performed at the bank or who her manager was. Anything like that at all."

I shook my head, leaning forward. "No, she didn't. You must understand that until I ran into Ella a couple of weeks ago, I hadn't seen her in over ten years. We were close friends at university and lived together for most of those years. But after we graduated, Richard and I got married, and we all went our separate ways."

At the mention of Richard's name, there was a flicker in Marcus' eyes. He frowned, leaning forward. "Your husband? Richard, did you say? I hadn't realised you're married, you don't have a ring on. Should he not be here with you?"

Just tell him quickly. "He, um, left our home—left me—about a year ago. I've not heard from him since, except through our solicitor. I doubt he would be worried if he did know."

I heard the bitterness and bleakness in my voice and had to stop talking. This time it was me swallowing hard and Marcus, watching intently, allowing me a moment to compose myself.

"Well, it sounds like this ex of yours is a prize roaster."

"A what?" I repeated with a shocked laugh, dispelling my dark thoughts instantly.

"Roaster, aye. The word for an idiot in my native Gaelic. You know, Soph, I haven't met this man, but it sounds to me like he didn't deserve you. If you're not treating your wife with the utmost love and respect and ensuring she never doubts you or your marriage, then, bottom line, you don't deserve her."

I stared at him, momentarily lost for words, moved despite myself. "Your wife was a very lucky woman, to be loved as such," I murmured.

He held my gaze, a hint of a smile on his lips, before breaking away to reach for his mug. I found myself doing likewise, feeling... what? Flattered, touched, wishing for more, wanting to know with an almost-feverish desire what it would be like to be loved like this.

"Anyway," I continued, clearing my throat, "Ella was always the popular girl. Everyone wanted to hang out and drink with her. Even the lecturers adored her." I gave a short, humourless laugh. "Needless to say, I didn't have the same effect on people. I was always amazed Richard went for me and not Ella, and when she graduated with honours, that took all of us by surprise, seeing as she was barely present at the lectures and was always asking me to help write her essays. Maybe she sweet-talked her way into getting the exam results—I'm joking!" I hastily added on to my ramble, seeing Marcus' expression.

"Mmm," was all he commented. "What happened after you left university?"

"Life. Life happened," I shrugged nonchalantly. "I guess those days of university are not real, not really. Sooner or later, real, gritty life comes crashing in."

I took a much-needed sip of coffee and found that each time it tasted surprisingly better. Marcus' mind appeared to be whirling around, his detective cogs no doubt turning as he took pieces from what I said to help him form a picture. I wish I knew what pieces I was giving, and why. Being kept in the dark was an uncomfortable place to be.

"When was the last time you saw her, before you met last week?"

That was easy to answer. "My wedding day. She was my chief bridesmaid, though she seemed to enjoy certain parts of her role more than others. Managed to get me very pissed on my hen party and kissed by a few blokes— not a nice experience, trust me on that. But when it came to actually organising the finer details and keeping everyone in line on the day... not so good. She was in a funny mood that day, distant," I recalled, shaking my head, my mind casting back to that fateful day I chose to marry a man who would not love me as my heart desired. "I never really got to the bottom of it. Ella drifted away after we got married, and, after trying for years to keep in touch, I simply gave up in the end. Richard told me I was wasting my time, and he was probably right. She could be so obstinate. In many ways, she hasn't changed one bit."

As I finished speaking, a renewed fear took hold of me. My eyes sought his for reassurance as my teeth anxiously bit my lip. "Do you think she's okay? What if she isn't answering my calls because she ca—"

His hand moved swiftly over mine to stop me saying what I most dreaded. "We have no reason to believe she's in any kind of danger," he said.

I tried to nod and smile, failing at both as I forced myself to take a further step into my darkest concerns. "And am I...?" I let the sentence trail off.

Marcus hesitated. And, by that one reaction, confirmed my fears.

"God help me." The words burst out of me, my body trembling with shock at being faced with this brutal reality I hadn't expected him to confirm. I covered my pale, cold face.

I felt the sofa sink next to me, his hands gently extracting mine from my face.

"Sophia, Soph, look at me."

When I complied, I was met with a firm, solid gaze that brought me immediate comfort.

"I won't let anything happen to you." The words were delivered with conviction and calmness, designed to reassure me. "That's a binding oath of a Scotsman who eats his porridge every day as long as he's remembered to buy milk."

On hearing my surprised laugh, he grinned before sobering again. "Keep trusting me and don't linger on anything else. I need you to stay your normal calm and level-headed self because I need you to help me solve what those numbers in the address book are. Think you can do that for me?"

I stared at him. "Am I... Am I allowed to help you in that way?"

Marcus smiled faintly in that way I had come to know so well. "I'm not meant to be doing many things I'm doing right now. What I should be doing is talking to you in the police station and having that address book sent off to our forensics team for analysis by the end of day today. I'm still planning to send it off in the next couple of days, along with a couple of other items from the safe. But my gut instinct tells me you can better understand these numbers than any expert we have on our team," Marcus said, jabbing a finger toward his chest.

"Because I'm a programmer?"

"Aye, exactly for that reason. You clearly have a head for numbers and codes to do the work you do. More crucially to me, even though you haven't seen each other in ten years, you still know Ms. Blair better than anyone here in Inverness. So," he took a short breath, held me in that gaze of his, "will you help me, Sophia?"

I felt like I was standing, once more, on the top of the mountain I stood upon yesterday. There, in front of me, was a higher, more challenging peak that would demand much from me if I climbed it. In contrast, below lay the flat valley, predictable and safe, a place I could easily run to. Which way should I go? What choice was right? Toward Marcus and all the stirring emotions he brought, but by doing so risking more than I could guess? Or toward home, away from the danger, but acknowledging I would never see Marcus again?

My choice alone.

"Ella? Ella, is that you?"

I stopped abruptly on the wet, shiny pavement, my hand covering my ear as I strained to hear her. Passers-by, heads bent against the falling drizzle as they made their weary way home, tutted as they swerved around me, jostling my arm.

"Thank God you're safe, I've been so worried!" I exclaimed. "Where are you? I've been trying to call you!"

Her voice was faint and muffled as if she was standing away from her phone. "I know, I know you have. It's... hard to talk," she said.

"Why? What do you mean?" My voice grew high in alarm. The rain was starting to fall heavier now, and I scarpered under the nearest doorway of a shop.

But as was her frustrating way, Ella chose to ignore my question and instead fire her own, one I had been expecting and dreading. "Is everything okay, no more break-ins? At least I know with you staying I don't need to worry. I should be back soon, and we can—"

"Wait, stop. I need you to tell you what's happened, and then you'll understand why I've had to involve the police—"

"*What?* Tell me I've misheard you and you haven't done the one thing you promised me you wouldn't do." Her words cut through me in shards of sharp guilt, just as she intended them to do.

"I had to," I hastened to explain. "Someone broke in and tried to get into the safe. There was no other choice, we had to see what was contained in there. So, Marcus and I—"

"Who are you talking about?!" she demanded. "Who's Marcus?"

"The DI I told you about." I heard a groan, a swear word. "No, no, it's okay, really. You can trust him. But you have to phone him, tell him you've got nothing to do with any of this and, more importantly, what the numbers next to the addresses in your book mean."

"What the hell were you doing looking through my address book?"

"I told you. Someone was trying to get into the safe, and we need to work out who. Please, Ella, listen to what's most important here! You need to come back now and talk to Marcus. I don't want you to be in trouble when you've got nothing to do with whatever Lyle and this burglar are involved in."

There was a long, drawn-out silence. I heard her soft breathing, then: "How do you know I've got nothing to do with any of this?"

My heart plummeted, palms growing sweaty. "Because... because you can't have," I stumbled out.

"Lyle, yes, but not you." No reply. "Ella, this isn't funny anymore. You're going to call Marcus the minute we stop talking—I'm texting you the number right now. You have to come home immediately to sort this out." Again, the ominous silence. "Ella, dammit, tell me you understand the gravity of this!"

The breath was tight in my lungs as I strained to hear what I was desperate to catch.

"I'm sorry," her voice whispered to me, before the line went dead.

No. No, I would not believe Ella was guilty. I wouldn't. She was scared, that's all, just scared. *I won't give up on you, Ella, do you hear me? I won't.*

I texted her Marcus' number with a plea to call him. But I wasn't deceiving myself.

Arriving back at the apartment, I let out an unconsciously held breath when the solid door was firmly locked. Dropping my handbag onto the floor, I flopped down on the plush but not overly comfortable leather sofa, stretching out my taut body. Almost unconsciously, my thoughts yearned for Marcus' worn but inviting sofa, on which I'd curled up only a couple of hours ago. Then for Marcus himself, until I gave myself a stiff telling-off. I was relying too much on Marcus, and it wasn't fair on either of us. He'd promised me nothing more than to keep me safe and that was the way it should be. I gave a soft groan as I thought back to how I'd pushed my way into his house. Yet, I didn't regret it; how could I? It had felt like… home.

Enough, Sophia! Enough. It was time to take action. I needed to know more about what Ella had gotten herself into before I looked at these numbers for Marcus. But how?

I pushed myself off the sofa with a renewed burst of energy and began to systematically go through any drawer I could find in the apartment that might give me some kind of clue. Rather frustratingly, most drawers held nothing more exciting than manual instructions on how to work the washing machine and dishwasher or a scrappy piece of paper wedged at the back with nothing more than doodled drawings on it.

The last drawer proved to be as poor in pickings as the others, with only a stray paperclip and an elastic band to show. Feeling a little defeated, I cast my eyes around the room. As I did, they fell on a tacked-up piece of flowered notepaper near the telephone.

Carefully, I walked across the room to unpin it, my breath catching in excitement.

For there, scrawled carelessly across the page, was a name with a phone number for the person who could help me the most, the one who knew Ella the best.

Mum: 01875 22556

"Hello? Hi, is this Mrs. Blair?"

"Um, yes, yes, it is," came the cautious reply.

I breathed out, forcing a relaxed tone to my voice so as not to alarm, "Hi Mrs. Blair, I'm not sure if you remember me, Sophia Meadows? Aneella and I were at university together—"

"Oh yes, yes, of course. My goodness, it's been such a long time since I last saw you. How are you, dear?"

"Good, thank you," I quickly replied.

I could hear her soft breath as if she was walking as she spoke. "What can I do for you, my dear? Only it's not really a good time as my Derek, Ella's dad, is doing quite poorly. He had a stroke, you see, and he's due for his medication."

My heart was troubled by her words. "I'm so sorry to hear that. I won't keep you, but I wondered if I could pop over tomorrow to see you. It's about Ella. Nothing to worry about," I hastened to add.

"Oh, okay. About ten, I think, would be best. Do you know where we live?"

After taking down her address, I hung up. I felt relieved to have made the call. Hopefully in the morning I would be able to fill in the very large gaping details of Ella's life. Ten years' absence was beginning to show itself starkly. How much had Ella changed in that time?

※

THE DAY WAS DESPERATELY TRYING to shine as I parked up outside a modest-looking terrace house, nestled amongst similar looking red brick homes. I had no idea Ella's parents lived in Inverness, having only met them on a few occasions, one being our graduation day. They certainly didn't have a Scottish accent. But now it made perfect sense as to why Ella had chosen to invest in an apartment so far from where she was based in London. This way, she was closer to her parents, who must be struggling if Derek was as poorly as her mum suggested on the phone.

I checked my watch—10:01 a.m. I took a mental breath in to prepare myself, acutely aware I had no clear idea of what I was hoping to achieve from talking to Mrs. Blair. Climbing out of my car, I carefully walked up to the bright red door with honeysuckle growing up around it, its sweet aroma hitting my senses as I waited for Mrs. Blair to answer my ring.

The door was opened some moments after I'd rang the bell. Mrs. Blair stood there, a confused look on her face as she looked at me. Her hair was tapered with grey amongst the rich brown, her figure round and homely. She wore a flower apron over her faded brown skirt and a light blue blouse. I gave her my brightest smile to help put aside any fears she might have opening a door to a stranger. My smile wavered as she hastened to say, "I'm sorry, dear, we don't buy from door knockers. Goodbye now."

"Oh, no, wait, Mrs. Blair," I rushed to stop her shutting the door in my face. "It's Sophia, Sophia Meadows. We spoke on the phone yesterday, do you remember? We made a time for me to come to yours at ten o'clock."

Comprehension began to dawn on Mrs. Blair's face, much to my relief. "Goodness, of course! How could I forget? And seeing you properly now, I can see you haven't changed a bit." She cast a glance at her silver watch. "And, look, it's ten o'clock now. You're very prompt."

I nodded, smiling as warmly as I could. We both stood there, awkwardly on my part as I wondered if I was going to have to ask my personal questions on the doorstep.

Thankfully, Mrs. Blair stepped back and said, "Come in, dear."

Dutifully, I followed her slightly swaying back as she led me down her flower-wallpapered hallway then into the lounge, all the while apologising unnecessarily to me, "I'm so sorry, dear, I forgot. With Derek poorly, you know, everything else slips my mind a little. It's a little messy, we don't get many visitors."

A little messy was perhaps an understatement; I observed the crowded, overflowing coffee table, chairs, and anything which had a surface. The contrast to Ella's flat was unbelievable. My heart lurched as I noticed a pale and weak man lying almost horizontally on the farthest chair from me, which had been pushed back into a reclining position. He had a blanket tucked carefully around him. One side of his body seemed more slumped than the other. I noticed him looking at me as I came in, though he said nothing. I smiled and nodded, "Hello."

"Derek, dear, this is a friend of Ella's. It's nice she's come to see us."

His eyes flickered as he caught his daughter's name, as if wanting to tell us something. I could see the frustration etched on his face. Deep pity swept over me. I'm not sure how you bear not being able to communicate or connect with the people living in close proximity to you.

"We're just going to have a cuppa in the kitchen so we don't disturb you. I'll bring you one through in a minute." Mrs. Blair walked over, tucked up his blanket a little more, and stroked his forehead. I stared, unable to tear my gaze away, a lump in my throat. That gesture, that simple gesture, was one of the most staggeringly intimate and loving moments I'd ever witnessed. She was devoted to her husband, in every sense of the word. Would I ever experience that same devotion to another? I thought I had that with Richard, but our love had not been strong enough to weather the harshest of storms when it hit us.

We came into a compact, slightly dated kitchen. She encouraged me to sit at the table, which was pressed up against the wall. Mrs. Blair bustled about making the tea while I discreetly looked around. Despite how cramped it was and the obvious need of a good tidy up, there was a homeliness to the room that I found relaxing.

"Is full-cream milk okay, dear? We don't seem to have any semi-skimmed."

"Of course, no problem," I reassured, wanting to put her at ease.

As Mrs. Blair warmed the pot, she turned to glance at me and said, "You were always such a lovely looking lady, my dear, and I see that hasn't changed. Aneella and I were always commenting on that."

I blushed. "Thank you, that's a very kind thing to say. I don't always feel that way about myself," I found myself confessing. "I feel much older than my thirty-one years sometimes."

"Nonsense, dear. You have many, many years yet to enjoy. Here you go. Do you take sugar?"

I shook my head as she handed me my cup of tea. "No, thank you."

Mrs. Blair settled herself down, letting out a breath, as if relieved to be resting her feet. *Looking after Derek must take every ounce of strength and energy she has.*

"Are you getting nurse help for Derek?" I gently asked. "To give you a break?"

"Oh, now you sound like Ella. No, no, I'm fine, really. Derek and I muddle through together. I've told the kind doctor at our surgery not to worry about us."

The answer came out a little too easily, like she had rehearsed it many a time. I wanted to say more but held back. It wasn't really my place. Instead, I tried to think how best to approach this conversation.

"Mrs. Blair—"

"Oh, please, call me Cathy. Otherwise, I think you're talking to my mother-in-law!"

I smiled. "Okay, Cathy, I hope you don't mind me coming here today out of the blue. I've been trying to get hold of Aneella. We are looking to have a reunion from our old university." The lie came a little too smoothly. Not my finest moment but better to lie than to have her worry herself sick over her only daughter's safety.

"Well now, what a lovely idea!"

"Yes. I wondered if you had an address for her and knew who else she's still in contact with."

I let the question linger in the hope it would encourage her to open up. And, hallelujah, it did the trick.

"I'll help you as much as I can, dear, but my Ella, as you know, is a bit of a drifter. She moves around a lot. She always tends to call us, rather than the other way 'round."

"Is she still in London working?" I pressed on, leaning forward. When Cathy gave me an odd look, I had no choice but to spin the yarn of my lie a little more. "We're just trying to think of a good, neutral place to all meet up in."

"Goodness me, I don't think so. I thought she was here in Scotland, at her flat. She phoned us last week, saying she had taken leave from the bank and would be catching up with friends. I don't think she gave me an address, I never thought to ask."

My heart sank. It seemed her mum was as much in the dark as I was with the whereabouts of Ella. I racked my brain to try and think of another angle.

"What about her boyfriend, Lyle? Do you see much of him?"

There was an immediate swish of confusion on Cathy's face, confirming what I already suspected. "I don't know a... Lyle, did you say?"

I nodded.

"Oh no, goodness me. I don't remember that name, I—"

Seeing her begin to look panicked, I was quick to allay her fears. "You know what, I must have got that wrong. My mistake. I'm always getting things muddled up."

I pushed out a laugh and was glad to see it do the trick as Cathy laughed in return while saying, "Don't worry, dear. Ella is always laughing at my misunderstandings. I thought her boyfriend was called Rob, Rick, Richard—see, I'm muddled myself now."

I faintly smiled and said, "I think you're confusing my husband—ex-husband—with one of Ella's old boyfriends. Mine was called Richard, not Ella's."

Cathy's hand flew to her face. "Goodness, I'm so sorry dear. How did I get that so wrong?"

I tried to give a nonchalant shrug, despite a heavy feeling coming over me at the mention of Richard's name.

Cathy must have sensed this, for her hands moved away from her face to cup my cheek, her eyes full of sympathy. The tender gesture was so unexpected, tears hit the back of my eyes.

"And I'm sorry you've suffered too, Sophia. Someone like you deserves to be cherished."

The words touched my heart and caused a few tears to slide down my cheek. Cathy brushed them away, gave my hand a squeeze, then allowed me a moment to compose myself as she pretended to be busy stirring her tea.

We chatted then about the old days of university, both relieved to move off sensitive subjects. In this, Cathy had almost a photographic memory, recalling anecdotes and funny stories from each of our friends, most of which I had forgotten, causing us both to laugh.

"Do you know, I think I still have the telephone numbers of some of your old friends. Shall I try digging them out for you when I get a moment?" Cathy asked me now.

At that moment, a hoarse voice from the lounge could just be heard. Instantly alert, Cathy quickly rose, as did I, while rushing out, "That would be amazing, thank you." Maybe they had heard from Ella recently. It was a long shot, but it was all I had right then.

A few minutes later, as I closed the front door softly behind me, I could hear Cathy whispering soothing words over Ella's dad. Once again tears clogged the back of my throat, but this time I swallowed them down.

[16]

There were two messages flashing on the answerphone when I walked in.

Ignoring them, I dropped my bag on the sofa and walked over to rummage in the fridge. A disappointed sigh escaped me when all that greeted me was some wilted lettuce, a crumb or two of cheese, and one solitary egg. Hardly much to satisfy a ravenous stomach like mine.

I grabbed the last morsels of cheese before closing the fridge door with a heavy sigh, then chewed while listening to my stomach growl angrily at me. Standing there, it hit me. I was tired of my own company. When before I had craved solitude, now I wanted nothing more than the stimulation of others.

Struck by this thought, my breath stilled. What had changed my determination to remain alone and reliant on no one? Or, more precisely, who had broken through my feelings of wanting to shut myself away from the world, which had been so overpowering to me only a couple of weeks ago?

The answer came immediately, and with it, a strong, overwhelming urge to call him. Did I dare? No way was this my normal behaviour, to boldly take the lead. But these were extraordinary times, a chance to define and change myself that I may not ever get again.

I dare.

Before common sense kicked in, I grabbed my phone, found his number, and pressed the call button. My heart raced a little erratically, like some schoolgirl with her first crush, and if I wasn't so nervous, I would have been mortified.

When he answered, his voice was full of concern. "Soph, is everything okay? Have you had another break-in? I've had my men doing patrols—"

"No, no, I'm fine. No break-ins or strange men running out of the door," I hastened to reassure, a soft teasing note in my voice.

"Oh, good," Marcus breathed out, causing a warmth to cover me. *He cares.* "Have you had any other leads or information come your way to help us?"

This was my chance. "Well, actually, I do have a couple of things for you to catch up on. I was wondering, if you're free, whether you wanted to chat over dinner?" No reply. I babbled on. "A little like your fridge situation, I've only got a sad piece of lettuce and a lonely egg in mine. My stomach is not impressed. I don't fancy eating out alone. I'd much rather eat with you," I added, surprising myself with my honesty.

I held my breath as I awaited his answer. There was a long silence, then, "Can you meet me at the police station in about half an hour?"

My eyes widened in surprise, expecting a no. "Yes, definitely! Shall I come up to your office?"

"Aye, aye. I'll... see you then."

With a quick goodbye, I ended the call before I babbled on anymore. All at once I felt lighter of spirit and my body eager. I darted into the bedroom to take a quick shower and change.

In my haste, I'd forgotten all about the two phone messages flashing at me.

⌒⋏⋏⌒

ACROSS TOWN, Marcus stood with the phone in his hand, staring at her photo as he seemed to do now countless times a day, instead of focusing on what he should be doing.

"Marcus, what are you doing?" he muttered as he put the phone down with some force. "What the hell are you doing?"

She continued to stare at him, her vulnerable eyes drawing him ever further in and reaching a part of him he believed was dead. He could feel himself wanting, needing, to seek her out and stay as close to her as he dared, so he knew she was safe by his side.

But it still came back to the same point again and again, driving him crazy: *Could he trust her?* Should he be solely relying on his gut instinct telling him she was innocent, instead of the circumstantial evidence stacking up against her, like unexplained calls to Ms. Blair's parents and even a visit?

Almost without conscious thought, his hand reached

out to stroke her face on his screen, before dropping hastily away. He stood there, eyes closed, breathing hard and gripping the desk, until he felt once more in control.

And then the call came in, disturbing everything.

⋀

AFTER ALL MY deliberation over what to wear, before settling on smart black jeans and a silky top, I was running late and had to walk fast to reach Marcus on time.

The police station, which never stopped or slept, was its usual hive of organised chaos. I was granted permission to enter through its guarded doors and found my way once more up to his office.

Marcus was standing, talking on the phone and turned slightly away from me. I paused, taking in his solidity and the strength he represented that awakened a desire in me. A desire that had me craving to feel his hands on me, to the point I could almost imagine it for real. But that wasn't all. I wanted to know the real Marcus, the one beneath his professional facade. I'd caught a glimpse of this the other day in his cabin, and I was hungry for more.

Feeling all of this, I walked toward him and knocked softly on the door.

He looked up and gazed at me for a moment, then smiled as his hand beckoned me in. I did as bidden, walking in and closing the door. Marcus motioned "one minute" to me. I nodded in understanding, and, to resist listening in on his conversation, I distracted myself by looking around. My eyes travelled to a working board. To my stunned surprise, I saw a photo of myself taken in the car park outside the apartment, alongside a grainy one of Aneella holding what looked like a suitcase. Hastily I looked away, not wanting to process why we would be on his wall like suspects to a crime I didn't remember committing. Perhaps I would ask him later when we were out, if my nerve held.

"Thanks, Kev. Call it a night," Marcus was saying now, unaware of what I had been looking at. "We'll speak tomorrow."

He hung up and turned to me. His eyes were dark and unsmiling as they studied me. Guilt at snooping around his office had me defensively saying, "What? Why are you looking at me like that?"

Marcus frowned, remaining silent for another agonising moment, which only heightened my guilt that much more.

"Have you had any calls today?"

That caught me unawares. It was not what I was expecting. Now, I was the one frowning when I said, "Not that I can recall. You mean on my mobile?"

"Possibly. Or on the landline at Ms. Blair's apartment."

That pulled me up short. *Hold on...*

"Actually, there were some messages on the answerphone I didn't get 'round to listening to yet," I answered as I stepped closer to Marcus, my mind in a whirl and my senses sharply aware of the unmasked concern in his eyes. "Why are you asking me this, Marcus?" I asked, my eyes determinedly holding his.

I sensed the battle wrestling within him, though his voice was calm and measured when he finally spoke. "We've had your friend's apartment under surveillance for some time." Hearing my gasp of surprise, Marcus was quick to continue. "We—I—wanted to make sure we could act quickly if or when your intruder came back. Today, my officer picked up on phone calls being made to the apartment, with the caller hanging up. We think it's the same man. We also spotted—"

"Hold on, just hold on!" I moved closer, my mind in a spin as I tried to process what he was saying to me. "Are you telling me that I've been watched, coming and going—"

"For your own safety, yes."

"—and that you're listening in on all the conversations I'm having?"

"Yes."

At his continued mild tone, I shook my head with pure and unbridled anger. "I don't believe this! You're standing there telling me that nothing I'm doing right now is private? You're making me feel unclean!"

Marcus continued to stand there poised and calm. "That's not my intention, I promise you, Sophia. I'm not watching you."

"Aren't you?" I challenged, my eyes hot and daring. I saw his jaw flinch, but nothing more. It only served to rile me further. "Why is my photo on your wall, then, if you're not watching me? Tell me that."

For a moment he looked uncomfortable, then he said, "It's not for the reasons you think."

"So, you don't consider me a suspect in whatever this unholiest of messes I've been pulled into is?"

Marcus chose to ignore what I said, saying instead, "You have to trust me."

"You keep saying that!" I protested. "I want to, but you're making it very hard when you won't give me anything!"

As we stood there, almost touching but not quite, something took a hold of me, draining the anger away to leave me with a sense of acute frustration at *this*, at Marcus. At me. The room seemed to be pulling us together. The air became alert. I became aware of his scent, his physical presence.

"How can you always be so calm, so controlled?" I breathed out, staring up at him.

There was a flicker of frustration across his eyes, just for a moment. His voice was laced with restraint as he forced out, "I have to be, there's no other option for me."

I could have left it there, stepped back, allowed him to relax the tautness and wariness I saw moving within him. I should have.

But I didn't.

"And me? Are you in control when I'm near you?" I softly said.

Marcus breathed in sharply. His pupils dilated and flickered. "I... what?"

I pushed on, unable to stop, needing to know if I was the only one feeling this undercurrent between us. "When I'm close to you, like this..."

"Sophia, Soph... don't." Yet his eyes told me otherwise.

"What about if I touched you, right now?" I breathed out, pushing us both to a place neither had dared to go before.

Marcus stared at me, his hands clenched at his sides,

his chest moving rapidly. I stepped a little closer still, reaching out to touch his chest. It felt solid and strong, like it could hold me steady against a storm. His heart thudded beneath my warm hand, and, in that moment, I understood. We both understood. His hand came over mine, holding it there, locking us together. Our eyes held, darkening with want and yearning. Need. My breath caught.

The door opened sharply without invite, shattering the air and us with it. His warmth instantly disappeared, leaving a coolness in its place.

"Sorry, am I interrupting something, Sir?" came the clipped female voice.

Morven Atkins stood there with her arms crossed and a look in her eyes that caused me to shiver. To stop myself, I forced a smile on my face. Marcus had smoothly transitioned back into his calm, collected self and was walking back behind his desk. "No, not at all. Did you need me for something?"

I purposely turned away, pretending to be engrossed in a *How to Keep Safe* poster tacked on the wall. I could feel her eyes burning into my back, and I was surprised my clothes weren't catching alight from the sparks.

"I was clocking off and wondered if you wanted to debrief over a drink," came her reply.

There was a moment of silence. Now, I felt both their eyes on me. I had a strong desire to vanish right through the wall and bit down hard on my lips.

"Could we do it tomorrow in the office? I need to meet with Soph—Ms. Meadows—now. Thanks, Morven."

It was a polite but firm dismissal. I dared to glance at

Morven. She was still looking narrow-eyed at me, suspicion seeping out of her every pore, like sharp lemon being squeezed out. But to Marcus, she summoned a smile.

"If you don't need me to stay as well... Fine, I'll see you tomorrow then," she said.

The door was closed more forcefully than needed. I couldn't resist turning and grinning at Marcus. After a moment, I was rewarded with one in return.

WE FOUND our way to a tucked-away Italian restaurant Marcus knew, aptly named Little Italy. My stomach growled in appreciation and was rewarded with an oozing cheesy pizza, complete with warm bread soaked heavily in oil. Marcus tucked in as greedily as I did into his hot pepperoni, stopping me from feeling embarrassed at my lack of politeness.

Easy conversation flowed happily between us. As I took a sip of wine, Marcus smiled at me. I returned the smile, then laughed as I spotted a trickle of red sauce on his chin.

"What?" Marcus protested with a laugh. Grinning, I reached across, risking my floaty top catching alight with the candle flame, to wipe away the smear with my napkin.

At my touch, our eyes connected and darkened. My hand hovered for longer than was necessary. Marcus' hand lifted as if to touch mine, before falling away again with seeming reluctance. I moved back into my seat.

"Thanks," he murmured.

"You're welcome. There's nothing worse than walking

around oblivious as to why people are giving you funny looks because no one's told you you've got food on your face," I grinned, picking up my one remaining piece of pizza.

"Too true," Marcus commented as he swallowed the last of his. "Maybe I should get you to accompany me to police events. What if all this time I've been walking around with bits of spinach or something stuck in my teeth and never realised?"

"You probably have," I teased, then let out a yelp as he flicked me with some water from his glass. The candle, in protest at being sprayed, fizzled out, leaving us with a small stream of grey smoke rising. We both watched it for a moment, inhaling its woody scent.

"Oops." Marcus grinned. "Your fault, lass," he said, only to have a taste of his own treatment as I flicked water back at him with bullseye precision, eliciting a girlie yelp as it sprayed his shirt.

Sitting there, both laughing hard, the thought came of how good it was to see him like this, relaxing, teasing. I yearned to lift away the dark cloud that had hung too long over him, like a long shadow stealing the rays of the sunshine. I wanted to be the warmth on his skin.

Dragging my thoughts away from these unsettling desires, I watched as he sipped his wine.

Marcus froze, murmuring, "Why are you staring at me like that? Beginning to feel a wee bit uncomfortable here."

"Sorry... sorry. I was thinking about your name, Marcus."

"My name?"

"Mm, isn't it from Roman origin rather than Scottish?" I asked.

Marcus leaned forward, smiling a little. "Hadn't put you down as a genealogist. As it happens, you're both right and wrong. Many people say the name derives from Mars, the Roman god of war, making it Latin. But make no mistake, here in Scotland we take pride in our own name origins and mine is as Scottish as it comes."

I smiled, "Alright I'll bite, tell me what it means in your country, Marcus Armstrong."

He grinned, "It's from the name Mac Mharcuis."

"Mac what?"

"Mharcuis. It means—now don't laugh—warrior."

I bit my lip, trying to keep my features steady. "Really? So, you're a Roman warrior god." A laugh escaped from me. "That's quite a lot to live up to."

Marcus raised his eyebrows, giving me a look that sent my pulse racing, "Oh, I'm more than able to live up to my name. My wee mámag knew what her boy was capable of."

"Mm, well, time will tell if that's true or if your mum was simply blind to the truth."

"Oh, you have quite the tongue on you, Sophia Meadows, for an English lass on Scottish soil."

Only when the rich, steaming coffee was placed before us and the restaurant was almost empty did Marcus once more turn back into the detective, as he began to probe me on what I had discovered in the last couple of days.

I filled him in on what Ella's mum had told me, promising to chase up the numbers of my old university friends from Cathy. All the while, I watched him process this new information, his eyes muted and giving me nothing. The urge to provoke a response out of him stirred me up.

"Do you trust me, Marcus?" I blurted out.

Swallowing his sip of coffee, Marcus eyed me warily over the table. "Aye, I'm beginning to. Why?"

"Then tell me what's going on. So far, you've revealed nothing about this case involving my friend, at least nothing of significance," I exhaled.

Marcus frowned, reaching towards me. "Soph—"

"You were already watching Ella," I said. It wasn't a question, and Marcus had the sense to understand this. "Why? *Why*?" I pleaded.

Marcus sat there, apologetic but unwavering. "I can't tell you. I'm sorry," he added softly. "I'm bound by confidentiality."

I closed my eyes, fighting to control an unfair anger toward him. Biting down hard, I half whispered, "At least tell me if you're now more concerned about Ella and whether I should be."

I opened my eyes, fixing onto his like a radar seeking its target, determined to hit. It found vulnerability in the flinch of his jaw and something unreadable lurking deep in his eyes as he quietly said, "I'm concerned for both of you."

Taken aback by this stark truth, I stared at him. The thrill of having him care for me fought against the reality that we were both in seeming danger. Marcus would not exaggerate, ever. He dealt with facts.

"Am I a suspect, Marcus?" I whispered, my eyes pleading with him. "Please, tell me honestly."

My plea reacted within Marcus. He shook his head, unconsciously mirroring my body language as he leaned closer, his voice soft and raw in a way I hadn't heard before. "If you were, do you think that I would be confiding in you like I am, breaking every damn rule I ever set for myself by becoming close to you? Would I be thinking about you like I am if I still suspected you? Tell me, tell me now, if I'm wrong to trust and confide in you."

His words moved me in a way I'd never known, as they weaved their way softly inside me. His eyes had me reaching across to take his hand in mine, my voice earnest and eager as I shook my head and said, "No, you're not wrong, you're not wrong to trust me. Just as I'm not wrong to trust you."

THE COOL NIGHT air hit our cheeks as we stepped out of the restaurant, causing me to shiver a little within my thin leather jacket. I turned to Marcus to say goodnight, expecting him to head straight off, but before I had a chance, I found my hand grasped in his and being gently steered along the path. I had a vague sense of where we were. Marcus, it appeared, had accurate precision as he weaved us around sharp corners and confusing, long, and shadowed streets.

As the streetlamps cast a strange unnatural yellow glow over us, I caught a tight frown between Marcus' eyes as he stared straight ahead. I could sense he wanted to get me home quickly, and yet, though that should alarm me, it had the opposite effect—I didn't want this walk to end.

Despite the lack of chatter, in spite of the cold biting hard at me, regardless of the dark, looming streets, I did not want to stop walking with him. With his hand against mine, I felt cocooned and protected. Alive. It was a heady mix.

So, with a sense of dismay, we walked briskly through the front door of the apartments and efficiently into the lift to take us up before I'd drawn breath.

Should I ask him in?

The dangerous, tempting thought had me darting discreet looks at his inscrutable profile. Sensing this, he turned to look at me, catching me out. I felt my cheeks flame a little, but I resisted turning away. There was a suspended moment as we both gazed at the other, as something tangible built between us, only to have the door lifts swish open to shatter the moment.

We both stepped out. As I went to push open the door, his hand enclosed over mine, and he said, "Let me go in first to check the place."

I stepped back, nodded, let him do what he needed to do, though instinctively, I knew there was no danger on the other side of the door. I was proved right.

"It's all good. Safe to come in."

As I stepped in, Marcus walked toward me, smiling, the first since leaving the restaurant. The effect was intoxicating. A relieved smile spread across my face to see his tension slipping softly away, like a coil of smoke losing its heat.

"Would you like a drink? Coffee, tea, something stronger?" My voice sounded a little breathless and unnatural. I swallowed hard, trying to compose myself.

He stopped and stared at me. Temptation to accept lurked there in his eyes, I could see it. The battle to remain professional against the desire to stay with me. I moved closer, silently urging him to accept.

"I... should probably head home," Marcus said, thrusting his hands into his back pockets. We both stepped back, the distance stretching out.

I swallowed down my acute disappointment and forced myself to say something, anything. "Of course. I'll look at those numbers from Ella's book for you tomorrow. See if I can decipher them."

"I'd appreciate that, thank you."

The politeness in our voices was killing me.

"Should I come to the station to look at the book?" I asked in a strained voice.

Pause, then, "Actually, it's at my home. Can you come over late morning?"

My head flew up, my eyes meeting his, startled. Had I heard correctly?

"Okay, if that's easier for you," I stumbled out quickly.

Silence, unbearable silence, before, "Aye, I think it would. Can you remember where I live?"

His eyes finally met mine. There seemed to be confusion in them, as if he couldn't understand why he'd just proposed this. That made two of us. But I wasn't about to let him off the hook by suggesting we meet elsewhere. His home was precisely where I wanted to be.

"I think I can, yes. I'll find my way to you."

The minute Marcus walked into his home after leaving Sophia, it hit him like a thunderbolt—he hadn't checked her answerphone messages. He should have got her to play them to him before he'd left. He should have been doing his job, dammit. A costly mistake.

No one needed to tell him his mind was distracted by the closeness of her, stirring him up. Every minute they spent together was only heightening this. He craved being alone with her. It was why he'd asked her to come to his home tomorrow. Here, they could be themselves with no watchful eyes of a sergeant on them. He could acknowledge that, at least.

But there was no excuse for failing to do his job properly. He had to think clearly and rationally, do what he must to bring this case to a close. After tomorrow, he would take a step back, withdraw from her. He must. There was a strong, forceful desire for her stirring within his gut, fighting to be let out and acted upon. It scared him, shook him up. He had loved Lucy, honoured her with his body, but never had he felt this intensity, deep within him, when they had first come together. It had been a gentle love between them, nothing like this wanting, desiring, dreaming of making love to Sophia—

Stop, enough! Enough. Just one day. He would allow himself one more day to savour every minute with her— then he would pull away, he would. No matter what it cost.

᠁

IT WAS ONLY when I was slumped on the sofa eating a bowl of cereal did I notice the answerphone again, still blinking furiously to indicate two new messages.

I was tempted to leave them; after all, they were hardly likely to be for me.

Yet, like a curse, the red flashing light seemed to grow larger and angrier at me, refusing to be dismissed.

Sighing, I put down my bowl and traipsed over to the machine to press play.

The first message started. There was silence, then the sound of the other receiver being put down without a message left. The sound filled me with an unexplained dread I forced down. Instead, I concentrated on the next message clicking in.

Ella's voice filled the room as if she were here with me. The air seemed as taken aback as I was.

"Sophia? Are you there?" her voice held frustration, annoyance. "I tried your mobile, but it wouldn't connect. Listen," her voice came breathless, agitated. I unconsciously leaned closer. "I'm not able to come back yet. I know I said we would spend some time together, but now you've involved the police—look, it doesn't matter. Just stay close to that address book you found, don't let it out of your sight. Do you understand? Do this for me, and I promise I'll get you out of this silly mess soon." Silence stretched out, and I was about to turn away, when, "I'm sorry, I've already taken too much from you. Maybe one day you'll forgive me."

The phone clicked, leaving only the long dull tone of the machine.

My feet couldn't seem to move from where they swayed.

I've already taken too much.

What? What have you taken from me, Ella?

I grabbed my mobile, knowing already it was fruitless but compelled to do it nonetheless. I pressed "Call" beside her name.

Her phone didn't even bother to pretend its owner would pick up. Aneella's demure recorded voice cut in before one ring had commenced, telling me she was unable to take my call and to please leave a message.

"Ella, it's me, Sophia. I got your message, and you're really worrying me now. I don't understand what you're trying to tell me. The only thing I know for certain is that we're both in danger. So, you've *got* to call me, then come home. We'll keep you safe. You can trust Marcus. You can trust me! Please, tell me what these numbers are, why somebody wants them. Just... call me, get here. It will be okay, I promise."

With reluctance, I ended the call, biting down hard on

my lip. It didn't feel like I was doing enough, not by a long shot.

———

IT WAS with a mixed feeling of buzzing trepidation and acute anticipation that I drove over to Marcus' next morning, my eyes watching every road sign leading to Loch Meikles. My poor old car was starting to expel some odd sounds. I badly needed a new one, or I would be stuck in Scotland forever. *Though, on second thought, is that such a bad thing?*

When I spotted the small turning for his place past the Loch, I couldn't resist a gleeful, happy dance behind the wheel.

I carefully parked the car on the makeshift driveway, made of old bricks laid in a precise order, and climbed out.

My finger hesitated for the briefest moment over the doorbell, before pressing against its coolness.

The door swung open, flooding me with sudden light. Marcus stood there in the doorway, a smile on his face, welcoming me in.

We walked into his lounge; this time bathed in morning glow rather than falling dusk.

"You found me okay." Marcus was a step behind, his closeness a hair's breadth from me.

I nodded and turned to smile at him over my shoulder, "I'm rather proud of myself." I shrugged my jacket off and found his hand ready to receive it. "Oh. Thank you."

"No worries. Take a seat… if you can find one." Marcus gave a short, rueful laugh to acknowledge the paperwork strewn haphazardly across his sofa. I raised my eyebrows, amused, then carefully moved some to the side so I could perch myself on the edge.

Immediately, my eyes were drawn to the name written on the case file before me. *Aneella Blair, case no. 324M5.* Bold as brass, tempting me to open it up and read more.

My hungry fingers hovered over it. The air felt thick, still. With the greatest willpower, I moved my hand away without giving in to temptation.

"I thought we could start with the address book and see what you could make of the numbers," Marcus said behind me, much closer than I had realised, making my body jerk in reaction. "How does that sound?"

"It sounds like a fine plan to me."

"First, though, tell me about the answerphone messages left for you," he instructed, frowning hard. "I need to know every detail. I'm sorry, I should have checked them last night. That kind of carelessness won't happen again."

I hastened to reassure him, stretching out a hand. "Don't be silly, there's nothing to apologise for. It was a message from Ella. Do you want to know the exact message she left?"

He nodded, still frowning hard. "Please."

So, I told him, watching a set of different emotions cross his face, though he refrained from adding his own opinion and views.

A FEW HOURS LATER, my eyes burned in irritation as I forced them to concentrate once more on the list of scrawled numbers, as if written in a rush, in Ella's book. Before me, on a pad marked with the police address Marcus had given to me, were my rambling thoughts: *Last digit of phone numbers? Addresses? Or some other form of numbers like codes? Maybe bank account numbers? Why four numbers on some, more on others? Are they in a logical order or just randomly written down?*

I felt Marcus' eyes on me from where he sat surrounded by paper. He said, "Any joy?"

I shook my head without looking up, frustration biting down hard on me. I was desperate to work this out, not just for me but for Ella also. And Marcus, of course for Marcus. "There are so many possibilities of what they could be. They're similar to the binary codes I use to create my programmes, though those are usually much longer in length. It could be bank numbers, sort codes, banking codes perhaps. Maybe phone numbers, but if so, for who and why shorter in length? On their own, they don't make a lot of sense. Oh, it's so infuriating!"

"Welcome to my world, Soph," Marcus commented dryly. "Most of the work I do is headache-inducing."

I half smiled as I lifted my head up. "And I thought that was just an infliction in *my* chosen career path. Looking at computer language all day, trust me, you start to ramble utter nonsense by nightfall."

The burst of deep laughter from him had me unable to resist joining in. Our eyes drew toward each other, held, the laughter fading away as I felt my breath shorten. His eyes darkened with untold words I wished he would reveal. Neither of us moved.

His phone cracked to life, breaking the moment.

Marcus put up an apologetic hand while moving out of earshot. I guessed it was a call from the police station.

Wanting to distract myself in a bid to curb the temptation to eavesdrop, my eyes caught on the photo of Ella and me, which we'd found in the safe alongside the address book. This time, I found I could look into the distant eyes of my ex-husband without having to turn away. That was surprising. Had I begun to come to a place of acceptance? Did I dare believe that?

I continued to gaze at Ella and me. In my mind, I saw again our former selves, when we believed the world owed us and nothing would stop us from achieving our rightful lot. How naïve we were. We never receive all that we desire and dream of, but we can receive something infinitely more precious: love, friendship, encouragement, loyalty, and peace. Now, I dreamed I would know the power of them all.

As I drew the photo closer to me, I caught the face of someone in the background I'd not noticed before. I narrowed my eyes as I stared at his unruly, sandy hair blown about by the wind, his black gown billowing as he stared at our carefree backs.

I knew him, I was sure of it. That had to be—

"You're staring at that photo so hard you could set it on fire."

Jolted out of my reverie, I swung round. Marcus stood, looking down at me. The detective instincts in him must have immediately kicked in because he was next to me in an instant, staring down at the photo now slightly bent in my hand. "What have you seen?"

I pointed to the hazy, unclear guy hovering in the shadows. "I swear that's Ella's old tutor!" I exclaimed excitedly.

"Okay…"

"No, no, you see they were close, very close… maybe a little too close."

That spiked Marcus's interest. He looked hard at me, frowning. "You mean, as in they had an affair?"

I breathed out, pulling a face. "They never admitted to it, so this is all my hunch, right?" Marcus nodded, encouraging me, so I said, "But Ella and he spent a lot, and I mean *a lot*, of time alone in his room, far more than with any other student. And I'm sure I've seen his picture in the safe." I began to search round the sofa for the other items we had found, my heart racing with adrenaline. "Do you have the other things?"

"Here." He handed me a standard brown manilla envelope with the words *Evidence* and a case number below in the top right corner. "Everything we took from Ms. Blair's safe should be here."

I hastily took it, turning it upside down to shake out the contents. A silver heart locket landed in my palm. At once I remembered holding this locket before. *Hold on, the photo inside—*

"See, look at this picture! That's the same man, right!?"

Marcus craned his neck closer to peer at the picture within the locket I'd prised open.

"The picture-quality is far from perfect, but, aye, I

think you might be right enough for me to look into it further." He looked into my grinning face and said, "All right, DI Meadows, you think you can find out the name of this tutor for me?"

"You better believe it," I said, grinning.

"I like your confidence."

"I keep telling you, you should have me on your team."

He laughed, shaking his head and said, "Maybe I will consider that."

Marcus' mobile beeped yet again. He glanced at it, frowned, then closed it without replying. The laughter in his eyes had died away, as if someone had come along and smothered it.

"Everything okay?" I quietly asked.

Marcus gave me one of those long looks of his that I had yet to decipher, as if weighing up how he should reply. His smile didn't quite reach his eyes as he stood up and said, "Listen, do you fancy going for a walk around the loch? We could grab whatever is salvageable from the fridge, to eat when we get to a suitable spot."

"Oh, okay, sure." I nodded, despite feeling confused by his sudden change of mood. "Sounds picturesque."

His hand reached down to pull me up off the sofa.

[18]

The air was different here from anywhere else I'd ever been, so fresh and pure. Even the soft mist swirling over the loch's shimmering water felt good against my skin. Sunbeams filtered through the ever-moving clouds, warming us enough to keep the coolness away as our feet crunched over the fallen green leaves beneath us.

With each passing step, Marcus seemed to relax further, the tension leaving his shoulders. When first leaving the lodge, he kept casting glances over his shoulder, then peering into the distance with a tightness to his face I longed to smooth away. I did dare to ask if something was wrong, only to have my concerns brushed aside with a noncommittal reply. For a while, we walked in silence.

Yet now, with his evident relief relaxing me in turn, I broke the silence. "I can't get over how beautiful and peaceful it is here!" I said, turning my face up to the sun, smiling.

"Aye, I know, it's why I can't leave this place," Marcus said, giving me an appreciative smile. "Even though it bleeds me dry on constant repairs, and it takes me an hour sometimes to get to work if I'm unlucky enough to get stuck behind meandering tourists stopping at every corner." Marcus grinned at my scoffed laugh. "I think you would have to drag me out of this house, kicking and screaming, when my time on this world is up."

"It's all right, I'll let you stay. No need for any kicking and screaming today."

"Thanking you kindly." He bowed.

"No worries, that's just the kind-hearted girl I am," I said with a grin. "How long have you lived here?"

Marcus turned to look back toward his home and said, "Lucy and I moved in here after we got married. About eight years ago now, I guess. Time slips by quickly, doesn't it?"

We came to a small grass area overlooking the loch, and by mutual agreement, stopped. Marcus pulled the rucksack off his back and produced, to my growing admiration, a checked picnic rug in highland colours of red and green. Having smoothed out the rug and made ourselves comfortable, we spread out some bread and cheese we'd brought along and hungrily tucked in. I could feel the tension within me melting away as I gazed over the calming water, Marcus close by my side.

"How did you find this place?" I felt compelled to ask —intrigued, yet so aware I was treading on a delicate, painful subject where his late wife was concerned.

Marcus gave a rueful laugh as he leaned back on one of

his elbows, one knee bent. "By accident or fate, depending on your stance. We'd come for a short break away from Glasgow, where we lived at the time. Just after we got engaged, it must have been. Anyway, we were staying at a hotel not far from here full of hideous pictures of the Loch Ness monster on all its walls." He shook his head in shuddering memory, causing me to laugh. "Oh, I tell you it was the place of nightmares, lass."

"Sounds very like a hotel Richard and I stayed in not so long ago. I didn't think I was going to survive the night!" I shuddered, remembering it all too well.

"That bad, ach?"

"And more," I groaned. "Please don't let me relive it. Anyway, carry on. You were telling me how you found yourselves living here."

"I was, but first do you want a wee dram of wine?"

"Hold on, you've brought wine? In the daytime?!" I stared at him.

Marcus' eyebrows shot up as he reached for his rucksack. "It was that or whisky, and I didn't really take you as a lass who drank that tipple. Does it surprise you I drink while the sun is still high?"

"Well yes, because…" I spread my hands out wide in his direction, trying to get the words out. "It's you—focussed, undeterred, a stickler for the rules, one or two whiskies on a Friday night after dark when off duty—"

"So, shall I not open this very fine bottle of red then, from what I believe to be a very good year, if, as you say, I'm not one to break rules?" he said, holding the bottle temptingly near me, challenging me.

"Look, I have no problem drinking wine. I just don't want you to put the blame on me for 'breaking those rules' or for your sore head later," I said mockingly, mimicking his tone of voice.

"If I promise not to blame you, can I please, for the love of God, open this wine?"

"Permission granted, Sir." I grinned. Marcus gave me one of his slow, building smiles, then proceeded to open the bottle and pour us both a glass of deep, ebony-rich wine. I took a small, conservative sip then closed my eyes in pleasure as it slipped down like velvet. "Oh, that's good," I murmured.

Marcus, taking a sip himself, smiled, a little sparkle in his eyes that I enjoyed seeing. I felt his eyes on me, watching me. I bit my lip, suddenly feeling a little nervous.

"You do that a lot, I've noticed. Bite your lip, that is. Is that a sign I should take note of?"

I felt my face flush. "Please don't," I muttered. "I don't really know when I'm doing it, or why."

"As long as I'm not making you uncomfortable?" he probed.

Every time you look at me, I feel something; something sweet yet dangerous. But uncomfortable? No, never.

My hand reached out to briefly touch his. "I promise you, it's not that."

His hand covered mine. "Good."

"Just do one thing for me," I ventured on.

He pulled his hand away to take his wine, "What's that?"

"Can you try to stop overanalysing me? I know it's part of your job," I rushed on as his eyes narrowed like pinpricks, "to scrutinise everything and everyone but it's quite…"

"Quite what?" His voice carried a note of low warning.

I forced my word out. "Intimidating."

That word might have been a little strong for what I felt inside, but my mind struggled to think of another under his intense look. I dared to look at him, preparing myself for what he would say in reply.

"Intimidating?"

"Uh, yes," I said and gave him an apologetic half smile.

"And overanalysing?"

"Yes."

"I see."

"Not all the time," I felt compelled to add. "Just occasionally, like now. Or when you're determined I answer your questions, or when—"

"Sophia?" He cut in, leaning forward. I found myself mirroring him.

I swallowed, "Yes?"

"Stop there before that hole you're digging swallows us both up."

"Got it," I mumbled, taking a large swig of wine, which promptly caught the back of my throat, sending my body into a coughing spasm, my eyes watering until everything became blurred before me.

The hard slap on my back shocked me so much it stopped my coughing right there and then.

"Th-thanks."

"No problem. Not too intimidating, I hope? It was that or watch you choke to death."

My eyes met his laughing ones, and this time it was me forcing a serious tone. "Shut up and stop laughing, I could have died!" I gave him a push on the arm, attempting to look stern, but his laughter was contagious, and I found myself laughing with him, both of us nearly spilling our drinks on the picnic rug.

A little later, Marcus persuaded me to my feet to teach me a traditional Ceilidh Scottish dance. As I clumsily attempted to copy his jig and reel moves, which reminded me of county dancing only with more intricate toes pointed, I felt a rich release of pure joy and excitement. Holding my hands tightly, Marcus spun me around giddily, grinning as I laughed so hard my sides felt like they were about to split apart, before pulling me closer to him.

The sun began to set into a glorious golden hue, teasing the water with its radiant reds and striking yellows, as if stroking the surface with its featherlight touch.

MARCUS WAVED the empty wine bottle at me, as the light gave way to the gathering dust. "I had no idea you were such a heavy drinker, Ms. Meadows."

I had been watching the colours dancing on the water as the sun finally sank down, and now dragged my eyes away to focus on him, raising my eyebrows. To be honest, I'd had no idea we'd drunk so much, but there was no denying I felt a little squiffy and very chilled. I stifled a yawn, which Marcus caught. "I think you'd find I was merely drinking out of politeness so you wouldn't feel like a billy no mates," I murmured.

"Such an honourable, selfless act."

"I thought so, yes." All at once, a shiver gripped my body. "Oh, you really feel it when that sun's not on you."

"Or, you're no longer warmed by the wine and dancing. Let's pack up," Marcus said before I could utter my protest, "and head back to mine. Here, grab this." The rucksack came flying toward me, nearly knocking me back.

"Steady on!" I gasped.

In the limited light, we managed to grab everything. I felt heavy with reluctance as I followed Marcus out. This tucked-away spot had reached a part of my heart, fulfilling a strong yearning I didn't know I had. I wanted to stay, I wanted to come back… with him.

"I hope you know where you're going," I nervously laughed as I stumbled, not so elegantly, after his own sure-footed boots crunching loudly in the now-gathering darkness. The moon was half eclipsed, lighting only the blue loch alongside me with its eerie white rays.

Marcus laughed shortly without turning around and said, "I would hope so too, ach, seeing as this is my homeland. Feeling concerned?"

"No, no, not at all," I exclaimed a little too brightly, gritting my teeth as my ankle bone collided with a tree root. I stopped to rub the painful spot. Unaware, Marcus carried on, and I had to risk tripping up to catch up with him, breathing hard to keep up with his pace. Marcus seemed determined to reach home as soon as possible, with a constant look all around him, whereas I would have preferred a slow meander back.

To stop myself from dwelling on whatever it was that lurked in the undergrowth—producing those weird noises, invading my ears and brushing against my skin—I said the first thing that came to mind. "You never told me how you and Lucy ended up living in this place. Oh, sorry," I gasped as I almost fell against him, my feet unable, it seemed, to walk in a straight line. He paused for a moment to turn and peer at me through the blackness. I couldn't read his expression, could only hear that his voice was concerned, if a little distracted when he spoke. "You okay?"

"Yes, yes, I'm fine, good. Just not as nimble-footed as you."

"I forget, sorry. But let's keep going, aye? It's not much farther," he encouraged.

On we walked, me trying to copy his every movement from behind. *Can't be too much farther, surely*, I reassured myself. Maybe I should get my phone out to use as a torch.

"To answer your question," Marcus began, as I felt inside my pockets for my phone. "After coming across this lodge while staying round here, we noticed it was up for sale and had clearly been for some time, as it was very neglected. So, we put in a cheeky offer. Mind this bit here, some loose rocks."

My hand pulled out my phone, distracting me from

what Marcus was saying, paying no attention as to where I was placing my feet.

The rocks beneath me moved suddenly under the burden of my full weight, causing my footing to give way with nothing for me to cling onto to stop myself from sliding. Arms flailing wildly, I screamed as I fell into the cold, dark water waiting to pull me down into its grasp.

19

The first thing you feel in a moment like this is the shock of the cold hitting your skin, which will have you sharply sucking in your breath, forcing you to swallow large mouthfuls of choking water as you become increasingly desperate for air.

My arms and legs flailed helplessly as the water dragged me under, my coat and boots now an oppressive weight. Even so, I frantically tried to push my way back up to the surface. All the time my mind was screaming, *I don't want to die! Push harder, Sophia, push hard.*

But as the seconds became minutes, my mind grew as panicked as my body. The water was determined, and it felt like I'd been battling against it for hours. My breath became shallower and my limbs weary. Time came to a standstill.

With my strength failing me, my eyes started to close, and my arms ceased flailing as a dull acceptance of my fate took hold. My body stopped fighting against the inevitable, and I began to sink into the darker depths below…

The strangest of sensations then occurred, as if I was being weightlessly carried up and up toward the water's surface.

It was only when the cold blast of air hit my icy body, jerking it out of its semi-consciousness, did my brain grasp that I was being half pulled, half dragged toward the edge of the loch. Arms were locked tight around my middle, and my legs were kicking hard against the force of the water.

He dragged us both onto the merciful soft ground, where we collapsed, coughing and shivering. Immediately, I could feel Marcus' hands upon my face, pushing back the wet strands of hair as his body arched over me. His ear came close to my mouth as he strained to hear my breath. "Sophia? Soph? Can you breathe? Are you hurt, lass? Do you know where you are?"

I tried to nod, my voice croaky as I forced myself to reassure him, "I'm okay, I…"

At my words, I was crushed hard against him. "Thank God," he breathed out. "Thank God. I never thought, I didn't think of this kind of danger…"

His voice trailed off, as if he was stunned. My arms wrapped themselves around him, and we stayed like that, until the inevitable shudders began to rack my body as the water from my wet clothes seeped like ice into my skin. Feeling them against his own wet body, Marcus pulled back.

"We need to get you out of these wet clothes before you get ill. Can you walk?"

"I-I think so," I managed to get out through chattering teeth.

"Take my hand and, for the love of all things, don't let go. I just need to find where I dropped my clothes."

Only then did I realise he wore only his underwear, his torso stripped of his T-shirt and coat. His skin glistened in the moonlight, as his strong back bent down to pick up his clothes and shoes. Taking the time to only slip on his jeans and boots, he wrapped his coat around my shaking shoulders, before taking my hand firmly in his grip to lead us home.

NEVER HAD THERE BEEN A MORE welcome sight than the light and warmth streaming from his lodge as we half stumbled, half crawled through the inviting door.

Our wet footprints left a trail over the wooden floor as we stepped into the lounge. By now, I was like a helpless child, unable to do anything for myself. I couldn't even find the strength in me to reach for a towel. Uncontrollable shudders ripped through my body as I stood there, drenched and dripping.

As if sensing this, Marcus treated me as if I was a child, dragging off my jumper and T-shirt, then easing down my jeans that stubbornly clung to my legs, until I stood in only my bra and knickers. If I hadn't felt so cold, I might have felt embarrassed, but the relief of having them away from my skin overrode any other emotion. I wouldn't have cared if he had taken off my underwear, but

Marcus had been quick to avert his eyes from my half-dressed state.

He gently propelled me to his bathroom. I watched him turn on the hot water tap for the shower, still looking anywhere but at me. He grabbed a towel from the cupboard then said, "Jump in, warm up. Fortunately, there's plenty of hot water. Here's a towel to use. I'll grab you some clothes of mine."

"But wh-what about-t you?" I stuttered.

Marcus was already moving past me, eyes determinedly ahead. "Don't worry, I'll go in after you. I'll be back in a minute." And with that, the door closed firmly behind him. Obediently, I stripped off the remainder of my clothes and stepped under the inviting, steaming water, willing it to quickly soothe and warm me. As the soft water trailed over my cold skin, an unexpected urge of shock, along with the desire to break down and cry, gripped me.

Don't be so silly, you're fine, you're fine. Pull yourself together.

Except I couldn't. I couldn't. I wasn't strong enough, right then. Without turning the water off, my eyes full of tears, I unsteadily climbed out of the shower and pulled the towel over me. Sinking down onto the bath rug, the emotions came in a way I had never allowed before. The shock of tonight had the effect of a dam exploding as it was forced to collapse. Repressed emotions from the last few weeks, combined with the hurt and pain I carried from Richard, began to leave me.

I was dimly aware of the door opening, the water being switched off, of being gently pulled into his arms. An immense feeling of protection and comfort warmed my body as I responded to his touch, clinging to him. The rhythmic stroking of his hand over my hair soothed me. The pressure of his legs resting against mine brought strength and reassurance.

In that defining moment, my heart began to heal and let go of the past.

In that life-changing moment, my heart began to love another.

I didn't know it, not then. It would only be much later before I would understand this, when my life would once more be threatened.

20

Marcus let the hot water caress and soothe his cold, aching muscles, strained from diving down and pulling Sophia out. His energy was now at its lowest, when just before it had been at its highest. Adrenaline had flowed violently through him from the minute he'd realised she had fallen in, through every second it had taken to drag off his clothes and dive in. All the while, urgently calling out her name through the suffocating darkness. That same adrenaline had kept him swimming down again and again for her, even though his chest had burnt with the need for air and the water had become an enemy to them both.

The intense feeling of relief when his searching hands touched her skin had given him the burst of power he desperately needed to pull them both out. He had feared the worst and had instead been rewarded with a breathing, talking Sophia. That was when he became overwhelmed, crushing her hard against him as he silently vowed never to let her go. When she had later cried in his arms, it felt as if his guts were being twisted up, and all he wanted was to take her pain and grief away.

Now, only lingering shock stayed with him.

He had nearly lost her.

And that changed everything.

THE SHIVERING in my body had finally faded away. I sat curled up on Marcus' sofa, dressed in his soft green V-neck jumper and jeans too large for my waist, the last of the shudders finally leaving my bones. I had no underwear on, having left them hanging on the bath to dry, and found myself worrying what Marcus would think. He must have noticed the rather plain white undies when he'd showered, but he made no comment as he padded barefoot into the lounge wearing faded jeans and a black sweatshirt.

I discreetly checked my eyes in the TV screen near me, praying the puffiness from my crying bout had gone down and my hair, prone to frizz, was calm as it curled in wet tendrils around my neck. I'd never been one of those ladies who look good after crying; all I could hope was that I was passable. Everything inside me felt different, like pieces of a puzzle had been moved into different holes. Was it because I'd had a glimpse of my own mortality and how fragile our lives really were? Or was it something more profound stirring my spirit? Still, a superficiality left me wanting to impress him.

I smiled at Marcus as he came round to sit beside me. I could feel those ever-piercing eyes on me, which missed nothing as they scanned my face, and I had to fight hard against the urge to avert my gaze. Whatever he saw must have reassured him, for he gave a small, satisfied nod and returned my smile.

"I made you a coffee," I murmured, pointing to the still-steaming mug of coffee resting on the coffee table, amongst the papers we left earlier.

"You did? Ach, thanks, I need this. Though I may need a wee drop of something." Marcus reached over to the table in front of us and picked up the bottle of whisky he kept below. He then added a "wee medicinal dram" to both of our coffees with a small smile. I made no protest and closed my eyes to savour the kick of heat trailing down my lungs as I took a large sip.

Marcus took his mug between his palms, taking a healthy swallow himself, then, letting it warm up as his body, gave a small shudder. "I knew there was a reason I've never gone swimming in that loch. It's cold enough to freeze the *fuar bàlaichean* off me, that it is."

"No idea what you said at the end, but rest assured there's no way I'm in a rush to fall back in," I said, hugging my arms round me tightly, the memory swamping over me of icy water pulling me under\. *Don't go there. Crying once was enough*. I attempted to smile at Marcus as he glanced across at me.

"Good to know. You've helped me earn my damsel in distress badge, a new one for me, but I'm in no rush to repeat it."

"I'm glad I was able to assist you in earning a brand-new shiny badge." Gratitude flooded me as I gazed at him. I wanted to wrap my arms tightly around him but settled for leaning my head against his shoulder for a long moment. "I never said thank you when you first pulled me out, risking your life for me like that. So, I'm saying it now." I looked up to capture his eyes, wanting him to know the depth of gratitude I felt. "Thank you, a million times thank you. I don't know many people who have that kind of bravery and courage within them, as you did."

Frisson crackled in the air. There was a new intensity in both our eyes, an awareness something important was taking place. His warm hand brushed against my cheek for a moment before sliding away, and he said, "You're very welcome."

In that moment, I felt incredibly close to Marcus. I craved more. I needed more. My trust in him was now at its greatest. He had shown that I could put my very life into his hands, and he would risk his own to save it. It was a heady feeling, one I thought should feel scary, but I found that instead it gave me a boldness and conviction to open up to him on a deeper level again. The line between professional detective and witness had long since been crossed, blurred into undefinable boundaries. We both knew this.

"When I felt myself being pulled under," I began, my voice croaky and a little stilted until it gained in strength. "I could feel panic hitting me, that blind scary-as-hell kind of panic like I've never experienced before. All I kept thinking was, what have I done with this life I've been given?" I shook my head, feeling again that damnation of having wasted so many moments and chances. "I've lived half a life by carrying around this huge weight of self-loathing for giving my love to a man I knew right from the start wasn't right for me, would never be right, that's the brutal, honest truth. How could it be a full life when he never really loved me? That's fourteen years of my life. Over half of it, dammit, that I've let slip away. And that could have been it, the story of my life, finito! I can't... I can't let that be it. It can't be my only story."

The fire burning in front of us crackled. I stared at it for a moment, trying to order my chaotic thoughts. Marcus sat quietly beside me, his body solidly beside mine, allowing me to talk, to understand myself. I knew with certainty he was listening intently to every word I said.

"I think that's why I cried like I did, back there in your bathroom. It was as if I could no longer keep all these feelings I'd been pushing down and down within. They had to come out." I turned from staring into the fire, to the steady man beside me. "Does any of what I'm saying make any sense, or do I just sound like some crazy nutcase who's about to set up home with fifty feral cats?"

Marcus shook his head with that faint smile of his. "You're not quite that crazy yet but, aye, give it time and —Ow! You've got a hard flick on you, lass. Too soon for jokes?"

"Too soon," I said.

Leaning forward to put his mug down, he swivelled on the sofa so he could look at me fully. He paused as he stared at something undefinable over my shoulder. I could see his mind had taken him to a place that was at once exquisite joy and excruciating pain. "When she got sick, really sick, I used to carry Lucy down to the loch where we've just been. I remember one time I found myself staring at my wife, this twenty-nine-year-old woman who should be setting the world on fire but instead was being ravaged and destroyed by this loathsome disease. I hated it with every fibre of my being, and this uncontrollable *rage* just grabbed me, hard, like a tight band thumping in my head. I had to run as far away as I could from her before I did something stupid. I don't even know where I ran, but with every step, I raged at God about the injustice and unfairness of it all. She loved God, you see, never blamed him for her illness. So, I was doing it for her."

Marcus swallowed, looking down. I took his hand between mine, waiting patiently as he had for me. He looked down at our hands, then turned his gaze up to me.

"When I finally felt calm enough to return to Lucy, she did exactly what you just did then—took my hand. I asked her how she could be so at peace and she said... she said, 'Don't blame God. He didn't give me this sickness, He hates it as much as you do. All our bodies fail eventually. I've accepted there's some things people can't change, no matter how much they want to. I can't change this. You can't change this. But what I can make sure is that every morning I wake up to see the sun rising, I won't let one minute of that day slip me by unnoticed.''

He broke off, swallowing, rubbing his thumb over my hand as if needing to feel another person's warmth. I pressed a little closer to him, my throat raw with unshed tears.

"You know, that was the moment I stopped raging

against the illness, stopped trying to fight against something I couldn't win. Instead, I made the decision I would watch the sunrise every morning by her side until the day came when it finally stopped rising for her. That's all we can do, Soph. Every sunrise we're given, we don't waste one single moment of the day that follows it."

[21]

I'd lost track of time but knew the hours must be slipping by. Lulled by the crackling fire and the music softly pouring from the speaker, my yawns became incessant. But the thought of getting up, changing back into my wet clothes, and leaving Marcus to drive back to the apartment was out of question both physically and mentally.

But I had to. Marcus had made no offer of a spare bed for the night, and I knew it would cost him, professionally speaking, to have me stay. Still it didn't stop me from desiring it.

A yawn ripped through me again, making Marcus' head swing up from where he crouched, prodding the last of the fire's ambers.

"You're tired. I'm not surprised; I am too. It's been an eventful last few hours, that it has."

He stood up, and I had no choice but to follow suit. "I'll just change back into my clothes, then be out of your way."

"What?" Marcus stared at me, flummoxed.

"So, you can get to bed," I expanded.

"I had presumed you were staying the night."

"Sorry?" Did I hear that right?

Marcus shook his head, walking toward me with an apologetic hand. "That came out wrong. What I mean is that I'm not happy letting you drive home in the dark by yourself, having had a near-drowning experience, not to mention a few wee glasses of wine and whiskey. All to then return to an unsafe apartment. There's no way you are going back there tonight." He looked at me with steely determination, and I couldn't help but smile, the roles reversed as Marcus babbled on.

I tried not to show the elation and excitement bubbling under my skin, by keeping my voice as neutral as possible when I said, "Where would I sleep?" *With you?*

"In my bed." My eyebrows shot up in surprise. He slapped his forehead. "For the love of all things! My damn brain must be waterlogged or something. What I meant is, you'll have my bed, and I'll take the couch. Of course, you will, naturally."

I really don't want you to take the couch. "Oh... Okay, if you're sure?"

"I am, aye, definitely. I uh... just need to go check it's presentable. All right to stay here for a minute?"

I nodded, watching him dash into his room as if the hounds themselves were after him. I let out a breath, trying to compose myself.

Sam Smith's voice echoed from the playlist, now singing only for me, his lyrics expressing what I was dying to say out loud. *Can I lay by your side tonight, Marcus, next to you?*

"It's all yours."

I spun round at the sound of his voice. Marcus hovered at the doorway of his bedroom, holding a blue blanket and pillow in his hands.

"Let me apologise in advance for anything unsavoury you find," he apologised, unnecessarily as far as I was concerned. "I've left a T-shirt out for you. Sorry I don't have pyjamas, I… don't wear them," he continued.

A vivid image of him asleep naked in his bed filled my imagination. My throat closed over, unable to ask him what I wanted to.

Marcus walked toward me, dropping his bedding onto the sofa, giving me a look I couldn't fathom. "Anyway, I guess we should get some sleep. Just call out if you need anything." Hesitation, then the briefest of kisses touched my cheek, over far too soon. Marcus turned away and started arranging his own bedding. The song began to fade away from us.

Come on, Sophia! Don't be a coward.

I grabbed his arm, harder than I intended, but it had the desired effect. His head swung back to me, surprise lingering in his eyes when he said, "Soph?"

"Share your bed with me," I whispered, taking in every detail of him.

I watched his Adam's apple move up and down as he swallowed. I saw desire fight against refusal. Beneath my hand, I felt his body tense. I watched it all.

"I… don't think that's a good idea. You, me, this is already complicated. We need to try and keep this at—"

"I'm not asking you to cross any more lines than you already have. I just need to feel safe tonight, in your arms.

That's all I'm asking, to sleep in your arms. No more than that." I could hear the plea in my voice yet felt no embarrassment. Not with him. I spoke the raw truth from deep within me. "Please," I softly added, as he stared at me, unable to turn away.

"Sophia," he breathed out. "Do you have any idea what you're asking of me?"

"Yes."

My hand slid down to grasp his.

⌇

I WAS ALREADY LYING on my side faced away from him when I felt the pressure of his body sink the bed down. I let out a breath I'd unconsciously been holding in as I had waited for him to join me. It had felt like an eternity from when he had hung back in the lounge, waiting for me to undress. I had begun to doubt that Marcus would come, the conflict of his actions becoming too much for him.

But here he was, as was I, and my heart raced. The bedside lamp was extinguished, and in the sudden plunging darkness, I sensed Marcus lying very still and controlled beside me. Reaching behind me, I felt for his hand and pulled it toward me so his hand rested on my stomach. His arm moved carefully around me, cradling me, until his chest pressed against my back. Instinctively, I pressed myself closer still, so his head rested close to mine, my hand covering his, our bodies mirroring each other, as if we had lain like this a thousand times before.

His mouth pressed a kiss against my hair before he softly whispered, "Sleep now, *mo leannan.*"

Despite the burning hunger for him tingling throughout my body, despite wanting to stay awake so I could somehow postpone daybreak coming, despite all of this, my eyes wouldn't stay open. My body gave in to the beckoning lure. Wrapped in his arms, his warmth softening my bones, I slipped away into a dreamless sleep.

IT WAS the rays of light dancing off the ceiling before touching my skin that finally dragged me out of my deep slumber. As I reluctantly opened my eyes, it took me a moment to comprehend where I was. In Marcus' bed. Alone.

Sitting up too quickly and making my head spin in protest, I looked around the room. No sign of Marcus apart from the slightly ruffled sheets where he'd laid. Straining my ears, I could hear a soft whistle coming from the kitchen area, and I closed my eyes in silly relief. Of course, he was still here. He wasn't the type to run away before any awkward questions were asked, though we had nothing to feel guilty about. I wasn't sure if I should be impressed or disappointed that Marcus had acted the perfect gentleman all night. Perhaps I'd mistaken the desire in his eyes last night.

Feeling the bird's nest that was my hair, I scampered quickly into the clean, blue-washed bathroom to try and make myself presentable. My mouth felt yuck, and I was tempted to use Marcus' toothbrush, before pulling a resigned face and rubbing toothpaste directly onto my teeth. Not ideal, but necessary. I knew I had some perfume and an emergency hairbrush in my handbag, which fortunately was sitting in the bedroom's doorway. My clothes, at least, were dry, though slightly musty and hardened. I grimaced as I dragged them on over my body after taking a quick shower, making my skin feel tight and uncomfortable.

I dared a quick look in the mirror (acceptable if not glamourous) before moving toward the sound of the whistling.

Marcus had his back to me as he bent over the cooker, frying two eggs, the sizzling hot oil in danger of burning him. He had on the same clothes from last night, and his hair looked a little unkempt. The desire to go and smooth it down itched at my hands.

"'Morning," I offered, smiling as he swivelled around.

"'Morning, sleepyhead," he replied, slowly returning my smile. I noticed there was a light sparkling in his eyes this morning. I moved closer to him, leaning against the counter alongside him.

"I know," I groaned. "Sorry. I probably should have been up hours ago, but I haven't slept that long and so well in such a long time. I guess I didn't want to stop."

"You look rested. You obviously needed it. How do you like your eggs? Ach, you wouldn't be able to butter that toast for me there, would you?" He pointed the spatula in his hand toward the toaster. Two pieces of toast, slightly burnt, had popped up.

Moving around him, I happily complied, spreading generous amounts of butter. "I like my eggs runny, to answer your question."

"Then you and I have the same taste." I could feel his

eyes on me, watching me, before he admitted, "You're not the only one who slept well. I don't think I've slept this good since... since Lucy died. I... didn't expect that."

I swung up to look at him. There was a puzzled frown on his face, as if his mind was trying to catch up with what his body instinctively knew. Without pause or thought, I reached up to kiss his stubbled, unshaven cheek, before pointing at the eggs, now hissing in protest at being left too long. "I think they might be done."

IT WAS the phone call not twenty minutes later that changed the mood, taking it from a laughing, teasing one, to a concretely serious one, at least on Marcus' part.

As he looked at the caller ID, Marcus' shoulders tensed, and his body stilled. Shooting me an apologetic look, he answered the call while moving away. I felt the rush of the outside air swoop in as he stepped out onto the veranda. Absently, I began to clear the plates, carrying them to the sink and filling up the basin to wash them.

Something in his manner took my mind back to yesterday, before my near drowning. Another phone call, us suddenly going for a walk, and something Marcus had said after pulling me out of the water. What was it? *What was it?* I could feel it coming back: *"I never thought... I didn't think of this kind of danger..."*

The feel of water slowly seeping onto my feet jerked me out of my thoughts enough to hastily turn the tap off. I grabbed the nearest cloth I could find and crouched down to mop up the small puddle forming on the wooden floor.

As I rose up, the wind must have changed direction, for now I could hear Marcus' voice from outside, his tone firmer and more direct than I had ever heard as he instructed, "I want this brought to a conclusion *now*! Do you understand me? This is a priority—"

The wind once more blew away from me, snatching away the last of his words. But what I had heard was enough. I stood there, gripping the towel so hard my knuckles turned white.

[22]

I still stood by the sink, not moving, when Marcus reappeared, his phone in hand.

He stopped short when I turned and faced him. There came an immediate look of resignation darkening his pupils as they met mine, and I calmly said, "You need to tell me what's going on, Marcus. I know something is. I sensed it last night though I couldn't vocalise it. I know *you*. Something has got you spooked." I shook my head, my teeth gnawing my lip. "And you don't get spooked."

There was a moment of suspended silence as we both considered the other. Then Marcus came up to me, gently disentangling my hand that gripped the tea towel before taking them in his.

"Trust me!" I implored, when still he hesitated.

Marcus nodded a couple of times, before he said, "Okay... okay. This is the situation. Yesterday, before we went for a walk, I got a call from a colleague to say they'd seen a man, possibly in his early thirties, very close to my lodge on the main path leading down this lane."

"Did they catch him?"

Marcus shook his head. "No, they didn't."

"Do we know who he is?" I urged on.

"There's no way of knowing for sure."

My hands gripped his tighter. "But could it be the man who broke into the apartment?"

"Possibly. Possibly Lyle or someone working for him. When I got the call, I decided it would be wisest for us to walk away from here for a while, keep a safe distance 'til I knew more. That was my plan. What I hadn't bargained on was you deciding to take a bath in the loch." A half smile played across his lips, almost enticing me to do the same. Almost.

I pulled a face and said, "Not funny. Do we know if this man came back last night or this morning? What did your colleague tell you then on the phone?"

Whenever Marcus paused, like he did now, my heart leapt in trepidation. I braced myself. "There's a possibility. Someone has certainly been tracking us both here and at your friend's apartment. A call was made to the station from her parents, concerned by a couple of what they thought were prank knocks and phone calls, the kind where no one is on the other end—"

"But which we know aren't prank calls at all. Marcus, we can't let anything happen to them with her dad so sick!" My voice rose an octave.

Marcus let go of my hands to cup my face. "Don't worry, I have one of my sergeants going to their house right now to check on them."

"I should check on them too," I said as I moved as if to do so right then. Marcus stopped me.

"Phone them, yes, but don't visit them." He raised my chin, so I was locking eyes with him. "Promise me you won't go by yourself." When I didn't reply, his eyes narrowed dangerously. "Promise me."

What choice did I have? I reluctantly nodded.

"Good. I know you'll keep your word, lass."

His hands still cupped my face, and I moved my cheek into his palm to seek comfort, closing my eyes before confessing, "I'm really worried. Not just for me, but for all of us."

Marcus pressed his head against my forehead, his breath coming out almost as a sigh. "Don't be, it's going to be alright. No one is going to get harmed. Hey, hey, don't cry on me again. Ach, I'm not good with tears." His fingers stroked away a solitary tear I didn't realise had fallen, before pressing his lips against mine on the salty trail left behind.

"I—"

Whatever words I was about to say got swept away in the sudden feel of his lips on mine, unexpected and all the more intense. I was still for a moment, taken by surprise, but then my body awoke with the thrill of his touch. I eagerly opened up to him, returning the kiss.

Marcus pulled back, intending to stop, to gain breath and perhaps some clear thinking. "I shouldn't have—"

"Yes, you should." I reached up to pull his mouth back down to mine, pressing myself against him, feeling his lips as he deepened the kiss, pulling me tight against him. I ran my hands down his firm chest, then around his waist, his own moving sensuously down my side and across my back, lingering in the low, deep curve just above my jean's waistband. I closed my eyes as his mouth moved down my neck, before finding mine again. We both wanted, needed more...

And we had to stop... Now.

We stood there, a little breathless, gazing at each other in half shock, half wonder. I laughed even while I gasped, "Great way to stop the tears, I must say, DI Armstrong."

Marcus let out a long breath as he half laughed, half groaned. "Thank you." He shook his head, closing his eyes. When they re-opened, I could see the guilt and confusion lingering there. "I shouldn't have taken advantage like that. I'm crossing so many lines, I don't know myself. I should get someone to take over—"

I shook my head violently. "No! No, don't do that, please!" I touched his face, urging him to reconsider and said, "You're the only one I trust." He remained conflicted, and I felt myself grow a little desperate. "I won't touch you again. You don't have to touch me." As I said the words, I dropped my hands, stepping back, and I could see from his face how almost impossible that would be for him, as impossible as it would be for me. Even now, my hands were itching to reach out and touch him again. I could still taste him on my lips, smell his scent on my cheeks. "See, we're not touching now. We can do this."

"Can we? You must be stronger than me." There was a bleakness to his voice.

"We can try," my voice whispered. "We have to."

Marcus ran his fingers distractedly through his hair. I could sense his mind racing, then he sighed. "All right, okay, for now I won't come off the case. But if I do have to, you need to know it's because of my own doing, not yours. I invited you here, kissed you because…"

"Because…" I softly encouraged.

He swallowed as he stared at me. "Because I can't bear the thought of anything happening to you, and I want, *need*, to be the one who's protecting you. You're becoming everything to me, *mo leannan*. Everything."

I PULLED up in Ella's assigned parking space, turned off the ignition, and waited. In my rear-view mirror, I saw Marcus park up at a discreet distance. Almost immediately, my mobile phone sprang into life, displaying his name. I pressed accept before it had rung once, a smile warming my chilled face from the cool, early morning air.

"Hey, you," I said.

"Hey, yourself. I'm sorry I can't come up with you," his deep voice said. "But…"

"Under the circumstances, we don't want anyone suspecting anything between us," I finished off.

"Aye, exactly. My men checked the apartment only an hour ago, and all seemed fine. They'll be right where I am now any minute and will keep their eyes right on the front doors, if they know what's good for them." The last bit was muttered in a dark tone that I only just caught.

"I'm not worried," I said, and it was true. I felt like I could take on the world right then. The feel of his body was imprinted on me, and I closed my eyes to savour it for a moment.

"That almost reassures me. I'll call you later this afternoon, but if you need me before—"

"Stop worrying!" I laughed. "I know how to reach you. Never had you down as a worrier, Detective Inspector Armstrong."

At last, I heard his laugh ripple down the line. "Nor me, Ms. Meadows, nor me. Ach, what is it you're doing to me?"

"I'll keep you posted on that. Now, go and do some work, part-timer. I'll speak to you later."

I was still smiling as I disconnected the phone and made my way up to Aneella's apartment, aware Marcus was watching my every step until I was safely inside the building. The thrill of his protectiveness over me was becoming more than a little addictive. I didn't want to contemplate what would happen when I was no longer in danger and he had no need to stay close to me. *Not yet.*

I had barely changed out of my clothes, grimacing at the smell of the loch lingering on them, when the doorbell rang.

My heart leapt in eagerness without any regard to my brain, which was trying to caution my haste. *Perhaps Marcus had changed his mind and decided to come up after all!* My fingers touched my mouth where his had been only a short time before. The taste of him still lingered there.

With a smile of anticipation, I opened the door.

As I stared at the man standing before me, my lips froze over and my heart turned cold.

[23]

"What the hell are you doing here?!"

The words came out more forcefully than I intended, but the shock of seeing him, coupled with the immediate intensity of unburied feelings he brought with him, had me behaving in a less than civilised manner.

"And it's nice to see you too, Soph."

His easy charm of a smile I'd succumbed to many times only served to rile me even further. "You don't get to call me Soph anymore. You lost that right the minute you walked out on our marriage."

Richard threw up his hands in defence, seemingly only to quell my anger. "I apologise. Can I come in?"

What choice did I have without sounding like a sullen teenager not getting her own way? Reluctantly, I moved aside to let him into the apartment. As I stared after him, watching him make himself at home on the sofa, all I could think was: *Why are you here when I've finally found some closure? Who gave you the right to come stamping all over me again?*

The shock was wearing away and, with it, my anger. I was glad, I wanted to look like I was in control. I still carried shame in the way I'd lost dignity and self-respect in those last dark days of our marriage.

I moved round to sit opposite him, as far away as I dared. I felt his eyes on me and averted my own, resisting the urge to see if his mouth still dimpled on his left side or if his eyes creased up in that way of his when he smiled. I stared instead at my hands and stubbornly held my tongue. No way was I making this easy for him. After a long, drawn-out silence, Richard finally gave in.

"How've you been? Still working all hours?"

My eyes flew to his. "Did you really come all this way to ask me questions you could have put in a text?"

"You've changed your number," he quipped back. "And your landline keeps ringing out."

And why do you think I changed my numbers?

I couldn't sit still. I leapt up and began to pace the room as my head throbbed with the suddenness of the situation.

"That doesn't really explain what you're doing here, and, more to the point, how the hell you knew where to find me."

"Why? Were you trying to hide from me?"

When I glared at him but said nothing in reply, Richard shrugged and calmly replied, "I'm sure you can guess who told me."

I stopped short. "Mum," I sighed out. Of course. Mum, who still believed that we could work through our differences and find a way out the other end.

Richard gave me that smile again, hitting me in the gut. I bit my lip and turned away.

"I see you still do that, that biting your lip thing when you're nervous."

I gasped, a reaction I couldn't stop as my ex-husband's words were almost identical to what Marcus had said to me not twenty-four hours ago. *No, don't think about Marcus. Keep alert.*

"Then perhaps you don't know me as well as you think you do," I replied as coolly as I could. "Because that's the last thing I'm feeling around you."

He sat forward now, frowning. "What are you feeling?"

"What am I feeling?" I repeated in disbelief, a surge of anger once more riding me. "All right, I'll damn well tell you. Right now, I feel disbelief that you have the audacity to turn up like this, acting like the last year never happened, angry that you can still rile me like this and—"

Hurt. I was going to say hurt. But there was no way he was going to know that.

Richard rose from the sofa and walked a little toward me. "And what?"

"It doesn't matter," I said, shaking my head, wanting to retreat, yet unable to move as if gripped in a battle where I didn't know whose side I was fighting for. I took a deep breath. "You walked out on me. On *me*, Rich, not the other way 'round. That means you lost the right to turn up and push your way back in."

Richard had moved closer still. If I reached out my hand, it would collide with his chest. I stuffed my hands into my back pocket.

"What if I wanted to walk back into your life, push my way back in?"

My head jerked up as his rich voice became like silken velvet, causing a reaction in me just as he intended, as he always did when he wanted me to do his bidding. His hand moved up to touch my chin. Again, my feet refused to move.

"Would you let me in, Soph? Would you give me another try?"

"Why? Why are you asking me this?" I whispered.

Richard smiled, his hand softly stroking my chin. I couldn't look away. "Because I want to be back in your life, in your bed. I want you to be my wife again."

[24]

For a full minute I could only stand there, staring at him. It was the oddest of sensations, hearing words that you desperately desired only a few months back, only for them to leave you conflicted by their very utterance.

I won't lie, the thrill of having them said to me, coupled with the touch of his fingers against my skin and his eyes full of hope as they gazed at me, was dangerous and intoxicating. It was almost like my body was wired to react to him, like a magnet drawn to a powerful source. The urge to reach out and touch him, and to feel his heart beneath my hand again, was building inside me.

My hand began to stretch out...

Until the knowing gleam in his eyes had me whipping it back. I violently stepped back, forcing his hand to drop away.

The gleam turned to confusion. "Sophia?"

"No, no," I said, my head shaking vehemently. "I'm sorry. You can't have me as your wife again."

Richard stared at me, his eyes like threatening slits. "I

don't get it. I thought this is what you wanted, what you begged me for—for me to come back. Now, it's a no?"

Shame washed over me. Had I really begged? Leaving my pride and respect shattered to pieces?

"Is there someone else?" he demanded when I didn't answer.

Marcus. There was Marcus. A flash of him, our kiss. All I wanted was to rush to him, feel his arms around me, pouring his strength into me. Strength I could now feel surging through me as he filled my mind.

I rose to my full height and faced Richard straight on. "That's none of your concern. I don't know what you thought you would achieve by turning up like this. I'm sorry you've wasted your time," I said, a deep breath escaping my lips. "But we don't love each other anymore, if you ever did. No, no, let me finish. There are things happening here that are literally using up everything I have, with nothing left over. Even if I'd wanted to get back with you, you couldn't have picked a worse time. You need to go home—"

"What 'things' are you talking about? Tell me." Richard attempted to move closer to me again. "Let me make it better. You know I can help." His voice was trying to caress me.

"Please! Go home. There's nothing for you here." My voice rose a little in despair. I needed him to leave before I began to fall into my old ways of letting him take control. I would not let that happen. No man was ever going to control me for his own gain again.

"I'm not leaving it like this," he said, his voice filled with a stubbornness I remembered all too well.

"That's your choice."

"Can I stay?"

"Are you damn well kidding me?" I stood there, flabbergasted by his audacity. "No! Go find a hotel, sleep in the car. I really don't care as long as you're far away from me."

I turned and walked to the front door, throwing it open. For a moment, I thought he wasn't going to take the hint, but at last he walked up to me. He tried to stroke my face, but I jerked it away from him.

His breath was close to me as he vowed, "I'm coming back, I'm not giving up. I know you still want me. You could never fool me."

And with those parting words, he was gone.

I sagged against the door, closing my eyes, shaken. I stayed like that until my breath and heart were steady again.

⁂

A DARK RED car roared angrily out of the car park, moments before the dark blue Volvo drove in, parking at its normal spot. The two cops settled down to watch, coffee cups and packets of crisps filling their hands. Neither of them wanted to mess up again, not with the DI breathing down their necks, increasingly so since the sighting near his lodge yesterday. No one dared to ask who the lady with him had been. But they had their suspicions, mostly founded by the attractive yet cold bitch of a sergeant, Morven. And no one was going to argue with her on that.

The whole team was on tenterhooks and feeling ill at ease. They needed a lead, and fast, or they would be too late to stop the fraud taking place. Once it had happened, it would be almost impossible to track the laundered money. Already, unexplained deposits were appearing then disappearing within minutes on the account. It felt like a ticking bomb getting ready to explode. These were clever and dangerous masterminds. After all, if they were able to locate a DI's house way off radar, what else could they do?

No one was out of reach. No one could predict what violent means these criminals would adopt if thwarted.

⁓

ALL DAY, despite my head whirling with thoughts of Richard and Marcus, one concern overrode everything else: my worry for Aneella's parents. I needed to know they were safe. With Ella, who knows if she was checking in on them, which meant the responsibility for them landed on me.

I longed to go over in person, but the promise I'd given Marcus weighed heavily on me. *But he hadn't said no to me phoning them.*

Putting down my steaming mug of coffee, I grabbed my mobile and called their landline. I sensed I was being listened to.

The phone rang and rang. I was about to give up when Cathy's croaky, hesitant voice answered, "Yes, hello?"

"Cathy? It's me, Sophia."

"Oh! Hello, dear. It's nice to hear your voice."

I pressed the phone closer to my ear, so I could catch her words.

"Are you and Derek okay? I heard that you'd been receiving some crank phone calls."

"Oh, goodness, did you?" Her voice sounded surprised. "Does Aneella know?"

"No, no. Have you heard from her?" I rushed on.

"Only a quick email a couple of days ago, but we don't really expect to hear much from her."

Disappointment laced through me. Two days. Too long to help me now in knowing she was safe. "You should tell her what's happening, Cathy."

"Oh, I don't want to worry her about some silly phone calls," she said, her voice hastening to reassure. "I was just concerned it would upset Derek, that's why I called the police. But now, don't you worry, dear. We're fine."

"If you're sure?" I bit my lip, reluctant to say goodbye.

"Yes, yes. Oh, hold on!"

"Yes? I'm still here," I quickly said.

"I almost forgot. I found an old telephone number for Anthony from your university days. I'll just go get it for you."

I heard the phone being put down. In the following silence, my mind tried to frantically shift through my memory files. *Anthony? Anthony...*

"Here it is, my dear. Anthony Andrews."

Andrews? Of course! Professor Andrews, Ella's university professor, and the background man in the photo.

"Have you got a pen?" Cathy was saying now. I reached out to grab my bag to source one.

"Yep, got one. Go for it."

"0131 788456. Shall I repeat that?" She asked.

"Yes, please."

Having got the number down, Cathy went to say good-bye. I hurried in with, "You have the number here, don't you, if you need to reach me?"

"Yes, yes, thank you dear. I must go, it's time for Derek's meds. Goodbye."

The line went dead. I slowly lowered the phone, while staring at the name and number before me. Should I call Anthony now or talk to Marcus first? *But what use is a number without some information to go with it?*

Within a split second, I'd made up my mind.

I dialled the number.

ACROSS THE STREETS OF INVERNESS, within the confines of the police headquarters, Marcus sat frowning behind his desk, tiredness and frustration at the lack of progress biting hard at his clenched jaw.

The various papers spread before him were no use in working out what the numbers in the book meant, or if they were putting Sophia in danger. Nor how they connected to the money laundering blatantly taking place right in front of him. The book was now with the forensics team, and the waiting game had begun, even while he frustratingly watched over the bank account, hoping desperately some slip up would occur. Something, anything! In his eyes, Aneella and Lyle remained high on the fraud suspect list, even though Sophia was adamant her friend was innocent. Perhaps she was right and he was wrong. His normal objective-driven and reliable mind was letting him down, no doubt about it. Nothing was as it normally was.

The words began to swim in front of him. Marcus rubbed his tired eyes, squeezing them shut. As he did, his mind flashed all too eagerly to Sophia, remembering with aching clarity the press of her against him as she had slept, the dip and curve of her hips beneath his searching hands, the softness of her lips against his—

The door swinging open without ceremony crudely snapped Marcus back to the present. He swiftly lowered his hands, fighting to compose his features. Morven stood there, giving him an odd look. He resisted the urge to curse out loud.

"You alright there, Sir? You look a little startled."

Marcus avoided answering this by asking one of his own, "Have you got a lead on the numbers for me? Please tell me you have."

Morven stepped in closer, shutting the door behind her, then pulled out a chair without waiting for an invite.

"Make yourself at home," commented Marcus, dryly.

"Thanks, I will," Morven leaned back, grinning, enjoying the power of the suspense.

Only Marcus wasn't in the mood to play her game, and his voice was more abrupt than normal as he said, "Cut to the chase. We're wasting time here."

Her smile wavered and fell away. She sat up, her eyes showing a brief spark of hurt before she concealed it. Marcus caught it, trying to pretend he hadn't.

"Sure, if that's what you want. The forensic techy guys have just come back after analysing them. They've ruled out the end of the bank account numbers, the obvious choice for fraud."

Marcus quietly swore under his breath. "I was hoping it would be that simple. Did they say why they've ruled it out?"

Morven shrugged and said, "Something about how they don't follow the banking code reference for account numbers. I didn't ask lots of details. Sorry." But she didn't sound sorry. It was evident she was still annoyed with Marcus.

Marcus spread out his hands. "Okay, all right, I'll check with them later. Have they got any other bright sparks of wisdom for us?"

"They said they're looking into the numbers being program codes."

"Like binary," Marcus nodded. "Makes sense. I'll call Soph—Ms. Meadows—and see if she can shed more light as a program designer. Thanks Morven, leave it with me."

Morven stood, yet didn't leave. Surprised, Marcus looked up at her. "Was there something else?"

"I was just wondering, Sir, why we're involving the help of a potential suspect in this case?" Morven dared to challenge, holding her head high. "Especially with another unexplained call to both Ms. Blair's parents and another unidentified man today."

His eyes flickered in surprise at this, but he forced his voice to stay neutral and calm when he said, "Ms. Meadows has been helping us with our enquiries."

"But, even so, we shouldn't trust her! What if she's involved—"

He cut in with a voice, hard and cold, "I'm sure there's

work you need to be getting on with. Don't let me stop you."

Shut down with no way to respond, Morven gave a curt nod, then marched out. The door shook on its hinges as if caught in a hurricane.

Alone again, Marcus rubbed his forehead, releasing a long sigh. After a moment, he picked up his mobile.

⠀⠀⠀⠀⠀⠀⠀⠀⠀⠀⠀⠀⠀⠀⠀⠀᠊ᢙᢦ᠊

I WAS JUST HANGING up from the call when my phone began to ring, its tone insistent. I glanced down at the name, and my heart lifted. *Marcus.*

"Hello," I smiled. "I'm fine, still alive for now, despite my best efforts and others around me."

"Not funny, Soph," his voice admonished.

"Sorry," I mumbled apologetically. "Poor joke."

"Mm, but glad you're okay." A sigh came down the line.

I frowned, holding the phone closer to my ear. "Are *you* okay? You sound tired."

"Aye. It's crazy stupid here, with nothing to show for it. I'm beyond frustrated by the lack of progress with this case."

"Have you had any luck with deciphering the numbers?" I pressed on. It had been bugging me, playing on my mind. The numbers felt familiar, like I knew them intimately.

"That's why I was calling. My guys have ruled out them being bank account numbers. They're now thinking about some kind of programming codes, perhaps binary."

As Marcus spoke, something began to click and whirl within my mind, like a piece of a jigsaw floating near its rightful place, yet somehow missing its landing position.

"I'm requesting a copy of the book to be emailed to me. Do you think you could take another look at them?" he said, forcing the jigsaw piece to slip once more out of my grasp.

"Sure, of course I can. But it won't be tomorrow," I rushed on. "I've just arranged to see Aneella's old professor to see if he can help us with anything. He's only a couple of hours away by car." There was silence from his end as he processed what I was saying, so I felt compelled to carry on. "You see, I'm certain he's the man in the background of that old university photo of Ella and I, as well as the man in her locket. I feel there's something he can tell me to help us."

"I'm coming with you," he said, voice firm, set, and determined. "What time are you meeting him?"

"About 11:00 a.m., but as much as it would be good to have you there, I need to do this alone," I rushed on. "He knows me, and I think he will open up better if I'm alone without a police detective staring him down. No offence."

"None taken, but I still don't feel comfortable about this."

"Let me do this," my voice cajoled. "I want to help you, and I'm desperate to get Ella out of all of this. Trust me with this. Please."

Another sigh, then, "All right, okay. Call me when you're leaving. Even better, meet me tomorrow evening, no arguments. I'll bring the copy of the numbers with me."

The smile crept back to my face. "You've got yourself a date, Detective."

I was rewarded with a short laugh. "How is it you keep managing to persuade me to go against my own rules? Don't forget to call me, Ms. Meadows. I'll be waiting."

25

The morning had not started well.

I managed to collide the back of my head with the bathtub after slipping on the shower mat, leaving a large tender bump. This was closely followed by the realisation that my hairdryer was not where I thought I'd left it. After a fruitless twenty-minute search, swearing under my breath the whole time, my hair now hung wet and loose around my shoulders, leaving a nice damp patch on my top. To add to this, my stomach was growling angrily at me on discovering not even a crust of bread in the offering, leaving me muttering angrily for forgetting to go to the shops. This disorganisation on my part was new to me. At home, I went to the supermarket every Monday without fail. No time now to go to the shops, I sighed to myself. I should have left thirty minutes ago to have any hope of beating the traffic.

As I grabbed my phone and keys to fly out the door, I heard an incoming text alert. It was from Richard.

. . .

I DON'T WANT to leave it like we did yesterday. Call me xx

I THREW my phone into my handbag without answering. There was no denying it felt good to have the power for once. But it wasn't the reason I didn't reply.

PROFESSOR ANDREWS LIVED on the outskirts of Edinburgh, convenient for where he was now, based as a tutor at the University of Edinburgh. He gave me very precise directions to meet him at a cafe near the university, in order to save me from having to battle my way into the centre of Edinburgh.

Fortunately, the drive was an easy one, and my car behaved, leaving me calm as I pulled up into their visitor car park. I easily found my way to the cafe he had suggested we meet in.

The cafe was bursting with students enjoying the relaxed life university had to offer. Some sat in groups, nursing a tap water or a small coffee grown cold hours ago, laughing and chatting. I smiled with fondness, remembering how we once did the same, then having to rush to make our lectures. Others sat alone with earphones plugged in, typing furiously onto a laptop as they made the most of free Wi-Fi with forgotten books half folded back without any thought to the damage inflicted on the binding. Perhaps if it hadn't been for meeting Aneella that first week, I would have been one of these students, sitting alone pretending to be okay with that.

A fairly tall man sat alone towards the back of the cafe, nursing a coffee, his age making him stand out amongst this young crowd. The sandy hair, now tapered with grey, was alone enough to tell me it was Anthony, but as he turned to look at me there was an immediate recognition on both our parts.

He gave me a smile and beckoned me over. I inched my way round the narrow passageways between tables and chairs, before coming up and smiling down at him as I held out my hand. "It's so nice to see you again, Professor Andrews. Thank you so much for agreeing to see me on such short notice."

Anthony looked a little taken aback by my politeness, half rising to shake my hand before we both sat.

"Please, call me Anthony. No need for formalities now. Would you like a tea or coffee?"

His manners were impeccable, his voice remaining courteous and friendly, though I could sense the curiosity bubbling below the surface. It felt odd to be talking to him as equals, rather than a professor I had looked up to, admired even. "A latte would be great, thank you."

He nodded and stood to walk over to the counter. I watched him as he ordered my coffee, taking the time to chat to the young girl serving him, who was perhaps one of his Literature students. Apart from a few more grey hairs, he seemed remarkably unchanged from the last time I'd seen him, just over ten years ago. I wondered if I seemed different to him.

Anthony wandered back with my coffee. I murmured

my thanks, taking a small sip before placing it on the table, all the while trying to buy myself time, so I could work out how on earth I could possibly begin this conversation. Launching in with *How come Aneella has your photo in her locket, was it because you were having an affair?* didn't seem quite the best way forward.

Anthony saved me by wading in with numerous questions about my job, where I lived, and everything in between. I answered him as best I could.

"And didn't you and... Oh, what was his name? The guy you were seeing—"

"Richard," I supplied, a little reluctantly.

"That's it, Richard! I thought I heard you two got hitched soon after you graduated. Our first official student wedding!" he exclaimed, grinning, as he took a gulp of his black coffee.

I remained silent, not wanting to talk anymore. Perhaps something in my eyes, my closed-off face, told him everything.

"Ah," was all he said, then proceeded to swiftly change the conversation. "Do you still keep in touch with anyone else from those days? I have fond memories of teaching you all."

Anthony's eyes connected with mine. A wistful smile played on his lips. This was my chance, perhaps my only chance. I inhaled a deep breath, then said, "Actually, funny you should mention that. I'd lost touch with most people over the years, you know how it is. But, to my surprise, who should I run into about a month ago, but Ella?" Seeing his blank look, I immediately realised my mistake. "Sorry, Aneella, I mean."

I watched him closely as I spoke. There was an instant reaction to hearing her name, like a muscle jerking, "Aneella? Really? I... haven't heard her name in a long time. How is she?"

"Not so great right now. She's in a little bit of trouble."

He sat forward, coffee forgotten, staring at me. "What kind of trouble?"

"The kind where she needs all the friends she can get." My smile was tight, worried. My plan to play it cool had vanished, as if a strong gust of wind had blown it right out of the French windows beside us.

"And you think I might be one of those friends?"

"Yes," I whispered. "I really hope you are."

Anthony looked away first. "Then I think you'll be disappointed. I wouldn't have called us friends."

He was withdrawing. I needed to salvage this, fast. "I appreciate you were her professor, but I know you were close, very close."

He turned sharply to me then, his frown hard. "What exactly are you implying?"

My heart began to hammer, but I forged on, "Please don't misunderstand me. I'm not saying something... inappropriate took place—"

"Good, you would be right."

"But you must still have been closer than, say, you were with me or the other students—"

"Why?" Anthony demanded, his voice rising, causing a couple of nearby students to turn and stare. Feeling their looks, he tried to lower his voice. "Why?" he repeated.

"Because..." I swallowed, then plunged on in a bid to

quell the sparks in his eyes. "Because your photo is in her locket."

He fell back against the chair, his face one of rigid shock.

26

"I don't know why she has my photo in her locket."

I found that incredibly hard to believe. "She must have at least looked up to you, saw you as more than a tutor," I persisted.

Anthony raised his eyes at me. There was a battle going on inside him, a desire to say more hindered by something inexplicable. My eyes pleaded with him while my voice echoed what was on my mind, "Please, anything you can share may help me. I'm very worried about her."

Something gave way then, in his eyes. "I'm not sure what I can tell you that will help, rather it may disappoint you in ways you can't imagine."

"I can take it. Please, carry on."

Anthony sighed softly before leaning forward. "Aneella started coming to me for extra tutoring. It was clear she was struggling, finding it hard to keep up with her studies. She was worried about her dad. I think he was starting to show the first signs of his illness. I agreed to help her on a one-to-one tuition, against my better judgement perhaps. I had a sense she was hoping I could be her saviour and make everything all right for her. I never thought for a minute she was trying to lead me somewhere."

Anthony halted, stirred his coffee. I tentatively asked, "Did she begin to develop feelings for you?"

Anthony's head swung up, nostrils flaring. "Sophia, as a student, you were always jumping to the wrong conclusion because you didn't listen carefully enough to what *wasn't* being said. It seems you haven't changed. It was not that, it was never that. I told you this already."

"Sorry," I apologised, feeling humbled and taken aback by his tone. "I won't interrupt again."

He let out that sigh again, before stating, "Your final-year exams were coming up, which would account for forty percent of your final grade. Despite all the extra hours I gave to Aneella, she either found it impossible or was not willing to memorise and understand all she would need to pass the exam. The night before she was due to sit it, she came to me and asked if I could 'help' her pass the exam. At first, I didn't understand. And then it clicked. Do you understand what she was asking of me?"

I could only stare at him, my breath drawing in. I knew, of course I knew, yet I didn't want to hear it. I'd asked him for the truth and now I had it.

"I can see you do. But to be clear, so there's no need for us to ever go over this again, what she wanted was for me to get hold of a copy of the exam paper. She wanted me to steal it."

I heard a gasp, then realised it was me. My hand flew

to my mouth. Ella was not a thief, a cheat, or a liar... *was she?*

Anthony carried on, wanting to end this now, wash his hands clean of his part in this dishonest behaviour. "Of course, I refused. I was angry at her, for putting me in this position, for breaking my trust in her. She failed me, and she failed herself in that moment. This she knew without my saying another word. She never came to see me after that, though she sent me emails asking me to not to think badly of her. I think I was the first person she had truly looked up to. Perhaps that's why she had my photo in her locket."

"But, but she passed!" I stumbled out. "How? I mean..."

Anthony raised his eyebrows. "Again, I think you know the answer. Someone else obviously had far fewer scruples than I."

I had to turn away. The thought that Ella had cheated and lied left me devastated, as if she had betrayed me. *Do I really know you, Ella? Have I ever really known the real you?*

Anthony was preparing to leave, jolting me back to the present. As he stood, he gave me an apologetic look. "I'm sorry your friend is not who you thought she was and that I can't help you find her now. Let me at least give you a warning. Tread carefully, Sophia. Don't believe everything she tells you. She's good at fooling you into helping her, knowing your weaknesses to use for her own gain. I learnt to my own cost that she can't be trusted."

With that, he walked out, leaving me sitting there, a hollow feeling in my heart.

Outside, the sky darkened as an incoming storm rolled in.

MARCUS STARED out of his tiny excuse of an office window, without really seeing the miniature-sized people hurrying past him three floors below. The wind kicked up a few stray pieces of debris and danced them along the pavement. The spring sun had been stolen away by the looming dark clouds now swelling with rain. As if to prove a point, the rain chose that moment to hit his window with force, startling Marcus with its ferocity. He turned and grabbed his phone, hoping to see a text from Sophia to say she'd arrived back. No message. He sighed deeply.

The phone on his desk rang. Marcus walked over to grab it. "DI Armstrong." He listened intently then, "I'm on my way now. Stay put."

Stopping only to grab his jacket and mobile phone, he flew out of his door, calling over his shoulder as he did, "Morven, you're with me. Now!"

THE JOURNEY HOME had been long and odious. The lashing rain had suited my mood exactly. All I wanted was to get back and change into more comfortable clothes, then flop on the sofa with a cup of tea. I didn't want to think, not yet.

As I made my way wearily up in the lift, I became

aware of raised voices coming from one of the apartments on my level. Only when the lift doors opened did it become apparent the voices were coming from my apartment. My pulse began to race in trepidation.

Carefully, I walked toward the door, scrambling in my bag for my phone. Edging closer and unlocking my phone in anticipation of calling Marcus, I leaned against the wall to peer around the opened front door. Three people were inside, one with his voice raised in protest as he was forced from kneeling on the floor into a stand-up position, his arms behind his back. My eyes widened.

Without waiting, I marched into the room, demanding, "What's going on?"

At my words, the other two turned to look at me. I ignored Lyle to stare at Marcus. Morven took hold of Lyle's handcuffed hands as Marcus walked quickly over to me, pulling me to one side, so we wouldn't be heard. He bent his head close toward me, intimately so, his hand brushing mine before moving it away. I could feel the stares of Morven and Lyle burning a hole into us.

"Are you okay?" His voice was barely above a whisper.

I gave a quick nod, my voice following his lead, keeping at a low whisper. "I'll fill you in later, but what's going on? Why is Lyle here?"

"He was seen entering by my men on patrol outside. They followed Lyle at a discreet distance and watched him let himself in after checking you weren't here. When Morven and I arrived, we entered." He cast Lyle a swift glance, as did I. "We caught him snooping around trying to get in the safe. He may well have his name on the lease, but until he can prove it, we can caution him for trespass, enough at least to bring him in for questioning. We won't be able to hold him for long, though," Marcus warned.

"But long enough to see if he knows where Ella is and why he wants these numbers?" I urged.

Marcus nodded. "Aye, I'll do my damnedest, see how hard I can push him—"

"When you've quite finished your cozy chat over there, can you get the hell out of my apartment!" Lyle's voice, loud and harsh, cut in. We turned to look at him.

"Be quiet!" Morven stormed. "You're in no position to make any kind of demands. Sir? Are we...?" She glared at us both.

"I'll call you later," Marcus murmured quietly, once more touching my hand before walking over to Lyle.

"Okay, Mr. Boyd, let's go have a chat about these supposed rights to this place down at the station, see if we can get everything nicely confirmed."

"Seriously? Hold on, you don't have the damn guts to arrest me! Sophia, tell your boyfriend I've got every right to be here. If not, you'd better pray they do keep me away, or I'll be coming back to see you personally." As he uttered the threat, Lyle stepped toward me, his eyes blazing with anger entirely focussed on me. My heart began to pound.

Instantly, Marcus twisted Lyle's cuffed arms, hard enough for Lyle to grimace. His voice was low and dangerous. "Threaten Ms. Meadows like that again, and you'll discover I more than have the guts to arrest you and throw everything at you. Want to try me out?" His steely eyes dared, until Lyle turned away without saying a word. "No, I thought not. Let's go."

They led Lyle out of the apartment. I ran to the door, watching them enter the lift. Just as the lift door was swishing close, my eyes collided with Marcus'. As he gazed at me, I felt a strong rush of emotion course right through my body, leaving me standing there long after the lift had descended.

27

Across town, Marcus sat facing Lyle in an airless, enclosed room, designed precisely that way to make people desperate enough to confess to their crimes, if only to escape from its suffocating confines.

Lyle's foot tapped impatiently on the floor, his leg jerking up and down. Marcus, unfazed, calmly flipped through the pages of the file in front of him, as if looking for something, when in fact he was stalling for time to give Morven a chance to come back with the information he needed. He was also taking advantage of this wait to unsettle Lyle. And it seemed that his strategy appeared to be working.

"Is this going to take much longer?" Lyle blurted out, unable to help himself.

Marcus raised one eyebrow. "Some place you need to be? Not at work, as you were fired from there a couple of months ago. Why was that again?"

"I told you this already. It was a difference of opinion. Why keep asking me?"

He was rattled, and Marcus was quick to jump on that. "Sure, it wasn't because you 'borrowed' some money from your company then forgot to pay it back?"

Lyle remained tight-lipped, looking away.

The door to the interview room swung open. Morven entered and slid into the chair next to Marcus. Without a word, she passed a piece of paper across to him. Written in bold letters were: *HE'S NOT ON THE TENANCY LEASE!* A triumphant smile danced around Marcus' face. At last! Something they could use against him.

Lyle's foot continued its tap, tap, tapping on the hard, cold floor, as if echoing the sound of a soldier's beating drum preparing to face the enemy on the war field.

"So, it seems you haven't quite been telling us the truth about your name being on the lease of Ms. Blair's apartment."

The tapping froze.

"I have it confirmed in writing here, which means you were trespassing on Ms. Blair's property, a criminal offence under the eyes of the law—"

Lyle half stood. "Now, wait a minute!"

"Sit down, Mr. Boyd." Marcus said calmly.

Lyle did but pointed his finger accusingly at Marcus. "No, I've got a key, so it can't be trespassing, right?"

Marcus leaned forward. "That's where you're wrong. If it were proven you got hold of the key without the key-holders permission, that's an offence we take very seriously here in Scotland."

"Of course she knows; she's my girlfriend. Ask her!" Lyle's face was growing red and sweaty.

"We would, Mr. Boyd, if the number you gave us for

her actually worked," Morven commented dryly. "How strange that it doesn't."

Lyle glared at them both. The foot tapping began again, with his hand joining in as it began to tap the table, declaring this battle far from over. Morven pursed her lips, annoyed. Eyes narrowing thoughtfully, Marcus watched him for a moment before trying a different angle. "Tell us about your girlfriend. What's she like?"

"What?" Thrown by the question, Lyle stared blankly at Marcus.

"For example, what's her favourite movie?" Marcus continued mildly, smiling at Lyle.

"I, uh, some girly flick I guess."

"Okay, what about her favourite meal, her go-to drink?"

"How should I know?!" Lyle spluttered.

"What's she reading at the moment?" Marcus continued with his relentless questioning. "Which side does she like to sleep on? Favourite flower—"

"Stop with all these damn stupid questions! What the hell does it matter what her favourite flower is? When are you going to let me go?"

Marcus raised one eyebrow. "As her boyfriend, you should know all these things. *If* you were her boyfriend."

Lyle's face filled with blind panic. He knew he had trapped himself by his own omission. Marcus silently counted to ten in his head. The silence stretched out, unbearably so for Lyle. He broke. The battle was over, defeated by a stronger opponent than him.

"All right, all right, you got me, okay?" Lyle spread his

hands out, trying to wipe his face against the restriction of the cuffs. "I'm not her boyfriend. We had a quick fling when we were work colleagues, but to be honest, she was too intense for me and hung up on some married guy. I—"

"Who was he?" Morven interrupted.

Lyle shrugged. "Don't know, didn't care enough to ask. Look, I've answered your questions, can I go now?"

Marcus gave him a dangerous smile, a smile that said *No way am I letting you leave now.* "Not quite yet. There's still the small matter of how you got hold of the key. That and, of course, what you were doing entering Ms. Blair's apartment on two separate occasions, searching through her personal possessions, both of which we have eyewitness accounts for. I think you need to get yourself nice and comfortable there, Mr. Boyd, as you'll be enjoying our hospitality for a while yet."

Lyle shrunk back into his chair. In a quieter, subdued voice he said, "I think I want a lawyer now."

FOR THE LAST HOUR, I had been wandering aimlessly around the quaint shops of Victorian Market, a beautiful building still standing strong as it resisted the modern world, while I waited for Marcus to call. The walls of the apartment had begun to press in and the need for fresh air had grown strong. I felt better outside.

I sat now in a quaint café behind Victorian Market, sipping a coffee. My phone was in front of me, taunting me with its silence. An email had come in earlier from my client, who was growing impatient with my lack of progress and delivery of their programme. Usually, this would cause me to grow alarmed. My clients were of vital importance to me, as was my reputation to deliver what I promised. But now it felt like a different life, a different me than the one sitting here biting her lip, desperate to talk to Marcus, while avoiding her ex-husband's ever-increasing number of texts and missed calls.

The clock nearby struck five. The cafe showed signs of closing up as staff began to wipe down counters and brush the floor. There was only me and one other customer left, and now they were gathering their shopping bags together to leave. Reluctantly, I finished my coffee and stood up, holding my phone tightly in my hand.

The air was cool on my cheeks as I stood outside. I could see the police station on the horizon and itched to walk toward it. Yet, I forced myself to turn the other way and go back toward the apartment, though my steps were slow and laboured. My phone grew warm within my grasped palm.

The moment I came on to the street of the apartment block, my phone began to ring. For a moment, my heart tightened at the thought of it being Richard.

But it wasn't, it was Marcus. My heart soared in joy. I rushed to answer it.

"Hi. I've been hoping you would call... Yes, I can meet you. How about at the Italian where we met before... Great, okay, see you in ten minutes or so... Bye-bye."

With a lighter step, I pivoted around and began to walk back the way I'd just come from, brimming with excitement and achingly glad to be rid of the lethargy that had gripped me all afternoon. I needed action, to be doing *something*.

I never noticed the man in the distance watching me, following my every step.

[28]

Marcus was already seated at a corner table in the relatively quiet restaurant when I walked in, staring into the glass before him, his mind seemingly whirling. The breadsticks beside him remained untouched. He looked troubled, and I yearned to stroke away the stress lining his face.

His head swung up as I approached. Once again that spark, igniting like an electric charge, rippled through me as we smiled intimately at each other. There was something unmistakable growing that neither of us could ignore, despite our vow of not touching one another. Our kiss had changed everything for me. I wanted more, so much more. I wanted to feel him pressed against me again, his hands and mouth on my skin. Why had I made that reckless promise to keep my distance?

He stood and bent to kiss me on the cheek. I closed my eyes for a moment, before reluctantly stepping back.

"You smell good," he murmured, a half-smile on his

lips, an unmistakable look of desire in his eyes as they willingly trapped my own.

He wasn't alone. As I took my seat opposite him, I felt my own lips curling in a seductive smile, my voice turning husky. "I'm glad you like it."

"I do, very much."

My breath caught, and my body tingled as he seduced me beautifully with his look alone. Never had I known a man to show such burning desire for me. Never had I felt more achingly wanted.

The Italian waiter materialised, flourishing the menus in front of us with a grand gesture and effectively dousing our ardour. I accepted with a polite smile, biting back a laugh while using the menu to fan my flaming cheeks. The amusement danced in Marcus' eyes as he also accepted his menu, though he made it clear it was more from the reaction he'd evoked in me. The keen waiter whipped the napkin with such force onto my lap I almost had whip-burn, then honoured Marcus with the same treatment. I had to bite down hard not to laugh out loud.

Only after we'd ordered drinks and some bread were we finally left alone, at last able to laugh quietly.

"You can't fault him for his enthusiasm," I commented, taking a few much-needed gulps of water. I wasn't alone, Marcus was necking down his water like he'd been stuck in the Sahara Desert for days on end.

"Aye, you can't. Wish some of my officers were as keen as him to impress me." Marcus gave me a rueful look.

"I'm sure I can think of at least one sergeant who's always trying to impress you," came my wry retort.

He had the grace to look a little sheepish, even as he exclaimed, "I'm pretty certain she isn't!" I snorted. "No, listen, she's just eager—"

"To please you," I ended, giving him a pointed look.

A deep infectious laugh burst out of Marcus as he leant forward to stroke my hand for an achingly brief moment. "Ach, okay, you got me. I'm trying to pretend it's not happening, in typical male fashion, with the hope Morven's crush soon moves on to someone else. It's a little... awkward."

At least I knew for certain now. It was one-sided, and not on Marcus' side. A giddy rush of relief flowed through me. "Oh, I'm sure it's *so* awkward to say the least, and not at *all* flattering for your ego. I think you might need to change your 'sticking your head in the sand' plan and develop a new strategy. If, of course, you want to lose your fan club..." My eyebrows arched.

Marcus' eyes narrowed. "You're enjoying this a little too much for my liking, Ms. Meadows."

Our bread arrived, halting the conversation. After the waiter insisted on telling us all the specials, we settled for two pastas off the standard menu, much to his acute disappointment. We barely managed to stifle our laughter until the waiter was safely out of earshot, once again reminiscing of his napkin skills.

"Ach, it feels so good to laugh." Marcus shook his head as he tore the soft white bread in half, dipping it into the delicious accompanying olive oil. "It's been a hell of a stressful day."

"Tell me," I urged as I too tucked in. "Or at least as much as you can."

He considered me, before nodding. I listened carefully as he told me what Lyle had finally confessed to: That he was not on the lease and had no right whatsoever to have been in the apartment in the first place. And, more crucially, they weren't in a relationship.

"So, let me get this right. He's now saying they had a brief affair but were never together?" I frowned hard, trying to get it clear in my head. By now our pasta had arrived, but I barely noticed eating it, despite its rich taste.

"Aye, that's right. Out of interest, did Aneella ever tell you Lyle was her boyfriend?"

With his question, my mind began playing tricks on me. Had she or hadn't she? Had she ever given me a straight answer on this, or in fact anything? Like a sharp blade cutting into my ever-moving memories, her voice came to me: *"Listen, Sophia, I don't have a boyfriend. I don't have a partner. If the police ask, that's what you tell them. Don't let Lyle back in."*

I gasped.

"What, what is it?"

"I remember!" I moved my hand to cover his apologetically. "I'm so sorry, I should have told you before, just with everything else since…"

Marcus covered my hand with his. "Don't worry, tell me now what you remember."

So, I did, watching as that intense, clever mind of his processed what I said.

"That tells me they're not working together on this, if she didn't want him near the apartment and presumably the safe containing this address book."

"Of course, she's not working with him!" I was quick

to defend, then stopped, confused, remembering what I'd learnt only this morning.

"You have that look on your face again. Plus, you're about to chew your lip off, and I'm growing rather fond of those lips. Tell me," his warm voice encouraged, stroking his thumb over my hand. Our half-eaten pastas were almost forgotten. I could sense our waiter's eyes on us, his disappointment in the air.

In truth, I didn't need Marcus to encourage me to open up. It was becoming the most natural thing in the world to confide in him. I barely remembered the closed-up woman of a few weeks ago, unable, or perhaps more accurately unwilling, to trust herself to another. Now, Marcus was the only one I truly trusted. Would he say the same about me? Did he trust me yet with his deepest thoughts and fears, with his feelings? *Trust me, Marcus,* I yearned to say, *trust me with your heart.*

With these thoughts whirling around, I forced myself to concentrate on the conversation I had with Anthony earlier. "You know I went to see our old professor this morning? Well, something he told me about Ella has completely thrown me, enough to make me doubt the kind of person she really is, as painful and hard as that is to accept..."

My voice trailed off as I became aware of a long dark shadow looming over us. Its presence prompted us to turn away from each other, simultaneously glancing up, our eyes meeting the figure before us.

"Well, this is cozy. Going to introduce us, Soph?" came a voice I knew only too well.

For a moment, my brain could not compute who stood there. When it did, all I could do was stare and stare as if to deny the stark truth of it.

My worlds were colliding, and I was ill-prepared for the fallout that would follow.

Without waiting for an invite, Richard grabbed a chair from the adjacent table and pulled it up to ours. He immediately gave me his direct attention, smiling dangerously at me. The glint in his eye was all too familiar and instantly had me on edge.

I could feel Marcus' questioning eyes flying between us. I withdrew my hand from his, unable to meet those all-seeing eyes of his. Instead, I forced myself to confront my ex-husband.

"What are you doing, Richard? How did you even know I was here?"

Marcus fell back against his chair. When I dared to give him a quick, darting look, I saw resigned understanding in his face now. He remained silent, watchful, with something flickering in his eyes as he looked at me, an emotion that I couldn't pinpoint. I forced myself to turn back to my ex.

Richard's mouth still smiled, but his eyes were hard and resentful. "I was on my way to see you again, as you seem to have 'forgotten' to answer my calls and texts. And as luck would have it, I happened to look into this charming restaurant window as I passed, and who should I see but my ex-wife and... Apologies, Soph appears to have forgotten her manners." Richard turned and offered a hand to Marcus, who accepted with reluctance. "Let me do the introductions for her. I'm Richard, her ex-husband, and you are?"

Anger building within me, I cut in, wanting to gain the upper hand by unsettling Richard with who Marcus was. "Marcus. He's a pol—"

"A friend of Sophia's."

I stared at Marcus, frowning. He shot me the barest warning shake of his head, intended only for me. My frown grew harder, but I played along.

"Yes, a friend."

Richard looked between us, suspicion oozing out of his pores. I made myself look him squarely in the eye, but he was now ignoring me, turning instead to Marcus.

"Are you a friend of Ella's?"

The question, from nowhere, threw us. Marcus' eyes narrowed thoughtfully, while I managed to stumble out, "Why-why would you ask Marcus that? Why are you bringing Ella into the conversation? What makes you think either of us has seen her?"

The smile slipped, the first sign of a chink in his smooth exterior. "You told me she'd been in touch with you, didn't you?"

"Did I?" *Had I?*

"Anyway, that's not important." Richard shook his head, ignoring Marcus completely again as he gave me a look of intimacy which once drove me crazy but now left me cold. "Can we have that chat you promised me? I'm sure your *friend* here won't mind."

I stared at him, beyond frustrated. "Your manners have not improved! No, we can't! I mind, even if Marcus doesn't. It's bad enough you've interrupted us—"

"If you hadn't ignored me then I wouldn't have needed to."

Other diners were beginning to stare, but I couldn't stop now. Never had I felt so riled by him. My eyes glared hard into Richard's glinted ones. "Where do you get off! Don't—"

"Listen, I'll go," Marcus's voice cut through. He stood up, avoiding my eyes as he put some money on the table. "Let you both... talk."

I jumped up, causing my chair to wobble precariously before Richard caught it. "No!" My hand stretched out to plead with Marcus, willing him to look at me. "Don't go, please."

That made him stop and look at me. His eyes took in my flushed cheeks, my wild desperate eyes that were filled with a raw emotion only meant for him. *Can't you see it's for you, not Richard?* For one blessed minute, I thought he understood as his own reflected mine, his hand within touching distance. For one wild moment, I believed he would take me by that hand and lead us out of here together, not allow Richard the victory. For one glorious and brief moment, I dared to believe.

"See you later then... mate." Richard grinned smugly.

I was a fool to believe.

Marcus turned from me, his eyes like slits as they

stared hard at Richard. His jaw clenched in anger as he uttered, "I'm not needed here."

Disappointment, hot angry disappointment, muted me from replying. I didn't trust myself to speak. I gave him a cold nod before turning away and sitting down abruptly. His body like a rigid rod, Marcus walked away from me. The restaurant door slammed hard behind him.

He walked away.

"Now, we've got rid of him, we can finally start our date. Hey, waiter," Richard called, waving at the hesitant man, "can you bring me a beer and the hottest pizza you've got."

"Of course, sir."

Richard turned back to me, sliding across into the chair Marcus had just vacated. For some reason that caused my stomach to turn. I pushed my own·food away from me, the sight of it now leaving a sick bile in my throat.

"Listen, I know I can't really say much about you going on a date with that guy, though come on, he looks like he could do with lightening up." Richard grinned, enjoying himself. "I mean, seriously, what does he do for a living; traffic warden or something? Anyway, you can let him down gently."

There was a knot, hard as lead, building within me at his absolute galling, arrogant presumption that I would fall back into his arms and be his humble, docile wife again. Never. *Never!*

"Let him down?" My voice was low, too calm and controlled. "Why would I need to let him down?"

In his arrogance of thinking he still knew me, he didn't

pick up on it. He let out a bark of laughter. "Well, I don't expect you to go on dates once you're living as my wife again. Naturally."

"Your wife… You think I want to be your wife again?" I gave a humourless laugh that touched on hysterical. I stood up.

"Where are you going?"

The knot exploded. I leaned over him, punching out my every word, watching his eyes widen in mute shock. "Understand this and understand it well. I am not, nor will I ever be, your wife again, in name, deed, or love. I'm not that woman anymore—the wife you knew died the minute you walked out on her. She will *never* come back. I don't love you anymore, Richard, and the thought of you touching me makes me feel physically sick. Go home, just go home, and live the life you so desperately wanted away from me. There's nothing for you here." I straightened up. Our waiter was hovering, nervously holding Richard's pizza. "Enjoy your pizza."

With that, I spun round, my body full of adrenaline. I walked out of there with my head held high and never once looked back.

There was only one place I was headed for.

"How could you walk away like that?!" I raged as soon as the door opened.

If he was shocked to see me standing there without invite, he hid it well. But what Marcus couldn't conceal was his instant reaction to fight back and cut as deep as I had, his accent growing stronger in his fury. "I could ask you the same thing, only mine would be why the hell didn't you leave him to walk out with me? Answer me that!"

"Because you couldn't seem to get away from me fast enough! You left me with him without a backward glance. You *left* me!"

We stood there, both breathing hard. Marcus swore in Gaelic under his breath, then yanked me in through the door, slamming it behind him.

I wasn't finished. My whole body was wound up like a coiled snake, heightened by my journey over here. We were a hair's breadth from each other. "Why? Why did you do that, walk away? Couldn't you see I wanted you to stay?" I exclaimed.

"For a minute, yes! But then that smug bastard got under my skin, and I had to get out of there. Aye, he seemed pretty certain that you and him were a couple again. What the hell am I meant to think, ach? You hadn't even told me he was here—"

"I've had no chance—"

"You want to know the truth?" His eyes blazed, his jaw tightening hard. "It was like being kicked here, right here." He hit his heart. "The way this ex of yours thought he had every right to walk back into your life, like he'd never done anything wrong to you, had never hurt you or caused you to mistrust everyone you meet. I don't know, maybe he does," Marcus said, spreading his hands wide. As his voice caught on the last word, I felt my anger turn to something new, something that had my pulse racing. He turned his head away from me. "I don't even know what I'm saying right now, what I'm doing. I'm acting like… a jealous lover. I don't—I don't have any right over your feelings, your decisions, who you love—"

"Yes, you do. You do! You have every right. Look at me," I softly commanded, turning his face to mine. "Look into my eyes. What are they telling you? Would I be fighting with you right now if I didn't care about you, about us?" I could feel tears at the back of my throat as I tried to explain what was burning within me. Words alone could be so restricting. He was looking at me with an intensity that spurred me on, giving me the courage to be vulnerable before him. "Don't you see? I'm not that woman who was Richard's wife anymore. I don't even recognise her now. She's dead to me, just like my feelings for him. I never want to go back to being her." His hand lifted to cover mine where I still cradled his face. He gazed at me with eyes full of emotion. "This new me is yours, all yours," I whispered, swallowing hard. "But I won't beg."

"I don't want you to beg." Marcus' voice was fierce as he threaded his other hand through my hair, cradling it. "Not with me, not ever. You already have me, every bit of me, good and bad. I trust you with my life, I'm trusting you with my heart. Will you do the same for me?"

My throat constricted with intense emotion. Right then, I couldn't have denied him anything. I nodded, fighting back tears. "Yes."

Almost immediately his mouth met mine, and we were kissing with an almost desperate need, wanting more, so much more. Marcus grabbed me hungrily, backing us up until I was pressed against a wall, his hands caressing me through my clothes. My own ran up and down his back, bringing him hard against my body before pulling his shirt out of his trousers, so I could feel his bare skin beneath.

Marcus gave a low groan, his mouth leaving a hot trail down my neck and the curve of my exposed skin above my silky top. He paused, then suddenly yanked it off over my head. I heard myself gasp as his hands moved achingly slow over my skin, his mouth following behind.

"We should probably... slow down," I managed to get out, biting my lip to stop myself from moaning as his mouth moved over my breast above my bra, seeking all of me. "As I'm... we..." I gave up trying to be rational. I wanted him too much. I pulled at the buttons on his shirt until they released, then pushed the shirt down over his shoulders onto the floor. Immediately, my hands were touching him, enjoying the feel of his broad, strong shoulders.

"We probably should," Marcus breathed out, closing his eyes as I pressed kisses along his collarbone, then further down his muscled chest, before trailing my way back up to meet his mouth. Our tongues met and teased, before we drew back, breathing hard. "But not yet. Not yet..."

He took me into a deep kiss while moving us as one to his bedroom, our half naked bodies pressed tight together, his voice caressing me. *"Mo leannan, mo leannan..."*

[30]

The sky was a startling mix of vibrant orange and ravishing reds, flowing in through the curtainless window as I slowly opened my eyes. The gentle rays bathed my skin, feeling warm and cozy. My mouth stretched into a content smile. The beauty and peace outside the window seemed to match exactly how I felt in this moment.

I stretched a little, shimmying my arm slightly from under a sleeping Marcus to bring sensation back to it. He lay half on his stomach, half on his side, his arm stretched out toward me. My heart contracted as I gazed at him, and I reached out to softly stroke back his hair, which had fallen across his forehead. The feel of it immediately took me back to last night when I had threaded my fingers through it, gasping in pleasure as he took me. Even now, this morning, my body felt tingly and alive, sated yet wanting more. I'd had little experience with men, Richard until now having been my only lover, but I knew enough to know that when Marcus and I touched, it was not ordinary. Never had I felt like this when Richard had made love to me. He had left me feeling underwhelmed, like I'd been a convenient body to use for his own pleasure. With Marcus, I felt beautiful and desired, like he was desperate for my touch, in the same way I craved his.

Before I acted on the urge to stir him awake, I slipped out from beneath the warm duvet, tiptoeing across the wooden floors to slip on his tartan dressing gown laying across a chair. I had no idea where my own clothes were and didn't care. But what I did care about was that I was starving and needed coffee, figuring Marcus would too when he finally stirred.

The kitchen was messy and a stark contrast to his office. I shook my head fondly, laughing quietly to myself as I attempted to bring some kind of order to the chaos. Hunting through the cupboards and fridge, I managed to find bread that was fairly okay, toasted and buttered it, then got the coffee going. By luck, I found some wild strawberries in the fridge and put those onto the tray, before carrying it back through to the bedroom.

Marcus lay in exactly the same position I'd left him in. Padding over to the bed, I gingerly put the tray onto my side, then climbed up and gently touched him on the face, softly saying his name. When that didn't work, I shook his shoulder, my voice a little louder. "Marcus, time to wake up." And when that failed to get a response, I gave him a big prod on the side as well as a good shake. "Oi! Wake up!"

Disorientated and startled, Marcus sat up so fast the

coffee pot wobbled precariously on the tray, and I had to shoot out my hand to grab it. "Woah, that was close," I muttered, placing it carefully down on the floor out of harm's way.

"What—what time is it?" He sat there rubbing his jaw and cheeks, his eyes still half asleep.

Enjoying the sight of his bare chest, I couldn't resist stroking it with my fingers. "A little after eight, I think," I said, grinning.

That woke him up. Panic had him trying to jump out of bed. "Bollocks, you're kidding me! I'm usually in the station half an hour ago—"

My hand reached out to yank him firmly back down. "Relax! I'm sure it's okay if you're a little late today. You are the boss," I teased. "Plus, I've made us breakfast, once I got past the mountain of washing up clogging the way."

Marcus cringed in embarrassment. "You cleaned my kitchen?" he groaned. "Ach, now I feel even worse. That wouldn't have been a pretty sight to greet you." He squinted at me. "Are you wearing my dressing gown?"

"I am. Funnily enough I can't find my clothes at the moment."

That brought the smile to his face. "Can't think why that may be. My gown looks better on you, lass. How come you're so awake? Mm, that coffee smells good." He took my proffered mug of coffee gratefully, taking a gulp that must have scalded the back of his throat.

"Do you always talk this much first thing?" I laughed, taking a more careful sip.

"I don't usually have anyone to talk to."

"Oh." His words hit me hard, right in my heart. "Me neither," I admitted.

We gazed at each other, then Marcus drew me into a soft kiss. His voice was earnest and husky as he murmured, "I'm glad you're here with me now."

"So am I." I reached up to kiss him again, stroking his chest. I couldn't seem to keep my hands off of him. As I did, his whispered words from last night came back to me. I pulled back a little, frowning. Marcus gave me a quizzical look, attempting to kiss me again but was stopped by my finger pressing against his lips. "What was it you said to me last night in your Gaelic language... mo lin, len..."

He grinned at my feeble attempt, pressing his lips to my neck as he corrected me. "*Mo leannan*. It means 'my sweetheart, my beloved, my... lover.'"

I felt my breath catch at the seductiveness of the words as he continued to kiss and caress me, igniting both our desires. His hands began to slide the dressing gown off my shoulders, until it fell in a heap around my waist, his mouth following as it travelled down my body.

"It sounds so much better in your language," I managed to gasp out, before we fell as one back against the bed, my legs straddling him as I urged him into me.

The toast was stone cold by the time we finally came to eat it, but nothing had ever tasted so good.

NEITHER OF US wanted to break our relaxed mood to talk about the elephant in the room—what was going to happen when we left the cozy bubble of his lodge.

Yet, the world wasn't going to stop for us.

After we were both showered and dressed, and time was pressing down on us, we stood together by his door.

It was me who spoke first, touching his shirt button, unable to look at him. "So, what happens now? I'm guessing nothing has changed for us?"

Marcus lifted my chin so I had to look at him. His eyes were full of earnestness, determination. "Listen to me. Everything has changed for me after last night. *Everything*. I don't fall lightly; I don't do one-night stands. You're the first woman I've been with since Lucy. The first I've let into my heart."

"I know, I know," I murmured. "It's the same for me."

"I don't regret last night for one minute, though I probably should."

"No, don't you dare!"

Marcus gave a short laugh at my indignity, before resting his forehead against mine. "I've never known it could be like that," he confessed. "Almost desperate for each other. I don't want to stop kissing you, touching you…"

"I feel the same. My heart is racing now just being near you. Can you feel it?" I brought his hand to rest between my breasts. He looked down at where our hands were joined.

"I can. It's racing. Like mine." Marcus looked up smiling, as he brought our hands to his chest. I gave a small laugh as I felt the pump of his heart beneath my palm. He sighed a little.

"I wish… I wish for more than snatched moments. I don't want you to believe I'm ashamed of us. I'm not, you must believe me, *mo leannan*. But I'm not risking your name being dragged into this case anymore than it already has or you being accused of manipulating the case."

"Can they do that?"

"Believe me, losing my job because of our relationship is nothing compared to what they could do to either of us." Marcus's face bore a grim look.

"Then this is a no brainer," my voice was firm now. "There's no way you're risking your career for me. No arguments. I don't care about myself, but I won't have you leave the force under a cloud because of me. You're an incredible detective, do you know that? The first time you walked into my life, it was like you could see right into the pit of my soul. It shook me up like nothing I've ever known before. Your instincts are what will close this case. And you must, you must close this case, for us."

Marcus nodded, his face serious with intent. "When I do, and I will, trust me, nothing will stop me from coming to you and asking you to stay and love me, and for you to allow me to love you as I desire to."

"Love..." I repeated, my pulse kicking up a beat. Sophia of old would have run for the hills if a man had said that to her after Richard. But this Sophia felt nothing but incredible joy and racing excitement.

"Aye, if you're up for that," Marcus commented mildly, grinning, though there was a vulnerability behind it.

I felt a grin spilt my own face. "I could be," I teased, before reaching up to kiss him with everything that was within me, which I couldn't express, not yet.

We reluctantly drew back, letting go of one another finger by finger, until it seemed we were nothing more than passing acquaintances. Marcus opened the front door, and we stepped outside to walk to our separate cars. We both chose not to look at the other, though everything urged us to do so. If we had, we both knew our resolve to keep apart would have fallen astray within seconds.

Three days passed. I hadn't seen Marcus in person, only snatches of conversation on the phone that left us both unsatisfied and desperate for more. I knew he was working every godsent hour to follow up leads coming his way. I'd filled him in on the professor and the doubt he'd cast over Aneella's character, though I had felt like I was betraying her in doing so. I knew Marcus was like a dog with a bone and wouldn't rest until he had thoroughly looked into her background. After all, she'd been on his radar long before I had entered his world, for what I now knew was suspected fraud, hence the intense look into the number codes and his original interest in the apartment. How little I knew of Ella, her innermost thoughts, fears, and demons.

Every night I religiously called Aneella's mobile to hear her recorded voice telling me she would return my call. *Not true, Ella.* Of Richard, I heard nothing. At least, on that score, I could relax. Why he'd chosen this moment to re-enter my life left me with a funny taste in my mouth, like something was off-kilter and not aligned as to how the world should be.

Stuck in an apartment I wanted to leave behind but couldn't until Ella returned and was safe, yearning for a man who was not yet fully mine, I threw everything into my work to distract myself and ensure my client didn't sack me without paying the fee. Despite my lack of enthusiasm, I still needed to eat and pay my flat bills.

As easily as breathing to me, I worked the programme until it began to create codes to run the computer system without my assistance.

All the time, something niggled at me, slipping just out of frustrated reach, until I eventually gave up trying to grasp it.

Such a costly, costly mistake on my part.

~

HAVING BEEN DRIVEN by the need for fresh air after hours sat cramped over the computer, I was returning to the apartment and turning the key to unlock the front door when I heard the sound of movement from the other side. I'd almost come to expect it. Yet, I wasn't quite so blasé that I didn't make sure my phone was in hand, unlocked, and ready to dial.

Carefully, I dropped my shopping bag on the floor and turned the key fully to release the catch. The door opened with a silent swoosh of air, unnoticed by the person sitting on the pristine sofa with their back to me, a laptop perched on their lap and a mobile in their hand with what looked like the camera app open. Their blond hair fell over their face, obscuring their view.

My breath stopped. For a long moment, all I could do was gape, stunned. Then, as the initial shock wore off, I managed to gasp, "Ella?"

Aneella spun round, startled, dropping her phone as she hastened to slam the laptop shut. "Sophia! You startled me!"

Utter joy of seeing her here, alive and unharmed, had me running around to pull her into a tight hug, her own arms returning the pressure after the longest of seconds.

"Oh, thank God, you're okay!"

⌂

MORVEN, taking advantage of Marcus being away from the office, was gathering her bag to nip out for an extended lunch, when her desk phone began to ring with a relentlessness that echoed throughout the empty bay. She was half-inclined to ignore it and had even turned her back on it. But guilt prevailed, and she picked it up with a sigh of annoyance. Her voice was clipped and impatient as she answered, "Inverness Police."

A male voice came over. "Can I speak to the person in charge of the case against Lyle Boyd?"

Attention caught, Morven sank into her chair, her bag dropping onto the hard floor. "DI Armstrong is not here at the moment. I'm his sergeant, can I help? May I take your name?"

A long pause loomed as Morven began to wonder if the man had hung up, then, "No, no name. But I have some information you should know. It's about Sophia Meadows and her involvement in this case."

Morven's eyes widened. Scrambling for a pen and notepaper, excitement coursing through her, she rushed out eagerly, "Carry on. I'm listening."

HAVING REPEATEDLY REASSURED me she was unharmed, Aneella gently disentangled herself and proceeded to make us both a coffee. Seeing her at ease in the kitchen, her kitchen, felt… disconcerting. I'd come to see this as my second home, despite the danger it had placed on me. But it wasn't, nor would it ever be. My home was in Buxton, even if I felt completely disconnected from it and already bid it goodbye.

It began to dawn on me, as I sat down on the sofa, that the laptop on the glass table was my own. Frowning, I opened it. My home screen blinked at me. No apps were open, nothing to say what she might have been using my laptop for. Despite it leaving me with an uncomfortable feeling, I made a mental note to wait until later to ask her. It couldn't be a priority with too many other pressing matters needing to be addressed.

Aneella walked round with our mugs. As I accepted mine, my mind flashed back to the last time we sat on a sofa together. I took a sip and discreetly watched her as she sat, composed and calm, unlike her normal louder-than-life self and high-energy demeanour. Something wasn't adding up. A strange, ominous feeling clutched my stomach and, as always, I couldn't stay quiet.

I put down my mug without touching it and leaned forward. "It's so good to see you're okay. But you could have called me to say you were arriving. I've been trying and trying to reach you; you must have seen! I've been really worried. I—"

Aneella gave a quick shake of her head, stopping me. "I'm sorry you've felt that way, but you don't need to worry about me. It's all getting sorted. That's why I've come, so you can see for yourself before you head home."

"No, no, don't fob me off like that, not this time! How can it all be sorted when the police are investigating you and Lyle—"

Once again, she cut me off. "The police are the least of our worries. They're harmless against—look, it doesn't matter," she said.

Was she actually saying these words for real? "Of course it matters. Listen to yourself, Ella! They have evidence against you both. They have your black address book full of coded numbers, for crying out loud! Lyle is still being questioned."

She dismissed my concerns like I was an annoying child, waving her hand as if to brush me away. "I'll get the book back and sort everything. Look, I shouldn't have let you get this involved. All you have to do now is pack your bags and leave."

"I'm not leaving." My voice was adamant.

For the first time her cool composure began to crack. "You must, you have to leave right now! I'm trying to help you. Don't be so stupidly blind and dumb!"

I stared at her, dumbfounded.

A WEARY MARCUS had barely walked into his office when Morven accosted him, her body twitching with excitement.

Marcus pushed away his immediate annoyance and arranged his face into a tight smile. "Any updates while I was gone?"

"You could say that, Sir."

She was enjoying the suspense, wanting him to beg for her to continue. How little she knew him. Instead he busied himself at his desk, drawing in his patience like he would with a suspect. He counted to ten in his head, his go-to method. By six, she had cracked.

"I got this call from a guy who wouldn't give his name but wanted to give some info about our case. Guess what he told me?"

She was practically bouncing off the walls now. Marcus sighed and played along, "What?"

Morven grinned, an ugliness to her lips. "He had information about the number codes and how they link a woman to our case, a woman who's *criminally* involved a lot more than she's let on. Guess who? I'll give you a clue, it's not Ms Blair, but you definitely know her. So, come on, who was he talking about?"

Marcus felt the room begin to spin, his breath growing shallow. He wanted to push Morven physically out of the room and tell her to shut up, because he knew, he knew whose name she was about to say in that arrogant, smug voice of hers. A quiet rushing was building in his ears, and he had to turn his face away as a wave of faintness passed over him.

"Okay, fine, I'll tell you—Sophia Meadows! It's *her* programming codes being used to commit fraud. I can even show you photos of her programming codes matching the numbers we found in the address book this guy sent me from her laptop. I've double checked them on your email copy. It's enough to charge her! See, told you we shouldn't trust her."

The quiet rushing turned into a raging roar. Scared he was about to pass out, his hand reached out to grip the desk, his knuckles turning ashen white. A bile of sickness rose in his throat.

"Sir, are you alright?"

Without a word, Marcus shot her one look before roughly pushing past her to get out of the room.

"Where are you going?" Morven shouted after his retreating back. She thought he would be grateful to her. Instead, he had looked at her like he loathed the very sight of her.

"I'LL HELP YOU PACK. Then you can be on your way this afternoon."

There was a franticness now about Aneella I knew only too well. She was hurrying toward the bedroom. In disbelief, I followed her, in time to see her begin to empty the wardrobe of my clothes.

"Stop! Just stop, Ella!" I rushed to grab her arm. She

shook my hand off, but I wasn't going to be put off. This time, I grabbed both of her arms until it forced her to stop and glare at me. "Why are you trying to get rid of me so fast? Tell me the truth, and I mean the absolute truth, something you can't seem to do very well." A flicker of guilt was in her eyes. "I know you cheated on your university exams—"

"How?" she gasped. "Only Anthony... Oh, I see. Been digging on me, have you?"

"Don't take the moral high ground with me! You think I want to find these things out about you? You disappeared on me and left me with your crap to deal with. It's not fun coming home to find a stranger in here. If it hadn't been for Marcus—" I stopped abruptly, aware I was about to say too much. But Ella was smart, she immediately pounced on my mistake.

"Just Marcus now, is it? Don't tell me you've fallen for him. Oh, Sophia, you foolish girl, I can see it in your eyes. Don't you know you can't trust any man? I know that to my own cost, loving and protecting a man I shouldn't."

I flushed, hating the sudden despair in her voice, too riled up to comprehend what she was trying to tell me. "How I feel about Marcus has nothing to do with you. Anyway, we aren't talking about him. You need to tell me why you're trying to get rid of me. My use has gone, has it?"

She shook off my hands to grab my clothes again, saying as if to convince herself, "You must go. You need to go, right now. Trust me on this, okay."

I grabbed my clothes off her once more. It would be comical if it wasn't so pitifully sad. "I'm worried about you—"

"I didn't ask you to worry about me," she tossed out, a defiant glare in her eyes.

I shook my head. "I can't believe you can say that. Please, just be straight with me for once!"

Aneella threw up her hands in rage. "Fine! Here's the truth. I'm trying to stop you from being arrested by your boyfriend. If you leave now, he won't find you. I'm doing you a favour, you stupid girl, can't you see that!"

Staggered by her words, I couldn't form an answer. I think I took a step back. She moved as if to reach for me, her face softening, when a loud insistent banging on the door caused us both to jump in fright. We slowly turned to face the direction of it. Another louder bang, shaking the very walls of the apartment.

"We're too late," she gasped. It was the genuine fear in her eyes that had me clutching my clothes stupidly to me, staring at her when she said, "Quick! Go answer but shut this door so he doesn't know I'm here."

My clothes slipped unnoticed out of my hands, hitting the floor. My eyes were full of anguish and despair as I whispered, "Ella, what have you done?"

[32]

Taut as a coil straining to be released, Marcus would not even look at me as he stormed passed. I felt an immediate sickness grip me, coupled with the acute feeling of floundering helplessly in the dark, the only one who didn't know what the hell was going on.

As I shut the front door after Marcus, I glanced toward the closed bedroom door before bracing myself for the onslaught. It came immediately, brutally, cutting straight into my heart with its velocity.

"Have you been playing me all this time? Tell me!" He spun round to me, his face tense and white, his eyes sparking with anger mixed with another emotion I couldn't read.

"No! No, I haven't," I replied as calmly as I was able to manage, walking toward him with my hands outstretched. "I would never do that. What's happened? What's wrong?"

Marcus shook his head violently. "You look so innocent as you say that. I could almost believe you."

"That's because I am innocent of whatever it is you think I've done. Come on, Marcus, stop pacing, and talk to me. This isn't you!" I tried to reach out to him, but he reacted like my touch was poison. Pushing himself almost violently away from me, his eyes swiftly moved to my laptop still sitting on the table from earlier. He grabbed it, stabbing it toward me like it was a weapon.

"Wonder what I would find if I looked on here, hm? Maybe some new programming codes designed for corruption and fraud, just like those ones we found in that little black address book you've been so helpfully trying to solve for me."

His voice was dripping in sarcasm, in a way that was not him. I hated that voice.

"I don't understand!" My voice despaired, beginning to feel afraid, like I was once more under that water in the loch, only this time Marcus wouldn't come to save me but leave me to drown. "They can't be my programming codes, they can't! How would they have them? How—"

"Seems to me there's only one way they could have them, Sophia. You gave the codes to them."

As his words hit me, accusing me of something I hadn't done, with it coming an overwhelming guilt that my codes were being abused in this way to destroy the country he loved, I wanted to go in and drag Ella out to explain. The way he was looking at me now—betrayed, hurt, bitter, loathing the sight of me—was like someone had thrown me into my worst nightmare. A stranger before me, when only three days before I'd lain in his warm embrace, feeling connected and intimate with him in a way I'd never felt with another. When he had still trusted me with his heart.

As we stood facing each other, breathing hard, I was hit by a striking realisation. Do I let this man, the whole of him, with all his vast goodness as well as his faults, into my heart and soul? Or do I let him walk away, let him believe what he wanted, without fighting to save something beautiful and tangible we had begun to create?

Suddenly, I was fighting, fighting hard with everything I had. "No, no, something is wrong here. I've been set up, somehow…"

He wasn't listening, too riled up to listen to reason. The anger had subsided, but somehow that made it worse as he said, swallowing hard, "I trusted you, believed your innocence. Now, I'm the fool. I got too close, lost my sense of objection, lost myself in you. My sergeant tried to warn me about you, but I refused to listen—"

"Stop, just shut up, and listen for a minute! I am innocent. *Innocent*, goddamn it! Do you hear me? You're right to trust me." I came close to him, my despair turning to a fighting anger that spurred me on. "Look me in the eye and ask me if I'm telling the truth. Go on, do it!"

I held my gaze as he hesitated, challenging him. All at once, he grabbed my face roughly in his hands, fierceness piercing his voice and said, "Tell me the truth, dammit. I need to know."

"Ask me, ask me right now. You're a detective, you'll know if I'm lying."

Marcus closed his eyes briefly, before fiercely saying, every word punctured out, "Are these program codes in the book created by you?"

"Yes, they may be my codes, though I pray they're not," I breathed out. "I would have to check them to know for sure. Now ask me another question, the one you really want to ask."

The dark intensity in his eyes was almost too much and the urge to turn away great. I could scarcely breathe, but I held his gaze, willing him on. He swallowed again, still holding my face, still delivering every word with a punch I hadn't known him capable of. "Have you ever knowingly given your programme codes to someone to use as an act of fraud?"

Without hesitation, bringing my own hands up to cover his, I vehemently said, "No, no, no. Never. Nor will I ever. I swear it on my life."

Trust me, Marcus, trust me, my eyes pleaded, urging him to believe me. I wanted, needed, the hurt and pain in his eyes, mirrored in my own, to fade away.

I could see the conflict in his eyes, his heart battling against his mind, before he squeezed them shut. For the briefest moment, his forehead came to rest against mine, his chest breathing deep and hard. Hope filled me. But in the next breath, he let go of me, as if he couldn't allow himself to hold me for one moment more. I heard a sob, realised it was mine, as a coldness seeped into my skin with the withdrawal of his warmth.

I turned to see him almost stumbling out of the front door, giving me no time to react. My greatest fear was realized: I was losing him before I'd had a chance to love him. I was left with such pain and fear that my next words exploded out of my mouth before my brain had grasped the infinite truth staring me in the face all this time.

"I love you, Marcus."

It was enough to stop him dead. I let my heart do the talking, raw and without constraint. "I want to see the sun rise with you every morning. I want to trust you with my whole heart as I already trust you with my life. Most of all, I want you to trust me again. So, I'm going to find out who stole my codes and bring them to you, and then you'll know I'm worthy of your love."

I willed him to turn around, come back to me, and for a moment I dared to believe he would as his body turned to me. There were tears in his eyes as I knew there were in mine. For the briefest of moments, we held each other's gaze, saying so much and yet not enough. If I'd been able to read his mind, I would have understood that everything within him wanted to come and take me in his arms, tell me he loved me, and that it was costing him greatly in not doing this. I would have understood that it was too raw and too soon for him to tell me any of this. I would have known, even if I'd have found it hard to accept, that his mind was full of doubts and uncertainties, and his head was ruling his heart right then.

But I couldn't read his mind. So, when all he said in a strained voice was, "I have to go," then turned away to walk out on me, grief struck me hard, worse than when Richard had left me. I had laid my soul bare to a man I knew had the capacity to love me completely, and I had lost. I had lost.

Like a tidal wave, the tears came up, almost choking me in their intensity. I sank down to the floor, weeping.

It was only the sound of the front door closing with a quiet thud that caused me to dully look up. Then, the realisation hit me like a lightning bolt that Aneella had bolted out of the apartment, instantly drying up my tears. In its place came anger, pure raging anger. And it was all directed at one person.

"Oh, no, you don't," I muttered, springing up with a vicious energy. Without pausing, I grabbed my keys and phone and sprinted out of the door.

E very fiber of him was beating hard, like a hammer being pummelled inside him. His body groaned with an excruciating pain, and he felt the overwhelming need to hit someone or something.

Grimly, Marcus crashed through the doors leading into the interview rooms, his eyes narrowed, and his mind set on one purpose—to make Lyle talk, whatever it took, whatever the cost. The truth was going to come out, even if he had to drag it kicking and screaming out of the man.

Lyle gave the impression of a caged tiger, restlessly pacing up and down his small, suffocating police holding cell, hating the itchy feel of the clothes they'd given him. They were holding him on charges of trespass and entering, as well as attempted fraud. So far, he'd refused to talk or reveal the names of those involved with him. But his lawyer was next to damn useless and he was beginning to panic, big time. He might actually go down for this. Which begged the question, why should he be the only one paying for this, the sore loser who didn't get what he wanted while the rest rolled around in their riches?

The sound of his cell door opening was such a relief, he almost cried. Two uniformed police officers stood there. He stopped pacing.

"DI Armstrong wants to speak with you. Come with us, please."

When Lyle got to the interrogation room, it appeared his pacing was contagious. Detective Armstrong was a perfect mirror of Lyle's movements not two minutes before, though the latter abruptly quit moving on his arrival. As they seated him, his hopeless bespectacled lawyer looking nervous beside him, Lyle noticed the young bitchy sergeant from before, the one who got off on the sound of her own voice. She was watching him with a gloating smile from where she sat diagonally opposite him. He had loathed her on sight. Now, he ignored her, giving the detective all his glares. He was determined to hide how unnerving it was having this sharp-eyed officer leaning over the table, looking at Lyle like he wanted to throttle him. Weird, because every other time, Lyle had believed this man to be practically subhuman, showing no emotion whatsoever.

"I hope you're here to tell me I'm being released," he goaded, sounding more confident than he felt.

The detective gave a short, edgy laugh that bordered on unhinged. Lyle swallowed nervously. "Released, funny. No, I'm here to tell you that you're going to tell me exactly who you're working with and how Ms. Blair had those programme codes to begin with. Aye, we know they're programme codes, so there's little point in pretending to be surprised."

"Can you sit down?" Lyle muttered, trying to give himself a moment to process what they knew. He needed to come out on top with the best scenario for him. The detective sat down, never taking his eyes off Lyle. It was like he could read Lyle's brain as it whirred and clicked, rearranging the pieces to make the best fit.

Lyle's eyes narrowed. "If I tell you what I know, what's in it for me?"

Marcus sat back and crossed his arms. "Let's see what you've got to tell me first, then maybe we'll talk about reduced sentences."

As soon as the lift doors opened, I flew out, racing into the car park. It was fairly quiet, and luck was in my favour. Her sporty car, distinctive by its bright red against a sea of silver and blue, was reversing out of a space. I could see her blonde hair whipping in her haste to be gone.

Thinking fast, I snapped a picture of the car and licence plate, then texted it to Marcus with,

Aneella's here! Trying to run. You need to stop her. This is her car licence.

She's leaving the apartment car park. I'll chase after her.

. . .

PRESSING SEND, I ran to my own car, determined to follow her and somehow force her to talk to Marcus. I cared little for my own safety. I had nothing to lose and everything to fight for.

"FIRST THING, let's talk about the other man seen running from Ms. Blair's apartment on more than one occasion, as well as following Ms. Meadows." Marcus fixed Lyle with a steely gaze. His body was still racing on adrenaline from the last couple of hours, his head a throbbing drum. Never had he felt sharper in his determination to get to the truth, right here, right now. He couldn't even allow himself to think of Sophia and the look on her face when he'd turned away from her, nor the growing fear that his mistrust of her had killed her tentative love for him.

Lyle gave a small shrug, as if it was unimportant who this man was. "A two-bit criminal who clearly wasn't very good at his job if he was nearly caught so many times. He was supposed to get the codes for me, but he never managed to get the safe open. Useless," Lyle muttered darkly.

"I need a name for this useless criminal."

Lyle shrugged. "I only know his first name. Daryl."

"Try harder, Mr. Boyd."

"I can't tell you what I don't know," Lyle protested.

Marcus' eyes narrowed. He leaned forward. "That's just the thing, you do know. And you will tell me."

He was about to say more, but at that precise moment

his phone beeped from where it sat on the table. *Sophia* flashed up, for everyone to see. Marcus' heart constricted painfully. Morven widened her eyes in surprise, then gave Marcus a pointed look. Ignoring her and the curious glances from Lyle, he abruptly reached across to turn the tape recorder off. He hesitated, then opened Sophia's text.

Morven watched Marcus' forehead crease, then his fingers rapidly text back, saving an image to his phone. Within seconds, he was attaching the image to a new text. In the next breath, Morven's phone beeped, alerting her of an incoming text from Marcus.

"Thought there was a no-phone policy," Lyle quipped.

"That's only for you suspects," Morven retaliated.

Marcus barely heard them, his mind too busy processing the chain of events Sophia had just set in motion. Gesturing with his hand for them to move outside of the interview room, Marcus waited for Morven to follow, before commanding, "I've sent you a photo of a car which is registered to Ms. Blair. I need you to send out some cars to go and apprehend her, then bring her in. Tell them to be careful. Soph—Ms. Meadows—is following behind. No harm is to come to either of them." Morven was staring at him, not reacting with any kind of urgency. Marcus bit down on his growing frustration with her. He knew Sophia, in her stubborn determination, wouldn't give up until she'd caught up with Aneella. An overriding, mounting concern that she was about to get harmed had begun to cloud his professional, detached judgement of the situation. This he was all too aware of, with an almost desperate acceptance of what he couldn't change. His jaw clenched hard. "That's now, Sergeant!" he barked out.

Morven flinched with the scolding, then turned on her heel with a dark scowl on her face.

Marcus watched her walk down the corridor, sent Sophia a rapid-fire text before walking back into the interview room. There was a genuine spark of fear in Lyle's eyes now, and Marcus wasted no time in pouncing on this to use for his own gain.

Very deliberately, he reached back across to turn the tape recorder on, then watched Lyle intently as he firmly assured, "Ms. Blair will be apprehended, mark my words on that. So, I suggest you start telling me everything before I hear a different side to the story. One that has no happy ending for you."

⌣⌣⌣

I HAD her in my sight, following with a dog-eared determination to finally make her stop. Stop this running, this web of lies. This chaos. Not anymore.

Marcus' text had come through a few minutes ago, simply saying,

POLICE IN PURSUIT. Don't do anything crazy.

TOO LATE FOR THAT.

Ella had crossed over the bridge from Inverness and was now storming around the bends of the loch near Kessock like she was driven by the devil himself, with no clear idea of where she was heading. Why drive into the

Highlands when you could head southward? I had to hold my nerve to keep up with her. Fortunately, the roads were quiet with only idling tourists enjoying the luscious scenery, wise enough to pull over to let some crazy drivers shoot past them. Using handsfree, I managed to text Marcus where we were heading. I sensed Ella knew I was hot on her tail.

Adrenaline bit hard at me. It felt like my whole future, everything that was important to me, rested on me stopping Ella from leaving. She had to confess, she had to!

For, of course, she was guilty and making me an unwilling accomplice Why else run? A sudden sharp pain at her betrayal burst through my chest. A small sob grew in my throat, but I pushed down on the emotions threatening to cripple me. Not now, not yet.

My foot pressed down harder on the accelerator.

⌢⌢

LYLE HAD HALF RISEN out of his seat, as if to symbolise his innocence. But with the stark warning from Marcus, he sank back down again, his head slumping as if all the fight in him had suddenly been sucked out.

"Look, I'm not the mastermind of this fraud job, or whatever you want to call it. It was Aneella who approached me while we were still working at the bank. I was pretty shocked she even came to me. We'd parted badly at the end of our affair, if you want to call it that. I would have called it a 'mutually satisfactory arrangement.'" Lyle looked up at the impassive DI, whose eyes were boring holes into him. He shook his head, hoping to still weasel out of this somehow. "Is that enough?"

"No. Carry on."

Lyle sighed, and began fiddling with a scratch on the nondescript worn table in front of him. "She told me that she had an offer I couldn't refuse. All I needed to do was get a guy in place who wouldn't mind getting his hands dirty, and she would pay me handsomely for the deed. So, that's what I did. I got Daryl." Seeing Marcus' raised eyebrows, Lyle sighed. "Baker, all right, Daryl Baker. Happy?" His foot began to tap on the floor again, his face turning bitter and twisted. "Shit. Something went wrong, maybe she panicked; I don't know what the hell happened. Whatever, she told me she needed to lie low, and it was all down to me to get the codes. Which is what I tried to do, 'til you and that damn Sophia got in my way."

Marcus leaned forward, "So, is Ms. Blair the mastermind?"

Lyle snorted, giving Marcus an incredulous look. "You're kidding, right? She doesn't have the cool head or the bollocks for that. No, it's not her."

"Then who is?"

Here, Lyle lifted his hands up, "Honest to God, I have no idea. I never asked, I never wanted to ask. As long as I got my share of the gold, that's all I cared about. But I'll tell you one thing, Aneella worships the hell out of him to the point of it being unhealthy, like she's almost afraid of him. I wouldn't want to cross this man, whoever he is."

At Lyle's words, Marcus felt a cold shiver go down his spine, like someone had trampled over his grave.

I WAS GAINING ON HER, her taillight almost within a hair's breadth. I flashed my headlights at her, indicating for her to pull over to the side of the road. Her startled face stared at me through her rear-view mirror. She sped up, I matched her, having no choice though my car groaned and began to make a horrible rattling sound.

The bends were getting sharper, and I was beginning to lose my nerve. My heart felt like it was going to burst out of my chest. Up ahead was a straight part of the road, with a crossroads looming in front of me. This would be my only chance.

Biting my lip, gripping the steering wheel until my knuckles turned white, I angled myself to overtake her, praying there'd be no cars coming the other way.

Yet despite my every effort, she still gained space away from me. My car just didn't have the power in it, I could feel it pulling back, choking itself. *No, no!* I felt like screaming and hit my steering wheel in bitter anger and frustration.

Wait, wait, I could hear sirens! Two police cars, coming toward us, gaining back the ground I'd lost. Daringly, they swerved in front of Ella, forcing her to make the choice to crash into them, or brake hard, tyres burning. Her car came screeching to a stop, skidding a little on the mud on the side of the road.

"Thank God, thank God," I whispered aloud, as I pulled in behind them, my whole body shaking. The police officers were already walking over to Ella, opening her door, telling her to step out of the vehicle. I threw myself out of my car to run up to them. As she stepped out onto the gravel road, our eyes met. One look, only one look to try and convey everything I felt inside—anger, disappointment, betrayal, pain.

One look was not enough. It was nowhere near enough.

She turned sharply away from me, her head held high, as if she knew her dignity was all she had left to cling to. I watched her climb into the police car, her face averted.

Our friendship was in tatters. It would never be the same again. But I couldn't let her go completely, not until we had faced one another.

I would force her to look me in the eyes and tell me the truth. I deserved nothing less.

[34]

The hour was late. Dark shadows loomed in the stripped-bare room, the cold, artificial light from the ceiling failing to cast them out. Somewhere a clock ticked—tick, tick, tick—each one sounding louder than the last. Aneella shuddered, hugging her hands around the cold, tasteless coffee given to her when they put her in this room, before leaving her here to stew.

Her thin, grey-haired lawyer, brought in from somewhere obscure, was writing notes, his pen scratch, scratch, scratching against the lined pad resting on the table. He seemed unconcerned by her dilemma, mute to her pleas, and uncaring about what happened to her. What use was he to her?

Dark, foreboding fear was slowly creeping up over her body and into her mind, crippling her. But she would not be a betrayer.

MARCUS HAD SEEN me hovering by the doorway as he met his officers escorting Aneella into the station. My heart beat hard as we looked at each other. I waited. I had no idea what to do.

Issuing instructions to the police officers to lead Aneella away, Marcus walked across to me. I watched his every step, until he was before me. For a long moment, neither of us said anything. Then Marcus gave a short shake of his head, looking at me with anger mingled alongside admiration. "You know you could have got yourself killed, chasing after Ella like that."

"Yes."

"Then why? Why take such a stupid risk with your life?"

"She needs to face up to what she's done, for burdening me with this guilt of knowing something I created has been used to destroy your country." Unwanted tears blurred my vision.

Marcus almost took me into his arms then, like it was the most natural reaction to my distress. Almost. His hands fell onto my arm for the briefest, briefest moment as if to pull me in, before abruptly falling away. "I'll find out the truth, and if she's guilty, I promise you she will face the consequences."

I nodded, biting my lip. I saw his eyes follow my move-ment, almost smiling. I tried to smile in return, before, "May I speak with her, after you have?"

"I'm not sure that's wise…"

My hand flew to his arm, pleading, "Please. I need this. I need to understand why. Why me. She's caused me to lose you. I can't just walk away. I can't…"

He didn't agree with me, but neither did he deny that I'd lost him. All he said, in that calm, controlled voice of his, was that he would find me as soon as he could. I watched him walk away, nodding to a female police officer, who then led me to a chair and asked me some questions.

Now, I sat on an uncomfortable plastic chair nursing a pale, milky tea I did not want, waiting, waiting, waiting...

MARCUS WALKED into the interview room, Morven right behind him. Aneella's head swung up, her eyes widening. Marcus gave her a smile as he sat down to face her across the table.

He had her phone in his hand contained within a plastic bag and could see her zero in on it, her features stilling, as if afraid that if she moved one muscle in her face it would give her away.

Marcus decided to come in politely, acutely aware that once she'd been a close friend of Sophia. "Thank you for your patience, Ms. Blair. I appreciate you've had a long wait."

Thrown, though desperate not to show it, Aneella gave a small, hesitant nod.

"Is there anything we can get you before we ask you some questions?" She shook her head. "Have you had a chance to talk with your lawyer?"

Aneella gave what sounded like a derisive laugh. The lawyer glanced up, his face impassive. "Yes, we've talked, if you could call it that."

"Good, now can you state for the record your full name and date of birth."

"Aneella Louise Blair, fourteenth June 1989."

"Thank you," Marcus smiled, hoping to put her at ease, to gain her trust. He could sense Morven looking at him oddly, aware this wasn't his normal procedure when interviewing suspects. Usually his style was to keep a small, impersonal distance, let them sweat it out. But what Morven had failed to understand was that nothing about the case was as it should be. How could it be when there was Sophia?

"Ms. Blair, you're here today because two people have testified that you are involved in an attempted fraud, using codes from a computer program created by Ms. Meadows, someone you've known since your university days. On your phone, we've found photos of the computer language written by Ms. Meadows, confirmed by her only a few minutes ago, which was taken from her laptop earlier today. We also have in our possession your black address book containing the last four digits of each line of the programming code on different pages of the book. Mr. Boyd has written a full statement testifying to this and remains in custody."

Aneella had sat immobile throughout all of this, stripped of emotion. Or so it seemed. As Marcus paused, she finally looked at him. Behind the defiance of her posture was the smallest sense of realisation—everything was crashing in on her. Sensing this, Marcus leaned closer, holding her eyes. "Ms. Blair, I need you to understand that we have enough evidence to prosecute you. But I'm giving you a chance to tell me your side of the story. Let me tell you why. I've been a detective for some time now, and you start to get a sense of people very quickly. I know the ones who are as much a victim as they are a criminal." Marcus paused. He had her in his grip and decided to press on. "When I look at you, I see you're one of those victims. Not for one minute do I believe you're the mastermind behind this, but merely a woman who's got herself caught up in a situation she doesn't know how to get out of. So, I'm giving you this chance to tell me, in your own words and from the beginning, what's happened, so I can try and help you."

He saw the conflict in her eyes, her need to confess and save herself fighting hard against the need to protect the man she worshipped. This man, whose identity had remained frustratingly elusive, was the one Marcus really wanted ever since he'd received a tip off that a large bank fraud was being planned with links to Scotland, specifically Inverness. It was meant to be a simple open and shut case to solve. But then Sophia had come to stay at the apartment and turned everything on its head.

He waited patiently, silently counting to ten in his head. This time, Aneella held out to nine, longer than Lyle. She gave a strange sigh, closing her eyes, before opening them to fix him with an intimate look. She completely ignored her lawyer who was trying to quietly encourage her to talk with him before proceeding. Meeting her look head-on, Marcus nodded, as did she. Morven pulled out her notebook, unnoticed by them, poised to make notes.

"I was working at Scriveners Bank, within the corporate department. Part of my role is, or was, to entertain our big investors, ensure they were greeted well, looked after, wined and dined, etc., etc., so that they never consider withdrawing their precious money from our bank. We needed them more than they needed us, and they knew that. It was exhausting work and long hours, with no personal compensation. I grew to detest it and those greedy, mauling clients who thought I was nothing more than a pair of legs, there to meet their every vile demand."

"They underestimated your skills. You resented them."

Aneella nodded keenly. "Yes, exactly. Resentment can be a dangerous thing, when left to fester. There was one client who liked to brag about dealings and how much money he was making. After a few drinks, his tongue would become very loose. One evening, six months ago or thereabouts, Mr. Hoskins, our client, was boasting about his whizz of a programmer currently writing him a program that, if put in the wrong hands, could be used for fraud, that's how clever it was. My interest soared. I was curious, so I plied him with more drinks to keep him talking. Apparently, his programmer had warned him to ensure it remained protected for this very reason and that he'd had to sign a witnessed declaration to say it wouldn't be used for fraudulent reasons. He said she'd wanted to pull the project because of her concerns, but he'd convinced her to finish writing it. Guess who the programmer was?"

Marcus had to swallow hard, his mouth suddenly dry, before replying, "Sophia."

She nodded, smiling a little. "Imagine my shock on

hearing that my old university friend from years ago is now some high-flying programmer."

His need to know for certain, beyond all reasonable doubt, that Soph was innocent in all of this was driving every other coherent thought away. His voice punctured out, "So, you're telling me that Sophia, Ms. Meadows, never knowingly gave this programme to your client to be used for fraudulent reasons? Is that correct? It's absolutely vital you're clear on this and give me an honest answer." He held his breath as he awaited her answer, his whole body tense.

Aneella gave him a faint smile, acknowledging what he could not say aloud. She in turn leaned forward, answering slowly and carefully as if talking to a child, "No, Sophia never knowingly gave Mr. Hoskins the programme to commit fraud. You're right to trust her. In fact, I think it's fair to say she did everything to ensure it wasn't used for crime. Poor deluded girl, how wrong was she."

You're right to trust her. As the words washed deep into his troubled soul, easing it instantly, Marcus breathed out an immense sigh of relief, unbridled joy lighting his face. They stared at him, taken aback by his reaction.

Now, he had to hope he hadn't lost her, that the damage by his moment of doubt could still be reversed. She must love him, for why else would she have chased after Aneella like that, determined to find out the truth and prove her innocence in all of this? He would never doubt her again, prayed she would trust his word on that. An urge to leave right then and find Sophia almost overtook him; in fact, he half rose out of his seat. But it began to dawn on him that Aneella was saying something and Morven was frowning hard at him. Reluctantly, he lowered himself down. He owed it to Sophia, his team, and himself, to bring this to a conclusion, once and for all. He forced himself to refocus on what Aneella was saying.

"I filled him with more drink and got him to show me the programme that was then still a prototype. When he was distracted and left the programme still open and running, I managed to get into the C++ language I remember Sophia showing me as students, write down the last numbers of each line of code on a menu card, which was all I had time to do. Even then, I only just managed to put his laptop back before he noticed. Later that night, I wrote them into my black address book, separating them onto different pages, then destroyed the menu card. I still don't know why I did that—took the codes I mean. I've never done anything like that before, you must believe me on that." Her hands spread out toward him to plead her supposed innocence.

Marcus nodded, let that last comment go. "What happened after you wrote these codes down?"

"I told a... friend about what I'd done."

"What friend?" he pressed.

Aneella remained stubbornly silent. Marcus kept the frustration off his face, keeping his features calm, not wanting her to have any reason to clam up on this outpouring of absolutely crucial evidence.

He decided to take a gamble on it being her lover. "Okay, so he came up with a plan?"

"He got very excited when I told him. I'd never seen him so animated. He convinced me we could make our fortune then start a new life somewhere else, far away from the prison of a job we were in, away from this dreary depressing country." Aneella looked down, as if ashamed, then continued, "I would have done anything he asked me. He always knew the best time to sweet talk me into his persuasive plans was when we were in bed together, scams that would always rob and cheat someone but didn't seem so wrong when he sugar-coated it so expertly." She looked up then, a faraway look in her eyes.

Marcus coughed to draw her back to him. "What happened then? With such a long time between planning this to where we are now, something must have gone wrong."

Her eyes narrowed. "Lyle, that's what happened. He got cocky, telling colleagues about how he was going to make his fortune with a brilliant scam—the stupid arsehole. We should never have involved him. Needless to say, our bosses got suspicious, sacked Lyle on the spot, and I only just talked my way out of it by promising to take extended leave. Lyle got nasty at this point, threatening me and demanding I give him the codes. Like I was going to do that!" She shook her head, paused to sip her coffee, only to grimace and push it away. "I knew I had to lie low, that there was no way we could carry out the fraud at that time."

Frowning hard, Marcus tried to put the pieces of the complex puzzle together. One thing was now becoming abundantly clear: Lyle had either lied to him about Aneella telling him to get the codes from the apartment after she needed to disappear, or Aneella was the one lying to him now. Tough call, but he was more inclined to believe

Aneella in this moment. After all, her motive was not greed but desire to please the man she misguidedly loved. Lyle was purely in this for selfish reasons and good at hiding the truth until forced into a corner with no way out.

"And when you visited Sophia..." his voice trailing off. One look into her eyes, and he had his answer. "It was purposely to bring her here."

For the first time, there was a spark of something in those eyes. Guilt, perhaps? A flush came to her cheeks as she nodded, almost smiling. "I needed her here to get the rest of the codes I hadn't retrieved the first time, but I had to bide my time. And ironically, who better to protect the book of codes than the author and creator of them? It wasn't hard to track her down. I knew she was very low after her divorce and therefore easy to manipulate. It was easy, almost too easy, to make it seem like I was doing it for her own benefit by inviting her to come and stay at my apartment. She was always malleable and soft."

He felt a swift anger stir within the depths of him. The thought that Sophia's trusting love for others had been taken advantage of, to the point her own life had been at risk, affected him greatly. Out of sight under the table, his fists clenched, until he forced them to relax. She must have sensed it though—perhaps he gave it away in the movement of his jaw or his eyes—for she moved a little back from him. It took every ounce of restraint he possessed to calmly say, "You played her, used her for your advantage."

"Yes," Aneella admitted. "Yes, we used her. She's a better person than I'll ever be. And stronger than I've ever given her credit for. I should probably feel more ashamed of myself than I do."

"On that, we agree. You put her life at risk the moment you involved her, especially with Lyle clearly determined to get those codes, one way or another."

Her mouth compressed into a thin, unattractive line. "I had no idea Lyle had tracked down my apartment, which he must have gotten from my HR records before he was sacked, or that he still had this criminal guy working for him. When Sophia told me Lyle had been in, and about the break-ins that followed, I was as shocked as she was. I had a feeling she would find the safe; that's why I wrote *I'm sorry* on the photo of us. You see, I do have some shred of decency in me." Marcus raised his eyebrows but remained silent, not trusting himself to speak. Aneella's eyes narrowed, growing defensive. "Look, the truth is I didn't think she would go to you, nor that she'd trust you more than she trusted me when I told her *explicitly* not to call the police."

Marcus shook his head and said, "You cannot be at all surprised Sophia did that. She was worried for your safety, Aneella, like any good friend would. Can you not see that?"

"I can see that you care for her, DI Armstrong, very deeply," came the challenge back, trying to rattle him it seemed. He changed tack.

"What made you change your plans and turn up here, when you were keeping a low profile?"

Aneella sighed. "He ordered me to come. Things were not working out as he hoped. It was all taking too long, getting too messy and out of control. I needed to get the codes another way. That only way was…"

"Through Sophia directly," he finished for her, nodding. "You needed access to her laptop."

There followed a moment of silence as they digested what had been said.

Aneella was growing restless in her seat, her need to be away from this room beginning to consume her. "Look, I've told you everything. I want to stop now." She gave her lawyer frantic looks, but he remained as nonreactive as ever. "Am I able to go home? You can get me bailed out, right? I don't want to stay here for the night."

Morven was beginning to make noises, like she was going to say something inappropriate that would cause Aneella to grow more agitated. Marcus quickly reached out a hand toward Aneella.

"Ms. Blair, listen to me. I know you've been cooperative. I understand you want to request bail, and all of that can be arranged. This is your first offence, and we can ensure the judge knows that this wasn't your doing, you were merely an accomplice. But," he drew in a breath as she finally grew still, "for that to happen, I need to know one last thing. I need a name." His eyes bored into hers. "I need to know who he is."

A frisson of fear overcame her, stripping her of her confidence and her attitude, leaving behind a pale ghost who could be swept away in a strong wind. "I– I can't do that. I can't. You don't know what he's capable of doing to get what he wants. I can't displease him, I can't. Please, understand," she pleaded, grabbing his hand.

It affected him, inhaling her fear like that. Pity and

overwhelming concern swept over him. Either she was a talented liar, or she really was scared.

His warm hand covered her cold, clammy one. "I'll keep you safe, I promise. He won't get near you. You have my word on that." He nodded, unwavering in his look as he caught her flickering one, keeping a hold of her hand.

A battle fought within her. She wanted badly to trust him and let go of this. Yet, the pull toward the manipulative love of her life was magnetic, powerful, and destructive. Tears clouded her vision for a moment, until she hastily wiped them away. Aneella found she couldn't look away from this kind, solid man before her with his intense, beautiful eyes. The man whom her friend loved passionately.

"I can see why Sophia loves you," she said aloud, swallowing hard. "Why she couldn't help but trust you with her life. Your love for her is pure and courageous. I wish I'd known love like that, perhaps my life would have turned out differently." She gave a short, humourless laugh. "But who am I kidding? I'm too selfish and messed up to love like that. You two aren't. She deserves to be loved by a true, honourable man. Don't let her go. Don't waste another moment not telling her how you feel."

Marcus stared at her, moved by her words speaking of the depth of his feelings for Sophia, which he hadn't truly understood himself, until now. Until faced with the very truth he should have believed from the beginning.

Alongside him, Morven was swamped with intense disappointment. She knew the truth now. Maybe she always had: that's why she'd been desperate to blacken Sophia's name. Bitterness would come, that was the god-awful reality, and there was nothing she could do about that. She turned her head away, unable to look at him, afraid she would say something she'd regret. Damned if she was going to give him reason to sack her by screaming at him. He wouldn't see her tears. No one would.

Marcus swallowed, before quietly promising, "I won't."

A radiant smile transformed Aneella as she nodded. "Good, good. At least in this one thing, I've made amends to Sophia."

A suspended moment, then, her face became overshadowed by an indescribable fear. As if overcome with the worst possible thought.

"But I still won't tell you his name. You can keep asking me, and I will keep on protecting him. I'm sorry, sorrier than you know. I wish I could trust you. I wish for a lot of things. But it's too late for me to change what is or isn't. Now, please take me to my cell."

[35]

At last, footsteps came down the corridor. I sprang up from the hard chair, knocking my unfinished now-cold tea over in my haste. Crouching down to wipe up the spill with some tissues, no one noticed me as they silently filed past. As I stood back up, their retreating backs were beginning to slide away out of my reach. Aneella was beside Morven, who had a hold of her arm as if she didn't trust Ella not to bolt. Marcus was in front.

"Ella!" I shouted.

She turned at the sound of her name. Marcus stopped and reached out to halt Morven, who shot him a glare. I rushed up in front of Ella, forcing her to look directly at me, make her see the pain churning within me at her betrayal.

"Why?" was all I said.

The silence was sharp and agonising. I could feel Marcus' pitying eyes on me, Morven's resentful stare, but the only ones I focussed on were Ella's. Were there any signs, even the tiniest, of remorse and regret, even sorrow? I searched her eyes feverishly, a part of me still willing and eager to forgive, for her to explain that it had all been a misunderstanding. I wanted to believe that she'd never meant for me to get hurt, never planned to set me up so that it would have been me who was questioned and charged by the man I loved, not her.

"Because I could," Ella said, the simple truth agonising in its starkness. "Because I knew you would never say no to me, just like when we were at university together, and you were always the one following behind, sorting out the messes I created. You always were a little gullible, Sophia." She cocked her head, a sad sort of smile on her face. "Always wanted to believe the good in people. But some people have no good in them, they're rotten through and through. It's time you grew up and realised that."

I couldn't believe what I was hearing, that I was the one at fault for trusting her, for wanting to be a good friend. Marcus stepped forward, as if wanting to shield me, saying a little roughly, "Okay, let's go." But I held my hand out to stop them, my dignity drawing up to give me the strength to say, "You're not the person you once were, Aneella. Then, you had something contagious, irresistible within you, like a light we all wanted to come close to. Now, I feel nothing but pity for you. I hope this man you're protecting is worth it, though I doubt it very much. No man worth loving would leave you here to face your punishment alone without turning himself in too. So, where is he? Obviously, he doesn't believe you're worth saving, and I can't say I blame him. Enjoy your time rotting away in jail."

My words came from a dark, bitter place in my heart, a

place I didn't like. Aneella gasped, her eyes misting up with obvious distress. I must have hit a raw part of her soul. She turned her head away, bowing. It was such a clear sign of defeat, I let out a quiet sob of guilt, stepping back, feeling a sudden, acute, despairing loss. "Ella, I didn't mean... I—"

Warm hands came onto my shoulder, gently taking me to one side.

"Sergeant Atkins, please escort Ms. Blair to the holding cell," Marcus said.

He turned to me, holding my face so I would look at him, only him. I could feel the sobs rising in me, the tears falling down my cheeks. "I'm sorry, so sorry. I didn't mean all of that. I don't know where that came from," I said.

Marcus shook his head, resting it against my forehead and said, "Don't be sorry, don't ever be sorry. You've done nothing wrong. Nothing." He wiped away my tears with his thumb, while sheltering me from the curious passers-by. "I don't want to leave you like this, but I can't leave the station yet. Will you wait for me at my lodge? Can you do that for me?" I nodded, closing my eyes for a moment. "Good. Here's my key," he said, reaching into his pocket and pressing it into my hand. "Drive carefully. I'll be there soon."

With that, he was gone, bereaving my body with its sudden emptiness. I stood there alone again.

But I would go to him, I would wait, even if it was to hear him say goodbye. I would take every last touch, every last whispered word, everything he offered me, no matter how it would leave me feeling when day broke. My heart and soul were in pieces, and I didn't know how I was going to build myself up again.

As I stood in the endless dark corridor, words I had first read in the university library many years ago, came back with aching, vivid clarity: *Every person we allow into our hearts and souls will change and define us. Some bring goodness and restoration to our souls, flooding them with light… Then there are the others, who bring nothing but darkness and despair to our hearts and try to blacken our souls until they are exactly like their own. But we must fight to rise up again.*

[36]

The night air carried an enticing, intoxicating scent that drew me out to it. Wrapping a blanket around my legs, curled up on the wooden seat, I closed my eyes to inhale the rich freshness of it as it invigorated and calmed me all at the same time. Though it was dark, the full moon bathed the scenery around me, lighting the path meandering down to the loch, where the water glittered like stars of the sea. The mountains' rugged, proud edges almost eclipsed the moon with their grandeur and height, visible in the night light.

I drew it all in, every scent, every noise, every beauty displayed, as if for my own private viewing. I stored them up, allowing them to wash away my earlier anger and bitterness. There was a peace here that surpassed all understanding, and I welcomed it, needing its soothing balm more than ever. A smile softened my face, restoring light to eyes that had dimmed. This place was healing me, despite the danger it had brought. Yet perhaps I needed both to awaken me from the emotionless life I had been walking through, afraid to let love into my heart again.

As though I had drawn him to me with my thoughts, Marcus' car drove in, its headlamps dimming as the engine was cut. I sat, a strange calmness resting over me, waiting for him to walk towards me and lead me in.

As we stepped inside, his eyes searched mine for the briefest of moments before breaking away. It was enough for me to see a wariness darkening the pupils, hitting me in my deepest, gut wrenching core. Had I already lost him?

"Can I get you a coffee or tea or something?"

The ordinariness of his question jolted me. He seemed unsure what to do with his hands, so to ease him I said, "A coffee would be good.".

While Marcus busied himself, I tried to hold on to that calmness I'd felt outside. The urge to talk was almost too much. I could feel his eyes upon me, but when I turned to him, his head was turned from me. Finally, he finished making the coffees and came toward me. He moved to the sofa, expecting me to follow. We sat down on opposite ends, reminiscent of my first time in his house when we were still cautious of each other. The gap between us now seemed wider than ever, and I wasn't sure how to bridge it. The thought made me want to weep.

"Sorry I took so long getting back. Lots of paperwork to sort out, with Aneella... Sorry, you probably don't want to talk about this—"

"No, no, I do," I urged. "Please, tell me everything before I go crazy with it all."

So, he did, matter-of-factly, as I would expect. When

he'd finished, anger at Aneella's insistence on concealing her lover's name shot out of me. "Why is she protecting him by taking the rap and allowing this man to get away with it?!"

Marcus shrugged and said, "Love can blind you, make you do stupid things. Don't worry, I'll let her stew overnight in our hospitality suite, allow the reality to sink in, then question her again tomorrow."

I stared at him, swallowing hard. "Have you ever let love blind you?"

There was a stirring emotion in his eyes as he gazed at me, causing my heartbeat to quicken, before he looked down, his voice quiet and strained. "I find it hard to love someone blindly. I need to know I can trust her completely, without question, probably to the point of unfairness."

As his words punched me hard in the gut, all that hope I had clung onto, all the dreams of staying here and being loved by him, came crashing down to almost strangle me. A choking sob escaped out of my lips, causing Marcus' head to swing up. I stumbled out, "You didn't trust me when you thought I'd given Ella the codes." I moved off the sofa, unable to bear this a minute longer, my throat tight and painful as I fought down the tears. "It means you'll never be able to fully love me or trust me—"

He jumped up, trying to reach for me. "No, no, that's not what I meant! That came out all wrong! Listen, I trust you, I do. I was a fool—"

"Were you?" I said dully. "Maybe you're right not to. What do I know about love? I didn't do a very good job last time. Why else would Richard have left me? Perhaps I didn't love him as he wanted." I reached out to tenderly touch his face, continuing, "You should be loved by someone better than me."

Before he could react, I pulled away and flew to the door to fling it open, knowing I couldn't bear being near him and not having his touch. His hurrying footsteps followed me as we were hit by the night air. Blindly, I stumbled toward my car.

"Sophia, Soph, wait! Stay, stay here with me. Please. You have my heart, don't you get that? *Tha gaol agam ort!* I don't love easily, but when I do, I love with everything that I've got. I want to give that to you. I want to love you like you deserve!"

His raw words were almost my undoing. I so desperately wanted to stop and run back to him, sink into his arms. But it was like my mind refused to allow it, fighting back hard. I was climbing into my car without really registering what I was doing. Marcus reached out to stop me closing the door.

"Please, let me go, Marcus!"

"Listen, I know you're scared, I'm scared too. I don't know what the future holds any more than you do. But if you walk away now, we'll never know what happiness awaits us."

Why was I panicking, fighting against him, when earlier all I dared to hope was that we could be together? I didn't know; I didn't know.

"I'm sorry," came my anguished whisper, before I pulled the door shut, forcing him to step back. I don't remember putting the car into gear, but Marcus' figure was becoming smaller in the darkness, and the gap between us ever larger.

MARCUS STOOD THERE, paralysed, as the car lights faded, unable to comprehend what had just happened. Then a swell of anger, all inwardly directed, gripped him in its agonising tight fist. He let out a roar of frustration, startling the night birds as they let out a loud shrill. Stones flew out around him as he kicked out, shouting, "*T-amadan!* Idiot! Stupid, stupid idiot! You've lost her!"

Only when the anger subsided did a wave of pure grief, like he had felt after losing Lucy, overwhelm him to the point his knees became weak. He stumbled back into his lodge, sank down against the wall, his head falling into his hands.

He had once again lost the woman he loved.

Only this time, he had no one but himself to blame.

I MADE it to the end of his lane, then the tears fell with a relentless force. I had the sense at least to pull over before I couldn't hold them back. His parting words played over and over in my head, taunting and accusing me, telling me I was being a coward. A fool. He was right. I was running away because it was easier than being hurt all over again, easier than risking my heart and my innermost feelings with another. Easier than exposing myself to him in my most vulnerable state.

But Marcus isn't Richard. The propounding, unequivocal thought came to me with startling clarity, cutting through into the deepest part of my soul. He loved me, all of me, every last tainted bit with no selfish demands on what I would give him in return.

Oh, I was a fool, such an idiotic fool. Why am I running? What are you doing, Sophia? What are you doing?

Abandoning it where I had stopped, unable to go on, I climbed out of the car. I wasn't sure if minutes or hours had passed. Once more the sweet night air embraced me, enticing me on. *Go, go, start walking,* it seemed to whisper to me, caressing my skin. And so, I did, taking a courageous breath as I walked back up the lane to his lodge.

The door was open, as if awaiting me. Softly, I walked in, closing it. For a moment, I wondered if I was alone, but a slight movement beside me had me turning my head.

There he was, pressed with his back against the wall, his bowed head resting on his arms, which cradled his knees. His shoulders were slumped in defeat.

Nothing could have prepared me for the electric jolt striking my heart on seeing him like this. In an instant, his pain became my pain, and I wanted nothing more than to ease it away.

Without hesitation, I knelt down beside him and

touched his arm, then his face, as it jerked up with the feel of my hand on his skin. Sheer disbelief that I was here before him drenched his eyes before the beginnings of hope and joy had him searching my face intently. "Soph?"

I stroked my fingers over his cheek, his hair, my voice full of love when I said, "You have my heart, you have it. You were right, I was scared. But no more. I'm not going to let my fear rob me of my chance to love you. And I do." I nodded, biting my lip. "I love you. I have never trusted anyone more."

I watched in delight as utter relief and happiness, then unbridled desire washed over him. He went to reach for me, but I pulled back a little. There was something I needed to know, something he had to tell me before we could go any further.

"Loving me isn't enough. You need to completely and utterly trust me, no room for doubt in any part of you." I breathed in, before, "Do you?"

Never had I felt more exposed as I awaited his answer, my whole body paused, holding itself still. The air, too, seemed to hold its breath.

Then Marcus broke into a radiant smile, his hands coming up to cup my face, his voice telling me earnestly, huskily, "With my very life, *mo leannan.*"

A sound broke out of me, half a sob, half a laugh.

Then, we clung to each other. He drew me into a deep kiss, whispering he loved me with those words I was coming to adore, the sound of *"tha gaol agam ort"* satisfying a deep hunger in me I never realised I had. I sank into his tender caresses as his hands moved over my body, eager to taste and feel every part of me. My body responded joyfully, returning everything he gave me, desperate to feel his bare skin against mine and have nothing separating us. Ripping our clothes off as quickly as we could, he lay me back on the floor, my legs wrapped around him, until, at last, we were one.

[38]

I woke up and turned to gaze out of the window. This time, the sky greeted me with dark, looming clouds, smothering the light. As I lay in Marcus' arms looking out of the bedroom window, a strange shiver came over me, despite the warmth of our shared heat in bed, and I instinctively moved closer to Marcus' sleeping form. Stirring, his arm came around me, pulling me close. I felt no desire to spring out of bed and make us breakfast like the last time. I did not want to leave his side, though I couldn't have told you why.

When he awoke, Marcus was full of smiles and laughter, teasing and kisses. I had never seen him so at peace with himself nor so relaxed with me. It was an addictive, powerful drug. The luxury to relax and enjoy our banter, the ease we had with each other as we made breakfast, eating off each other's plates. Marcus was full of wild plans and ideas for us, wanting us to take time off together to travel around the rest of Scotland, then take me to his hometown of some Scottish name I couldn't pronounce, much to Marcus' amusement. I readily agreed, in no hurry to go back to Buxton or the life I'd left behind. It wouldn't take much persuading on Marcus' part to get me to agree to move here permanently, and I wondered if he knew how much he'd become the centre of my world.

I was clearing up our breakfast plates, enjoying the feeling of pottering around in his kitchen, when two arms came from behind to circle my waist and a mouth began to gently nuzzle my neck, causing little shivers to run through me. Smiling, I turned in his embrace until we were face to face. His hair was still wet from the shower, and I reached up to smooth it back from where it fell against his brow.

Marcus grinned and bent his head so he could kiss me. When we drew back a few moments later, he gave a soft groan. "I really don't want to go to work. Can we just pretend I've got man flu or something?"

"That works for me. Actually," I reached up to feel his forehead, pretending to look concerned as I pressed against him, "you do feel quite warm, Detective Inspector Armstrong, and you have had a strenuous night. Perhaps, I should take you back to bed."

Marcus shook his head, eyes narrowing, even while his hands ran slowly and temptingly up my back. "Oh, you are bad, very bad, Ms. Meadows, and far too tempting for your own good. I'm going to need another shower at this rate."

Laughing, I moved against him again, raising my eyebrows suggestively. Unable to resist, he pulled me into a hot kiss that left me breathless, before purposely pulling back to arm's length, so we could both take a deep breath.

"Okay, okay, just stay there for a minute," Marcus warned. "Do not come any closer, otherwise we really will be spending the day in bed— No, don't you dare," he groaned with a strangled laugh as I moved toward him. "I have to close this case, for you as well as for me. That way we can move on without anything hanging over us. Agreed?"

How could I argue with that?

"All right, you win." I sighed. "I'll walk you to your car, then hang around to tidy up before heading over to the apartment to pack my things."

"Pack your things?" He arched his eyebrow.

I hesitated, then plunged in. "Well, clearly, I can't stay at Ella's apartment anymore—"

"Clearly." There was amusement in that voice of his that made my eyes narrow even while my cheeks burned.

"So, I was thinking maybe I could stay here with you... until we work everything out, that is," I finished with a bit of rush, biting my lip.

Marcus stepped right up to me, even though he'd only ordered me to remain at arm's length two seconds ago, smiling softly as he touched his finger to my mouth. "Were you now, lass? Well, there's no need to bite that kissable lip of yours off. I'm sure I can find some space in my vast wardrobe for you." And with that, grinning widely, he drew me into a tender kiss.

I couldn't resist teasing him back, murmuring against his lips, "I thought we weren't allowed to kiss, otherwise you'll never get 'round to closing our case."

"Smart arse, aren't you, *mo leannan*? But aye, you're right. Escort me to my car then."

Arm in arm, we opened the front door and stepped out onto the porch, moving toward his car, which was parked near mine.

A branch cracked as if it was being stepped on. I was about to say something when Marcus suddenly froze, stopping us both.

"Get behind me," he told me in a low voice, moving in front of me, his hands spread out to protect me.

"What—" my startled voice died away, as my eyes followed what Marcus' eyes were fixed on, like a bird of prey about to swoop down on its victim.

From the shadows, a man in a dark jacket stepped forward, his face partly concealed by a black scarf, his posture poised to attack. On seeing us, he reached up and gradually pulled down the scarf until his face was revealed. As he grinned maliciously, enjoying his moment of glory, my voice gasped in sickening horror.

There stood Richard, and within his hand was a cold, steel knife. Its sharp-edged blade glinted in the light, reflecting the hard look in his eyes as they narrowed in on us.

[39]

For one suspended moment, we stood there like puppets, unsure of who was in control and what the hell was happening. It was like someone had pressed pause while the audience tried to catch up. Except Marcus and I *were* the audience, and no one had told us the plot. Why was Richard here, threatening us with a knife? Nothing was making sense.

What hit me first was that this wasn't the man whom I'd married, the man I had shared my bed and life with for over ten years. This man's eyes were hard and slightly feverish as he took a few steps toward us. The knife seemed even more deadly as it loomed closer.

"Richard," Marcus was saying now, still standing in front of me, his voice calm and measured as he was trained to be. "You need to put that knife down, and then we can talk about whatever it is you want to. You've got our full attention."

The words only seemed to cause Richard to brandish the knife more, moving ever nearer toward us. "Why would I want to talk to you?" he demanded, before jerking his hand toward me. "I just need you to do one more, little thing for me, Soph darling, then I'll be out of your life for good. You and the little detective here can skip merrily hand-in-hand through the glades as much as you like. After you've given me what I want."

"Put the knife down, and then, *only* then, can you ask your favour of Sophia." Marcus' jaw was clinching hard, as his hand reached back to reassuringly squeeze my shaking one.

Without warning, Richard marched up and pointed the knife's tip into Marcus' chest. I gave a small scream as Marcus stiffened.

"You are really starting to piss me off now! Just give me the damn codes, and no one needs to get hurt."

Codes. At his words, everything began to fall into place like a stack of cards dealt heavily and violently from above. Aneella's lover. Aneella's mastermind. Aneella's jailor using her for his own gain, exactly as he had with me.

"It's you," the words gasped out of me even while my brain lurched wildly with the appalling truth. "You're the one she's protecting."

"What?" Richard demanded in a distracted voice, his knife tip still pressing against Marcus' heaving chest, as Marcus fought to remain calm against the threat that was my ex-husband.

The man I once loved was endangering the man I now loved. And that I could not allow.

Without thinking, acting purely on instinct, I stepped out from behind Marcus, giving him no time to react. Calmly, I came in front and took Richard's wrist in my grasp, making him lower the knife whilst I caught him by surprise. In my defining moment, my perfect storm, each of my senses became aware of the smallest, most infinite detail. The distant cry of a wild, eager fox. The soft, rippling sound of crystal water stirring within the loch. The sweet scent of a pine tree moving lazily in the wind. The acrid, metallic taste in my mouth as I forced away the dryness. Marcus' warm breath on my neck, stirring the tendrils of my hair and sending a tremor through my body. The cool air stirring our clothes and the leaves on the ground beneath where we stood.

As I stared into Richard's cold terrifying eyes, I knew it was down to me to save us.

"How long have you planned this with Aneella, using my programme codes for crime?" Before he could answer, words continued to spew out in a bid to stall him. "You know, I don't even care now that you and she have been having an affair, and that it probably started in our university days. I know it's you who helped her cheat on her exam." The flicker in his eyes confirmed this. "I know you've somehow convinced her to throw herself on the mercy of the court so you can get away scot-free—"

"You think I'm getting away scot-free?" Richard's eyes grew wide, viciously yanking his arm free from my hold. As the knife began to wave dangerously close to my skin, I fought hard against the overwhelming need to run. Only knowing Marcus stood solidly behind me gave me the courage I needed to keep facing my dangerous ex even as my heart raced painfully against my ribcage. "When I've got nasty bastards after me for these codes, who won't bat an eyelid while disposing of me if I don't produce the goods? What does it matter how long we've planned this? I need them now." There was a wildness to his pupils now, an edge of mania I should have adhered to. But I was too wound up, my body screaming for release.

"You're a fool, Richard! You think we're going to give them to you? Tell me, did you ever love either of us? Why did you marry me?" Unwelcome tears pricked my eyes. Angrily, I wiped them away.

"Don't do this to yourself," Marcus whispered in my ear. I was dimly aware he had his phone in his concealed hand behind my back, calling for backup with a special red alert code.

"Why did I marry you?" Richard unexpectedly touched my chin, which I savagely pushed off, hating the feel of it. He shrugged. "Because you worshipped me, and you were sweet. I thought you deserved something for your loyalty. Then, you had something I really needed, but when it came to your work, you never let me close. So we thought if I left you, then came back begging for forgiveness, you would do anything for me."

"Except I didn't fall back into your arms, did I?" My voice shook, but I stubbornly kept my eyes on Richard. I was trying hard to give Marcus time to act by distracting Richard for as long as I could. I sensed Marcus preparing to act by the hard tightening of his muscles in his arm against my hands.

The knife came a little closer to me as if to stroke my skin. There was a fever about him as his eyes widened unnaturally. "Chrissake, you were supposed to fall apart when I left you, not drop your knickers for a cop of all people."

"You make me sick," I spat out, pushing down the taste of bile in my mouth. "You don't even know what love is."

Something dangerous sparked in his eyes at my loathing of him, triggering a violent reaction in him. "Give me the codes!" he screamed, as he shoved me back into Marcus, almost knocking us both over.

Marcus caught me in time, steadying us, as he fought to reason with him. "We can't do that, Richard. We don't have them. You need to drop the knife. Don't make this any worse on yourself than it already is—"

"*What?* No, no, no, you have to bloody have them! They'll kill me, don't you get that? Are you listening to me?" There was a desperation to him now, his eyes beseeching as they turned wildly to me. "Soph, you have to help me! You loved me once; you don't want anything bad to happen to me."

He went to grab me, pulling me to him before Marcus could react. There was a glimpse of the old Richard as he stared at me, momentarily confusing me. "Please, Soph, I'm begging you here!"

I swallowed hard against the fear this change brought to my control. I carefully touched Richard's arm, imploring him, "Then let Marcus help you. He can protect you if you tell him who these men are, the ones threatening you."

Sweat was breaking out on Richard's forehead. He gave a short, bitter laugh. "You're so stupidly naïve. You just don't get it, do you?"

"I do, really, I do. Please, let me have the knife." I moved my hand down his arm to where his hand grasped it. I kept my eyes locked on his, praying that somehow the part of him that cared for me remained. "This isn't you, it's not you. You don't need to be scared anymore."

Without warning, Richard yanked me hard against him, pressing his mouth on mine. Repulsed, I instinctively reacted, pushing him away, while at the same time Marcus moved swiftly toward Richard to grab him, his fists raised, ready to strike.

～～

TOO LATE, far too late, Marcus realised his mistake. In his blind rage at seeing Richard force himself on the woman he loved, he had moved too hard, too quickly, and unbalanced Sophia. Unable to stop herself, she flailed and stumbled, falling toward the hand that Richard brandished the knife in. Horror, pure terrifying horror, filled him. Marcus cried out a sharp warning as he tried to pull her back to him, only for the sound to become stuck in his throat as the cold steel plunged straight into her side without mercy or relent.

～～

EVERYTHING BEGAN to swirl and mist around me, slowing down time. For one minute, the world became soft, blurry. Then came a sharp, sharp coldness in my side that ripped out a scream of pain from me. I looked down, pressing my hand against my side, staring in disbelief as red blood began to stain it. My knees gave way, as if all the strength had gone. I slid down to the ground, my face brushing against the soft leaves as they cushioned my fall. Their voices drifted above me with no connection to the soft earth now clasping around me, wanting to take me for its own.

"No, no! Soph, Soph, I'm sorry, I'm sorry! I didn't mean to hurt you—"

"Don't you touch her! You stay away from her! Yes, yes, I need an ambulance. Now! My girlfriend has been stabbed in the right side, she's... bleeding. Oh, God, help her..." Marcus' voice came closer, I could hear it, as his arms came around me, pressing hard against my side, cradling me. Yet, my body couldn't seem to feel his touch. "It's going to be okay, *mo leannan,* stay with me, don't close your eyes now. I love you. *Tha gaol agam ort.*" His lips pressed against me, kissing my cold temple, again and again. "We're going to see the sunrise tomorrow, you hear me. We're going to watch it rise up over our loch. Oh, come on, where the hell are they? She's bleeding out, fast!" His voice caught on a sob, battling against the panic threatening to undo him. "That's it, keep those beautiful eyes open for me. I need you to keep them open for me for just a little bit longer..."

I tried to do as he asked, but the need to sleep was overwhelming me. I felt shivers run through my body. *So cold, so cold.* I looked up and saw the grey clouds move over me, raindrops beginning to wash my face. Was it rain? Is that why Marcus' face was so wet as he cradled me tight against him, rocking me? Soothing me, just like my mum did when I was little. I wanted to tell him I loved him, but my mouth refused to comply. Why was everything so hazy? Had night-time come early? I must close my eyes. *Just for a minute…*

"No, no! Don't you dare leave me, Soph!" His hands were shaking me, and I wanted to moan and tell him to stop. "I can't lose you, too. Oh, God, save her, I'm begging you. Come on, *mo leannan*, sweetheart, stay with me, don't let go of me, of us. Look, I can hear the ambulance! They're coming, they're coming…"

His voice became fainter and fainter, as if we were on different worlds that were not aligned. I couldn't pull myself back to him; I didn't have the strength.

Darkness enveloped me, extinguishing the light and pulling me deeper and deeper under its spell.

I was swimming underwater, my arms and legs stretching out, embracing the cool, fresh water of the loch. The sun's rays danced above me, warming me. The water muffled the loud noises of the outside world, cocooning me within its safe haven. My body felt free and without constraint, my limbs strong and without tiredness. Nothing or no one could harm me here.

A shadow moved across the water, the water stilling as if commanded to do so. A hand reached down, beckoning me to grab hold of it. The shadow's face—at first obscured, then sharpening into focus—was smiling down at me, enticing me to break through the water's surface to reach it.

I paused, conflicted. The water felt good, purifying, and weightless, keeping me nestled tight within its safe embrace.

But his eyes were filled with love and urging me to him. Come, come, he seemed to say, come see the sunrise with me again. There's beauty still waiting for you.

How could I refuse? The water would always be here, but he would not.

My hand reached up, farther and farther, until my fingertips clasped his. At the touch of my hand, his own wrapped itself around mine, and, with one fluid movement, he pulled me out of the cool water…

MY COLD HAND clasped within his warm one was the first sensation I noticed as I opened my eyes. Immediately, I blinked hard against the harshness of the artificial light, despite being dimmed for evening time. Monitors flashed at me from where I lay on a bed I didn't recognise. I was dressed in a gown that was itchy and smelled of antiseptic.

I shifted a little, trying not to panic at the unfamiliar surroundings. As I did, pain shot through my side, making me flinch and gasp softly. Letting my free hand move cautiously down, I gingerly felt around until I encountered a large bandaged area, sore and tender beneath my tentative fingers. Biting my lip, I moved my fingers away, letting them drift until they became entwined with soft, thick hair.

Lifting my head awkwardly, I looked down. Marcus lay uncomfortably with his head on the bed, while the rest of him was half sat, half slumped on an old, worn-looking chair. His hand held mine tightly, even in his restless sleep. A smile touched the edges of my lips as I gently stroked his hair.

It was enough to stir him from his slumber. His head

jerked up, his eyes confused and dazed. Creases from the bed sheet left impressions on his cheek. His T-shirt was crumpled, and his hair stuck up in funny little quiffs. To me, at that moment, he had never looked so good.

"Hi," I managed to croak out.

With that, his whole body straightened, his eyes now wide awake, staring at me, as if they couldn't quite believe what they saw. "You're awake. You're..."

"Have I been asleep for a while?"

Marcus broke down, bringing his head against my neck, clinging to me. I soothed him as best I could, stroking his head until he was calmer. He finally raised his head, stroking my cheek tenderly, eyes wet with tears. "I've sat here for the last three days, praying and pleading with God to spare you, to bring you back to me."

"And He has." I smiled, covering his hand, which cradled my face, with my own.

"Yes, yes, He has." He bent to kiss me softly on the lips. "I should call the doctor."

He went to press the button, but I stopped him. "No, not yet, in a minute."

"Whatever you say, *mo leannan*, whatever you want."

"There is one thing I need to know." I closed my eyes for a moment, then forced the words out. "Did you catch Richard?"

His jaw clenched. His voice held a fierce note as he gave a quick shake of his head. "No, he escaped while I was cradling you. But trust me, I won't rest until I do. He will never come near you again, that I vow to you—"

Marcus broke off and looked away, as if shame had hit him. Frowning, I moved my hand to bring his face back to mine. The raw emotion and distress I saw in his face caused me to draw in a breath. "What is it? Tell me," I urged.

His head hung down, his voice was low and filled with self-disgust. "I let you down. Worse than that, I let that bastard hurt you, nearly kill you. I promised you I would keep you safe, and instead, you nearly died... I'm sorry, I —" his voice caught.

"You listen to me, Marcus Armstrong," I said, my voice fierce, determined. "Don't ever talk such crap again, and don't you dare blame yourself. No, no, don't turn away like you're ashamed of yourself. Look at me." I took his head firmly in my hands, so he had no choice but to look at me. The deep pain caught up in the shame in his eyes almost destroyed me, telling me of the seven kinds of hell he'd been going through these last few days I lay unconscious. "I was the one stupid enough to step out from behind you and into that knife, instead of letting you protect me. You've saved me so many times, and you will keep on protecting me. This I know with utter certainty. Please, believe what I'm saying to you."

Marcus pressed his forehead against mine. I could feel tremors racing through his body. "I want to believe you; I want to feel that. But all I feel right now is that I'm not worthy enough for you. You deserve more, a better man than me to love you."

Despair hit me. How could I reach down deep enough into his troubled soul to make him see that without him I would have nothing? I closed my eyes for a moment. As I did, vivid memories of the dream I'd had while lying here unconscious brought me our salvation. "I had this dream while I was sleeping," I began, slowly opening my eyes. "I was underwater in our loch. The water was so beautiful I wanted to stay there. But then your hand reached down to pull me out. You beckoned me back to you. And I couldn't resist, didn't want to resist. Your love brought me back," I whispered. "It's enough, it's more than enough. No one else can love me like I need, only you."

Marcus drew back to look at me. A number of emotions crossed his face until, at last, I saw what I was desperate for—an acceptance, but not quite peace yet. With time and reassurance, that would come. He nodded, once, twice, as if to convince himself.

"I love you," I murmured, my lips moving close to his.

"And I you," came his response, before kissing me with an intensity that made me hungry for more.

As we broke apart, Marcus brought my hand up to his lips, held it there. The gesture was so intimate, so beautiful in its honouring and adoration, my heart contracted. I pulled him into my arms, ignoring the pain the movement caused.

We stayed like that, holding each other, until dawn broke through, the sunrays once more cast their mesmerising light over us.

[41]

F ive months later

WE SAT WRAPPED in each other's arms, watching the
sun rise over our loch, lifting away the gently swirling
mist. The aura of colours, from ruby red and burnt orange
to ochre yellow and faint wisps of midnight blue, took my
breath away with its stunning display put on for us alone.

Learning to be patient during my slow recovery and
returning strength over the last few months, I had come
to appreciate more and more the staggering beauty we
witnessed every single day on our earth, in all its many
wonders. From the sapping of a new bud to the gentle fall
of rustic autumn leaves, from the call of the eagle soaring
high in the sky to the tiniest of dragonflies floating lazily
over the loch, every new sense and sound I drew into my
soul was like seeing it for the first time in its miraculous
existence. Everything had taken on a new vividness and

clarity, like a camera lens turned to its sharpest focus so not one detail would be missed.

I had been given another chance with life, and I wouldn't waste it, I promised you this.

Ella and Lyle awaited trial. She had tried to contact me, but I wasn't ready to talk to her. Not yet. Richard still remained on the run, despite Marcus working relentlessly to find him. I knew he wouldn't rest until he had caught Richard and stopped the fraud gripping this country he loved.

Marcus turned to smile at me, his arm bringing me close to him, stroking my finger now bearing his wedding band engraved with the words *"s leatsa mo chridhe"*—"my heart belongs to you forever". I rested my head against his shoulder, his strength, as ever, all I needed. There was no need for words. We understood what the other was feeling. We knew the promise of the sunrise, the hope that it brought, and all the ones to follow. While there was still breath in our bodies, we would not take one single day for granted.

I had faced my perfect storm and not only survived it but became a stronger person for it. The darkness could not touch me now.

TO BE CONTINUED.

Book Two

Follow the author, Marie Jones, for updates about book two in the series.

THANK YOU FOR READING.

Thank you for reading *Those We Trust*. Please consider leaving a review so that other readers can find this title.

Did you know that reviews from readers like you help bookstores ell the book and other readers find their next favorite novel?

OTHER GENZ ROMANCES YOU MAY LIKE

Escaping to the Country by EA Stripling

Infamous by Allison Stowe

Animal Attraction by Kathryn Halberg

Made in the USA
Monee, IL
08 July 2021

73213037R00187